FIRST LOVE

&

SPRING TORRENTS

First Warbler Press Edition 2024

First Love first published in *The Reader's Library,* Saint Petersburg, 1860
Spring Torrents first published in *The Herald of Europe,* Moscow, 1872

Translation by Franklin Reeve first published in *Five Short Novels* by Ivan Turgenev,
Bantam Books, New York, 1961
Reprinted in accordance with U.S. copyright law.

Letter from Joseph Conrad published in *Turgenev: A Study* by Edward Garnett,
W. Collins Sons & Co., London, 1917

"First Love Is Exactly Like Revolution": Intimacy as Political Allegory in Ivan
Turgenev's Novella *Spring Torrents* © 2021 Alexey Vdovin, Pavel Uspenskij. Published
by Cambridge University Press on behalf of the Association for Slavic, East European,
and Eurasian Studies in *Slavic Review,* Dec 13, 2021
Reprinted with permission.

Biographical Timeline © Warbler Press

ISBN 978-1-962572-47-7 (paperback)
ISBN 978-1-962572-48-4 (e-book)

warblerpress.com

FIRST LOVE

&

SPRING TORRENTS

IVAN TURGENEV

TRANSLATION AND NOTES BY FRANKLIN REEVE
FOREWORD BY JOSEPH CONRAD
AFTERWORD BY ALEXEY VDOVIN AND PAVEL USPENSKIJ

CONTENTS

FOREWORD
by Joseph Conrad

DEAR EDWARD[1]—I am glad to hear that you are about to publish a study of Turgenev, that fortunate artist who has found so much in life for us and no doubt for himself, with the exception of bare justice. Perhaps that will come to him, too, in time. Your study may help the consummation. For his luck persists after his death. What greater luck an artist like Turgenev could wish for than to find in the English-speaking world a translator who has missed none of the most delicate, most simple beauties of his work, and a critic who has known how to analyse and point out its high qualities with perfect sympathy and insight.

After twenty odd years of friendship (and my first literary friendship too) I may well permit myself to make that statement, while thinking of your wonderful Prefaces as they appeared from time to time in the volumes of Turgenev's complete edition, the last of which came into the light of public indifference in the ninety-ninth year of the nineteenth century.

With that year one may say, with some justice, that the age of Turgenev had come to an end too; only work so simple and human, so independent of the transitory formulas and theories of art belongs as you point out in the Preface to *Smoke* "to all time."

Turgenev's creative activity covers about thirty years. Since it came to an end the social and political events in Russia have moved at an accelerated pace, but the deep origins of them, in the moral and intellectual unrest of the souls, are recorded in the whole body

---

1   Edward Garnett, author of *Turgenev: A Study* published by W. Collins Sons & Co., London, 1917. This letter appears as the foreword to the aforementioned book.

of his work with the unerring lucidity of a great national writer. The first stirrings, the first gleams of the great forces can be seen almost in every page of the novels, of the short stories and of *A Sportsman's Sketches*—those marvellous landscapes peopled by unforgettable figures.

Those will never grow old. Fashions in monsters do change, but the truth of humanity goes on for ever, unchangeable and inexhaustible in the variety of its disclosures. Whether Turgenev's art, which has captured it with such mastery and such gentleness, is for "all time" it is hard to say. Since, as you say yourself, he brings all his problems and characters to the test of love we may hope that it will endure at least till the infinite emotions of love are replaced by the exact simplicity of perfected Eugenics. But even by then, I think, women would not have changed much; and the women of Turgenev who understood them so tenderly, so reverently and so passionately—they, at least, are certainly for all time.

Women are, one may say, the foundation of his art. They are Russian of course. Never was a writer so profoundly, so wholesouledly national. But for non-Russian readers, Turgenev's Russia is but a canvas on which the incomparable artist of humanity lays his colours and his forms in the great light and the free air of the world. Had he invented them all and also every stick and stone, brook and hill and field in which they move, his personages would have been just as true and as poignant in their perplexed lives. They are his own and also universal. Any one can accept them with no more question than one accepts the Italians of Shakespeare.

In the larger non-Russian view, what should make Turgenev sympathetic and welcome to the English-speaking world, is his essential humanity. All his creations, fortunate and unfortunate, oppressed and oppressors are human beings, not strange beasts in a menagerie or damned souls knocking themselves about in the stuffy darkness of mystical contradictions. They are human beings, fit to live, fit to suffer, fit to struggle, fit to win, fit to lose, in the endless and inspiring game of pursuing from day to day the ever-receding future.

I began by calling him lucky, and he was, in a sense. But one ends by having some doubts. To be so great without the slightest parade and so fine without any tricks of "cleverness" must be fatal to any man's influence with his contemporaries.

Frankly, I don't want to appear as qualified to judge of things Russian. It wouldn't be true. I know nothing of them. But I am aware of a few general truths, such as, for instance, that no man, whatever may be the loftiness of his character, the purity of his motives and the peace of his conscience—no man, I say, likes to be beaten with sticks during the greater part of his existence. From what one knows of his history it appears clearly that in Russia almost any stick was good enough to beat Turgenev with in his latter years. When he died the characteristically chicken-hearted Autocracy hastened to stuff his mortal envelope into the tomb it refused to honour, while the sensitive Revolutionists went on for a time flinging after his shade those jeers and curses from which that impartial lover of *all* his countrymen had suffered so much in his lifetime. For he, too, was sensitive. Every page of his writing bears its testimony to the fatal absence of callousness in the man.

And now he suffers a little from other things. In truth it is not the convulsed terror-haunted Dostoevski but the serene Turgenev who is under a curse. For only think! Every gift has been heaped on his cradle: absolute sanity and the deepest sensibility, the clearest vision and the quickest responsiveness, penetrating insight and unfailing generosity of judgment, an exquisite perception of the visible world and an unerring instinct for the significant, for the essential in the life of men and women, the clearest mind, the warmest heart, the largest sympathy—and all that in perfect measure. There's enough there to ruin the prospects of any writer. For you know very well, my dear Edward, that if you had Antinous himself in a booth of the world's-fair, and killed yourself in protesting that his soul was as perfect as his body, you wouldn't get one per cent of the crowd struggling next door for a sight of the Double-headed Nightingale or of some weak-kneed giant grinning through a horse collar.—Yours,

J. C.

PREFACE TO *FIRST LOVE*

W RITTEN IN THE first three months of 1860, dedicated to Annenkov and published a few years later in Druzhinin's magazine the *The Library for Reading, First Love* provoked a warm response from Flaubert. He wrote Turgenev that all old romantics should be grateful for such a moving story, such an exciting figure as Zinaida—so real and ideal at once. Turgenev himself regarded it as one of his favorites among his own work and freely admitted its extremely autobiographical nature. In fact, according to all the evidence and Turgenev's own subsequent correspondence, the story may be read as virtually "literally true."

From the age given his father in the story and from the events described, it would seem that the incidents narrated took place when Turgenev was just about thirteen (he gives his age as sixteen in the story). The story itself clearly proceeds from a list of characters, beginning with the triangle "I, my father, my mother." The affection of both father and son for the same girl shapes another triangle, imposed on the first. The outcome of the affair deeply affects the narrator, who tells the story from the point of view of a middle-aged I man—which, of course, Turgenev was when he wrote it.

The whole story is intimately connected with Turgenev's own biography. In one letter, he writes that the knife episode in which the boy was set to kill his rival, is an actual account of what he himself did because of intense jealousy; in others, he refers to his hatred of unattractive hands and of the deep impression women's hands make on him—in the same way the whip across Zinaida's made such an impression on the young boy. And, finally, for all his other affairs, both physical and Platonic, Turgenev's most lasting attachment was

a kind of self-castigating devotion to Pauline Viardot. The self-effac-
ing, humiliating, but ecstatic devotion little Voldemar offers Zinaida
expresses better than letters or commentary the relation between
Turgenev and the famous singer. At the end of his life, the impos-
sibility of their long "affair" frequently filled him with despair and
fury. He was aware that she had never cared for him as he had for
her. An exquisite hopelessness of just this sort is the tone of "First
Love."

First Love

(for P. V. Annenkov)

T HE GUESTS HAD left long ago. The clock struck twelve-thirty. Only the host and Sergei Nikolaich and Vladimir Petrovich remained in the room.

The host rang and ordered the left-overs from supper cleared away.

"And so, it's decided," he said, sinking back in the arm chair and lighting a cigar. "Each of us must tell the story of his first love. It's your turn, Sergei Nikolaich."

Sergei Nikolaich, a rotund man with a chubby, blond-bearded face, looked first at his host and then up at the ceiling. "I never had a first love," he said finally; "I began immediately with the second."

"How so?"

"Very simple. I was eighteen when I first flirted with a very pretty young lady, but I courted her as if the whole thing wasn't new for me at all—just the way I courted others later. Strictly speaking, the first—and last—time I fell in love I was six...with my nurse. But that was very long ago. The details of our relationship are blotted out of my memory, and even if I remembered them, who would be interested?

"Well, then," the host began, "there's not much of interest in my first love, either: I didn't fall in love with anyone until I met Anna Ivanovna, my present wife—and it was all smooth sailing for us. Our fathers arranged our marriage; we very soon took a liking to each other—and got married without dallying. My story is told in two words. I must admit, gentlemen, that in bringing up the question of a first love I was counting on you, I won't say old—but also, not young—bachelors. *You* will entertain us with something, won't you, Vladimir Petrovich?"

"My first love was, actually, somewhat unusual," Vladimir Petrovich answered with a little hesitation; he was a man of about forty with black hair turning grey.

"Ah!" the host and Sergei Nikolaich said simultaneously. "So much the better. Tell it."

"If you want...or no, I won't tell it. I'm not an expert at story-telling; things come out dry and short, or long-winded and false. But, if you'll let me, I'll write down everything I remember, in a notebook, and I'll read it to you."

At first the friends did not agree, but Vladimir Petrovich insisted on having his own way. Two weeks later they met again, and Vladimir Petrovich kept his promise.

This is what was in his notebook.

I was sixteen at the time. It happened in the summer of 1833.

I was living in Moscow with my parents. They had rented a dacha near the Kaluga Gate across from Neskuchnyi Park. I was preparing for the university, but I was studying very little and was in no hurry.

Nobody hampered my freedom. I did what I wanted—especially after I parted with my last French tutor, who had never been able to get used to the idea that he had fallen "like a bomb" *(comme une bombe)* into Russia—and with an embittered expression on his face used to lie in his bed for days. My father treated me with indifferent kindness; my mother paid me almost no attention, although she had no other children besides me: other cares absorbed her. My father, a man still young and very handsome, had married her for her money; she was ten years older than he. My mother led a sad life; she was continually upset, jealous, angry—but not in my father's presence. She was very afraid of him, and he kept himself stern, cold, remote... I've never seen a man more elegantly composed, self-confident, and tyrannical.

I'll never forget the first weeks I spent at the dacha. The weather was wonderful. We had left town May 9th, right on St. Nicholas' Day. I would take walks—sometimes in the garden of our dacha, sometimes through Neskuchnyi Park, sometimes beyond the Gate. I'd take some book along, Kaidanov's lectures, for example, but I seldom looked through it; rather, I usually recited verses, for I knew many by heart; my blood fermented in me—and my heart ached, so sweetly and ridiculously. I was all the time expecting, and shying away from something, marveling at everything; and was always ready. My imagination dallied and flitted quickly around the same notions—like martins around a church tower at sunset. I would get lost in thought, grow sad, and even cry; but even through my tears, even through my sadness, provoked sometimes by a melodious verse, sometimes by the beauty of the evening, there broke out, like spring grass, the joyful feeling of young, bubbling life.

I had a horse. I used to saddle it myself and go riding alone to some place rather far away, used to gallop and imagine myself a knight in a tourney (how gaily the wind whistled in my ears!) or, turning my face up to the sky, let its shining light and its azure fall on my open heart.

I remember, at that time, the figure of a woman—the image of a woman's love—practically never arose in my mind in definite shape; but in everything I thought, in everything I felt, there lay hidden a half-conscious, half-ashamed premonition of something new, ineffably sweet—feminine.

This premonition, this expectation went through my whole being; I breathed it, it coursed through my veins in every drop of blood. It was fated soon to come true.

Our dacha was a wooden manor house with columns and two low little wings. In the wing on the left a tiny, cheap wallpaper factory had been set up; I often went there to watch how a dozen skinny and disheveled boys in greasy smocks and with hollow faces continually jumped up and down on the wooden levers that pushed down the quadrangular blocks of the press and, in this way, by the weight of their frail bodies, were squeezing out the motley designs of the wallpapers. The little wing on the right of the house stood empty and was up for rent. One day, about three weeks after May 9th, the shutters on the windows of this little wing were opened, and women's faces appeared in them; some family had moved in. I remember, that same day at dinner, my mother asked the butler who our new neighbors were, and, hearing the name Princess Zasekina, said first, not without a certain respectfulness, "Ah! a princess," but then added, "A poor one, suppose."

"They came in three cabs, ma'am," the butler remarked, serving a dish respectfully; "they don't have their own carriages—and the furniture is the plainest."

"Of course," my mother retorted, "but still it's better." My father glanced at her coldly: she fell silent.

Actually, Princess Zasekina could not be a rich woman: the little wing she had rented was so decrepit, and so small and low, that people who were even just a bit well-off would not have agreed to move into it. Anyway, at that time I turned a deaf ear to all this. The princely title had little effect on me: I had not long before read Schiller's *The Robbers*.

II

I had the habit of wandering through our garden every evening with my rifle and lying in wait for crows. For a long time I had felt real hatred for these careful, predatory, and cunning birds. On the day which I've started talking about, I set out for the garden as usual— and having gone through all the pathways to no avail (the crows had spotted me and only cawed sporadically from far off), I happened to come to the low fence separating our property from the narrow little string of garden stretching out behind the little wing on the right and belonging to it. I went on, my head down. Suddenly I heard voices. I looked over the fence—and was petrified: I saw a strange sight.

A few steps away from me, in a clearing among green raspberry bushes, stood a tall, slender girl in a striped pink dress with a little white kerchief on her head. Four young men crowded around her, and she was tapping them in turn on the forehead with those little grey flowers (I don't recall the name, but children know them well)—those little flowers which form small sacs, and burst with a crackle when you strike them on something hard. The young men were offering their foreheads so eagerly—and in the girl's movements (I saw her from the side) there was something so enchanting, so authoritative, so gentle, so mocking and kind, that I almost cried out in surprise and pleasure; and, I think, I would have given everything in the world right then and there if only those lovely little fingers would have struck my forehead too. My gun slipped to the grass, I forgot everything. My eyes devoured the slender figure and little neck and beautiful hands—and the slightly tousled blond hair under the white kerchief and those half-closed deep eyes and those eyelashes and the soft cheeks beneath them…

"Young man, oh, young man," suddenly somebody's voice beside me said, "is one allowed to stare so at young ladies one doesn't know?"

I shuddered all over, I was stupefied. Next to me—on the other side of the fence—there stood a man with short-cut black hair; he was looking at me ironically. At that very same moment the girl herself turned toward me. I saw big grey eyes on a mobile, animated face. This whole face suddenly quivered, burst into laughter, its white teeth flashed, the eyebrows were somehow amusingly raised. I blushed all over, grabbed my gun and, pursued by a ringing, but not malicious, boisterous laugh, ran to my room, threw myself on my bed, and covered my face with my hands. The heart in me was really leaping. I was very ashamed and happy: I felt an unknown excitement.

Having rested, I combed my hair, cleaned up, and went down to tea. The image of the young girl went along before me, my heart stopped jumping, but somehow ached pleasantly.

"What's the matter with you?" my father suddenly asked me. "You killed a crow?"

I was about to tell him everything, but I restrained myself—and just smiled inwardly. When I went to bed, I, not knowing why myself, spun around on one foot three times, pomaded my hair, lay down—and slept all night like a log. Before daylight I woke up for a moment, raised my head, looked around in delight—and again fell asleep.

III

"How can I get to meet them?" was my first thought as soon as I woke up in the morning. Before breakfast I went out to the garden, but I didn't go too close to the fence and didn't see anyone. After breakfast I walked up and down the street in front of the dacha several times, and I looked at the windows from a distance...I seemed to see her face behind the curtains, and I hurried away faster in fright. "However, I must get to know them," I thought, walking back and forth confusedly on the sandy flat piece of ground along Neskuchnyi Park. "But how? That's the question." I recalled the smallest details of yesterday's meeting: for some reason I saw clearly how she had laughed at me...But, while I was all upset and was figuring out various plans, fate had already had its conference on me.

In my absence my mother had received from our new neighbor a letter on grey paper, sealed with brown wax like that used only on post-office notices and on the corks of cheap wine. In this letter, written in ungrammatical language and a slovenly hand, the princess asked my mother's patronage. My mother, according to the princess, was well acquainted with some important people on whom her fate and her children's fate depended, since she was involved in very important lawsuits. "I turn tyou," she wrote, "as a lady to lady, and besides Im gladd to tak advantuj of this oportunity." In ending, she asked Mother for permission to call on her. I found my mother in an unpleasant frame of mind: Father wasn't home, and she had no one to talk this over with. Not to answer "the lady"—a princess besides—was out of the question; but how to answer, my mother was at a loss. To write a note in French seemed inappropriate to her, and Mother was not very good at Russian spelling (she admitted it herself)—and she didn't want to be compromised. She was delighted with my coming in, and immediately told me to go over to the princess's and tell her that my mother says she is always ready to render Her Highness whatever service she can, and begs her to call about one o'clock. The unexpected, quick fulfillment of my secret desires both delighted and frightened me; however, I didn't betray the embarrassment which had come over me—and, as a preliminary, went off to my room to put on my newest tie and little coat. (At home I still went around in a short jacket and turn-down collar, although I felt very restricted by them.)

IV

In the cramped and untidy vestibule of the little wing, which I entered trembling hopelessly all over, I was met by a grey old servant with a dark, copper-colored face, piglike, sullen little eyes, and deep wrinkles on his forehead and temples such as I had never seen in my life. He was carrying the bare skeleton of a herring on a plate—and, kicking the door shut that led into the next room, he said abruptly: "What do you want?"

"Is Princess Zasekina at home?" I asked.

"Vonifati!" a jarring female voice shouted from behind the door.

The servant turned his back on me without speaking, exposing the terribly frayed back of his livery—with a solitary, rusty, heraldic button—and went off, having put the plate on the floor.

"Did you go to the police station?" the same female voice asked. The steward mumbled something. "What? Somebody's come?" the voice said. "The young man next door! Well, ask him in."

"Please, come into the living room, sir," the servant said, having reappeared in front of me—and picking the plate up off the floor. I straightened my coat and went into the "living room."

I found myself in a small and rather untidy room with meager, seemingly hastily placed furniture. By the window, in a chair with a broken arm, sat a woman of about fifty, bare headed and homely, in an old green dress and with a gray worsted kerchief around her neck. Her little black eyes were fixed on me.

I went over to her and bowed.

"Have the honor of speaking to Princess Zasekina?"

"I'm Princess Zasekina; and you're Mr. V's son?"

"That's right, ma'am. I've come with a message from my mother."

"Sit down, please. Vonifati! Where are my keys, did you see them?"

I told the princess my mother's answer to her note. She heard me out, tapping her fat red fingers on the window sill, and, when I had finished, stared at me again.

"Fine; I certainly will," she said finally. "And how young you still are! How old are you, if I may ask?"

"Sixteen," I answered with an involuntary stammer.

The princess took some dirty pieces of paper, all written on, out of her pocket, put them right up against her nose and started sorting them.

"A good age," she suddenly said, turning around and fidgeting in her chair. "And, please, don't be formal. I live very simply."

"Too simply," I thought, with involuntary disgust looking her unattractive figure up and down.

At that moment the other living room door was flung open and the girl I had seen in the garden the evening before appeared in the doorway. She raised her hand—and an ironic smile flitted across her face.

"And here's my daughter," the princess said, pointing to her with her elbow. "Zinochka, the son of our neighbor Mr. V. What's your name, if I may ask?"

"Vladimir," I answered, standing up and stammering from nervousness.

"And your patronymic?"

"Petrovich."

"Fine. I used to know a police chief. He was Vladimir Petrovich too. Vonifati! Don't look for the keys! They are in my pocket."

The young girl kept on looking at me with the same ironic smile, squinting a little and tilting her head a little to one side.

"I've already seen Monsieur Voldemar," she began. (The silvery sound of her voice ran through me like a sweet shiver.)

"Please," I mumbled.

"Where was that?" the Princess asked.

The young princess did not answer her mother.

"Are you busy now?" she asked, not taking her eyes off me.

"Not at all."

"Do you want to help me wind some wool? Come this way, to my room."

She nodded to me and went out of the living room. I set out after her.

In her room the furniture was a little better and was arranged with more taste. Besides, at that moment I could hardly see anything: I moved as in a dream—and felt a kind of intense, almost foolish, well-being all over.

The young princess sat down, got her bundle of red wool, and, motioning to me to sit down in the chair opposite her, carefully undid the bundle and put it on my hands. She did all this without talking, with a sort of amusing slowness, and with that same bright and cunning smile on her barely parted lips. She began winding the wool onto a folded card and suddenly looked with such bright, quick glance that I involuntarily looked down. When her eyes, usually half-closed, opened up wide, her face completely changed—as if light were spilling over it.

"What did you think of me yesterday, Monsieur Voldemar?" she asked, a little later. "Probably you criticized me?"

"I...Princess...I didn't think a thing. How could I—" I answered in embarrassment.

"Listen," she said. "You don't know me yet. I'm very strange; I want to be told the truth always. You're sixteen, I heard; and I'm twenty-one. You see I'm much older than you, and therefore you must always tell me the truth—and obey me," she added. "Look at me— why don't you look at me?"

I grew even more confused; however, I looked up at her. She smiled, only not with that earlier smile, but with a different, approving one. "Look at me," she repeated, tenderly lowering her voice; "it's not unpleasant for me. I like your face; I have a feeling that we'll be friends. But do you like me?" she added slyly.

"Princess..." I began.

"First of all, call me Zinaida Aleksandrovna, and secondly, what sort of habit is it for children"—she corrected herself— "for young people not to say what they feel? It's all right for grown-ups. You know you like me, don't you?"

Although it was very pleasant for me that she talked to me so candidly, I was still a little hurt. I wanted to show her that she wasn't dealing with a boy and, having assumed as best I could a worldly and serious expression, said: "Of course, I like you very much, Zinaida Aleksandrovna; I don't want to hide it."

She slowly shook her head. "Do you have a tutor?" she asked suddenly.

"No, I haven't had a tutor for a long time."

I was lying: less than a month had gone by since I had parted with my Frenchman.

"Oh! Indeed! I see—you're completely grown up."

She tapped me lightly on my fingers. "Hold your hands straight!" And she diligently set to winding the ball.

I took advantage of the fact that she didn't raise her eyes, and began looking her up and down, at first furtively, then more and more boldly. Her face seemed to me even more charming than the evening before: everything in it was fine, intelligent, and kind. She sat with her back to a window hung with a white blind; a ray of sunlight, falling through the blind, covered her fluffy, golden hair, her virginal neck, sloping shoulders and tender, tranquil breast with a soft light. I looked at her—and how dear and how close she became to me! It seemed to me that I had known her for a long time—and that, before her, I had known nothing and had not lived…She had on a darkish, faded dress with an apron; I think I would have gladly caressed every pleat of that dress and that apron. The tips of her shoes looked out from under her dress; I would have bent down to those shoes in adoration. And here I'm sitting in front of her, I thought: I have really met her—my God, what happiness! I almost jumped up out of the chair from excitement, but I only dangled my feet a little, like a child in delight.

I felt fine, like a fish in water—and I would have stayed in that room forever—would not have left that place.

She raised her eyelids calmly—again her bright eyes shone caressingly before me, and she smiled again.

"How you look at me!" she said slowly, and shook her finger at me.

I blushed. "She understands everything, she sees everything," flashed through my head. "How could she not understand and see everything!"

Suddenly something made a noise in the next room—a saber clanked.

"Zina!" the princess called out from the living room. "Belovzorov has brought you a kitten."

"A kitten!" Zinaida exclaimed and, jumping out of her chair in a rush, she threw the ball in my lap and ran out.

I, too, got up and, having put the hank of wool and the ball on the window sill, went into the living room and stopped in bewilderment: A striped kitten lay in the middle of the room, its paws spread wide; Zinaida was kneeling in front of it and carefully lifting its face up. Beside the old princess, covering almost the whole wall space between the windows, stood a blond, curly-haired young hussar with a rosy face and bulging eyes.

"It's so funny!" Zinaida was saying. "And its eyes aren't grey, but green, and the ears are so big! Thank you, Viktor Egorych! You're very kind!"

The hussar, whom I recognized as one of the young people I had seen the evening before, smiled and bowed; as he did so he clicked his spurs and clanked the little rings of his saber.

"Yesterday you were pleased to say that you wanted a striped kitten with big ears—so I got it. Your word is my law."

And he bowed again.

The kitten mewed feebly and began to sniff the floor.

"It's hungry!" Zinaida exclaimed. "Vonifati, Sonia! Bring some milk."

The maid, in an old yellow dress and with a faded kerchief around her neck, came in with a saucer of milk in her hand and put it down in front of the kitten. The kitten shivered, blinked, and began lapping.

"What a rosy little tongue it has!" Zinaida observed, bending her head down almost to the floor and looking at it from the side under its very nose.

The kitten had all it wanted and began to purr, mincingly moving its paws. Zinaida got up and, turning to the maid, said with indifference, "Take it out."

"For the kitten, your hand," said the hussar, grinning and jerking his whole mighty body, held tightly in his new uniform.

"Both," Zinaida said, and held her hands out to him. While he kissed them, she looked at me over his shoulder.

I stood motionless and didn't know whether to laugh or not, whether to say something or to be silent. Suddenly, through the open door to the hallway, I caught sight of our valet Fyodor. He was making signs to me. Automatically I went out to him.

"What is it?" I asked.

"Your mother sent for you," he said in a whisper. "She's cross that you haven't come back with an answer."

"Have I been here long?"

"Over an hour."

"Over an hour!" I repeated involuntarily, and, having returned to the living room, began to say good-bye, and click my heels.

"Where are you going?" the young princess asked me, glancing up from behind the hussar.

"I have to go home. So, I'll tell her," I added, turning to the old woman, "that you'll call on us at two o'clock."

"Do tell her, young man."

The princess hastily reached for her snuffbox and took a pinch so loudly that I winced. "Do tell her," she repeated, blinking tearfully and clearing her throat.

I bowed once again, turned, and went out of the room with that feeling of awkwardness in my back which a very young man feels when he knows that he is being watched from behind.

"Be sure, Monsieur Voldemar, to come and see us," Zinaida called, and again burst out laughing.

"Why is she always laughing?" I thought, going home accompanied by Fyodor, who didn't speak to me at all, but moved along behind me disapprovingly. Mother scolded me, and was surprised: what could I have been doing so long at the princess's? I didn't answer her, and went off to my room. I suddenly felt very sad. I tried hard to cry…I was jealous of the hussar!

V

The princess, as she had promised, called on Mother—and Mother didn't like her. I wasn't present at their meeting, but at dinner Mother told my father that this Princess Zasekina seemed to her *une femme très vulgaire,* that she was very much fed up with her pleas to intercede for her with Prince Sergei, that she was involved in some sort of litigation and business dealings—*des vilaines affaires d'argent*—and that she must be a colossal intriguer. Mother added, however, that she had invited the princess and her daughter to dinner the next day (having heard the phrase "and her daughter," I buried my nose in my plate), because, after all, she was our neighbor—and with a name. In response to this my father informed Mother that he now remembered who this woman was: that when he was young he had known the late Prince Zasekin, a man excellently educated but empty-minded and cantankerous; that in society he was called *"le Parisien"* on account of his long residence in Paris; that he was very rich, but lost all his fortune; "and for some unknown reason, maybe even for money—however, he could have chosen better," my father added and smiled coldly—"married the daughter of some clerk, and, having married, began speculating—and ruined himself completely."

"Let's hope she won't ask to borrow money," Mother observed.

"Possibly she will," my father said calmly. "Does she speak French?"

"Very badly."

"Hm. However, it doesn't matter. I think you told me you invited her daughter too; somebody assured me that she's a very sweet and educated girl."

"Ah! Then she doesn't take after the mother."

"Nor the father," said my father. "He was educated, too—but stupid."

Mother sighed and became lost in thought. My father fell silent. I felt very awkward throughout this conversation.

After dinner I went out into the garden, but without my gun. I had just about sworn to myself not to go over to the "Zasekin garden," but an irresistible force lured me there—and not for nothing. I hadn't even come close to the fence when I caught sight of Zinaida. This time she was alone. She held a little book in her hands and was walking slowly along the path. She didn't notice me. I almost let her go by, but suddenly changed my mind and coughed.

She turned around but didn't stop. She brushed back the wide blue ribbon of her round straw hat with her hand, looked at me, calmly smiled, and again turned back to her book.

I took off my cap and, having hesitated a little where I stood, walked away with a heavy heart. *"Que suis je pour elle?"* I thought, (God knows why) in French.

I heard familiar footsteps behind me: I looked around—my father was coming toward me in his quick and easy gait.

"Is that the young princess?" he asked me.

"Yes, it is."

"Do you know her?"

"I saw her this morning at her mother's."

My father stopped—and, turning sharply on his heel, went back. Having caught up with Zinaida, he bowed to her politely. She greeted him in the manner, not without some amazement on her face, and lowered her book. I saw how she followed him with her eyes. My father always dressed very elegantly—strikingly yet simply; and he had never seemed to me more graceful, his grey hat had never sat more beautifully on his slightly thinning curly hair.

I was about to go over to Zinaida, but she didn't even glance at me. She raised her book again and moved away.

VI

I spent the whole evening and the following morning in a sort of despondent numbness. I remember I tried to work, and took up Kaidanov, but the scattered lines and the pages of the well-known textbook flashed before me meaninglessly. Ten times over I read the words: "Julius Caesar was distinguished for military courage"—I understood nothing and dropped the book. Before dinner I again pomaded my hair and again put on a coat and tie.

"What's this for?" Mother asked. "You're not a student yet, and

God knows if you'll pass the examination. And didn't you just get your jacket? Don't throw it away."

"Guests are coming," I whispered, almost in despair.

"Nonsense! What sort of guests are they!"

I had to give in. I changed from my coat into the jacket, but I didn't take off my tie. The princess and her daughter appeared half-hour before dinner; the old woman had thrown a yellow shawl over the green dress which I had seen, and had put on an old-fashioned cap with fiery-colored ribbons. She immediately started talking about her debts, sighed, complained about her poverty, whined, and didn't put on "company manners" at all. She snuffed tobacco just as loudly as ever, turned around and wriggled in her chair just as freely. It never seemed to occur to her that she was a princess. Zinaida, on the other hand, was very reserved, almost haughty, like a real princess. An expression of cold immobility and arrogance came over her face—I could hardly recognize her, the way she looked at me, her smile—although even in this new aspect she seemed to me beautiful. She had on a light wool dress with a royal-blue design; her hair fell in long ringlets down along her cheeks, in the English style; this hairdo went with the cold expression on her face. My father sat beside her during dinner and, with his own particular elegant and tranquil courtesy, entertained his neighbor. From time to time he looked at her—and from time to time she looked at him; but so strangely, almost hostilely. Their conversation was in French; the pureness of Zinaida's pronunciation, I remember, surprised me. During dinner, the princess, as before, letting herself go, ate a good deal, and praised the meal. Mother obviously found her heavy going, and replied to her with a sort of sad scorn; my father sometimes frowned very slightly.

Mother didn't like Zinaida, either. "She's a high-stepper," she said the next day. "And high about what—*avec sa mine de grisette!*"

"Clearly you've never seen a *grisette*," my father pointed out to her. "And thank God!"

"Of course, thank God—only how can you judge them?"

Zinaida paid me absolutely no attention. Soon after dinner the princess started saying good-bye.

"I'll hope for your support, Maria Nikolayevna and Pyotr

Vasilevich,"she said in a singsong voice to Mother and Father. "But what can you do! There was a time, but it's gone. And here I am—an illustrious lady," she added with an unpleasant laugh, "but where's the honor if there's nothing to eat!"

My father bowed to her respectfully and escorted her to the door of the vestibule. I stood there in my short jacket and stared at the floor, as if sentenced to death. Zinaida's treatment of me had crushed me completely. What, then, was my astonishment when, going by me, she whispered to me hastily and with the previous tender expression in her eyes, "Come to our house at eight, do you hear? Without fail…" I just threw up my hands—but she had already left, having thrown a white scarf over her head.

VII

Exactly at eight o'clock, in a frock coat and with my hair brushed up in front, I entered the vestibule of the little wing where the princess lived. The old servant looked at me glumly and reluctantly got up from his bench. Gay voices could be heard in the living room. I opened the door—and stepped back in amazement. In the middle of the room, the young princess stood on a chair, holding a man's hat in front of her; five men were crowded around the chair. They were trying to thrust their hands into the hat, but she was raising it higher and shaking it hard. Having caught sight of me, she cried out, "Stop, stop! A new guest; we have to give him a slip, too." And she jumped lightly down from the chair and took me by the cuff of my coat. "Come on," she said, "why are you standing here? Messieurs, allow me to introduce you: this is Monsieur Voldemar, our neighbor's son. And this," she added, turning to me and pointing to the guests one by one, "is Count Malevski, Doctor Lushin, the poet Maidanov, Captain Nirmatski,retired, and Belovzorov, a hussar, whom you've seen already. I beg you join together."

I was so embarrassed that I didn't even bow to anyone; I recognized Doctor Lushin as that same swarthy gentleman who had so pitilessly put me to shame in the garden; the rest I didn't know.

"Count!" Zinaida continued, "write out a slip for Monsieur Voldemar."

"That's unfair," said the count, with a slight Polish accent. He was a very handsome and modishly dressed dark-haired man, with expressive brown eyes, a thin white little nose and an elegant little moustache over a tiny mouth. "He didn't play forfeits with us."

"Unfair," echoed Belovzorov and the gentleman called the retired captain, a man of about forty, pockmarked to the point of deformity, as curly-haired as a Negro, round-shouldered, bowlegged, and dressed in an unbuttoned military coat without epaulettes.

"Write out a slip, as you were told," the young princess repeated. "What sort of rebellion is this? Monsieur Voldemar has joined us for the first time, and today the rules don't apply to him. There's no point in grumbling, write it out; that's how I want it."

The count shrugged his shoulders; but, bowing his head obediently, he picked up a pen in his white hand adorned with rings, tore off a scrap of paper, and began writing on it.

"At least let me explain to Mr. Voldemar what it's all about," Lushin began in a mocking voice, "for he's completely lost. You see, young man, we're playing forfeits; the princess has to pay the penalty—and the one who pulls out the lucky slip has the right of kissing her hand...Did you understand what I told you?"

I merely looked at him and continued standing there as if dazed, but the princess again jumped up on the chair and again began shaking the hat. Everyone reached out toward her—I with the others.

"Maidanov," said the princess to a tall young man with a lean face, little dead eyes, and extraordinarily long, black hair, "you, as a poet, must be magnanimous and give up your slip to Monsieur Voldemar, so he'll have two chances instead of one."

But Maidanov shook his head and tossed his hair back. I thrust my hand into the hat after all the rest, took out a slip, and unfolded it...My Lord, what happened inside me when I saw on it the word: *kiss!*

"Kiss!" I shouted involuntarily.

"Bravo! He won!" the princess joined in. "How glad I am!" She got down from the chair and looked into my eyes so brightly and sweetly that my heart leaped. "And are you glad?" she asked me.

"Me?" I stammered.

"Sell me your slip," Belovzorov suddenly blurted out beside my ear. "I'll give you hundred rubles."

I answered the hussar with such an indignant look that Zinaida clapped her hands together and Lushin shouted, "Well done!"

"But," he continued, "as master of ceremonies, I must see that all the rules are obeyed. Monsieur Voldemar, kneel down! That's the way we do it."

Zinaida stood in front of me, tilted her head a little to the side—as if the better to look me over—and grandly extended me her hand. My eyes became blurred; I meant to kneel down on one knee but I fell onto both—and I touched Zinaida's fingers with my lips so awkwardly that I lightly scratched the end of my nose on her nail.

"Good enough!" cried Lushin, and helped me get up.

The game of forfeits continued. Zinaida had me sit down beside herself. What penalties she thought up! She suddenly decided, among other things, to be a "statue"—and she chose as her pedestal the ugly Nirmatski, ordered him to lie flat, and even to tuck his chin into his chest. The laughter did not die down for a single moment. All this noise and racket, this too familiar, almost wild gaiety, these fantastic dealings with people I had never met before—all went to my head—me, a solitarily and soberly educated boy brought up in a staid, noble household. I simply got drunk, as if from wine. I began to laugh and chatter louder than the others—so that even the old princess, who had been sitting in the next room with some clerk from the Iverskie Gate called in for consultation, came out to look at me. But I felt so happy that I didn't care—and didn't give a hoot about anybody's gibes or anybody's sidelong glances.

Zinaida kept on showing preference for me and did not let me leave her. For one penalty, I had to sit right beside her, both us under one silk kerchief, and I had to tell her *my secret*. I remember how both our heads were suddenly in a stifling, semi-transparent, fragrant haze, how her eyes shone near and softly in that haze, and her parted lips breathed hotly, and her teeth gleamed, and the ends of her hair tickled and singed me. I kept quiet; she smiled mysteriously and slyly, and finally whispered to me: "Well?" but I only blushed and laughed and turned away, and could hardly breathe.

Forfeits bored us; we began playing hands-on-the-string. My God! What ecstasy I felt when, not paying attention, I got a strong, sharp blow on my fingers— afterwards I tried to pretend I was staring vacantly, but she teased me and would not touch my preferred hands!

What else didn't we do in the course of that evening! We played the piano, too, and sang and danced and pretended we were gypsies. Nirmatski was dressed up as bear and given salted water to drink. Count Malevski showed us different card tricks and finished up, having shuffled the cards, by dealing himself a whist hand with all the trumps—for which Lushin "had the honor of congratulating him." Maidanov recited excerpts from his poem "The Murderer" (the thing was in the height of romanticism), which he intended publishing in a black cover with the letters of the title the color of blood. The clerk from the Iverskie Gate had his hat stolen off his knees— and they made him, as ransom, dance a kazachok. Old Vonifati was decked out in a woman's little cap, and the young princess put on a man's hat…There was no end to it. Belovzorov, alone, frowning and annoyed, stayed mostly in the corner. Sometimes his eyes became bloodshot, he grew flushed, and it seemed as if he were right then and there going to rush at us and scatter us, like chips, all around. But the young princess would look at him, wag her finger at him, and he would hide in his corner again.

We finally ran out of energy. The princess was, as she herself would say, ready for anything—no shouting dismayed her; but even she felt fatigue and asked for a rest. Supper was served at midnight and consisted of a piece of old, dry cheese, and some sort of cold pirozhki with diced ham, which seemed to me tastier than any pâté. There was only one bottle of wine, and a strange one at that: dark, with a distended neck, and the wine in it tasted of pink coloring; nobody drank it, though. Tired and happy to exhaustion, I left the wing. Saying good-bye, Zinaida squeezed my hand tightly and again smiled enigmatically.

The night brushed heavily and damply against my flushed face. A storm seemed to be coming up. The black clouds grew bigger and bigger and crawled across the sky, visibly changing their smoky outlines. A light air restively shivered in the dark trees, and somewhere far off beyond the horizon, thunder growled angrily and hollowly, as if to itself.

I went to my room by way of the back entrance. My valet was asleep on the floor, and I had to step over him. He woke up, saw me, and informed me that my mother had become angry and again had wanted to send someone after me, but that my father had restrained her. (I never went to bed without saying good night to my mother and without asking her blessing.) There was nothing to be done about it!

I told my valet that I would undress and get to bed myself—and blew out the candle...But I didn't undress, and I didn't lie down.

I sat down in a chair and stayed there a long time, as if enchanted... What I felt was so new and so sweet. I sat there hardly looking around and not stirring, breathing slowly, and only from time to time either laughing silently, remembering, or going all cold inside at the thought that I had fallen in love, that this was it, that this was my love. Zinaida's face calmly swam in front of me in the dark— swam before me but not by—her lips still smiled enigmatically, her eyes looked at me a little from one side, questioningly, thoughtfully, and tenderly, as at the moment when I left her. Finally I got up, tiptoed over to my bed, and carefully, without undressing, laid my head down on the pillow, as if afraid of alarming by a sudden movement all that filled me.

I lay down but didn't even close my eyes. Soon I noticed that some sort of pale reflections were continually falling into my room. I raised myself up and looked out the window. The mullions stood out distinctly from the mysteriously, vaguely whitened panes. A storm, I thought—and indeed, there was a storm, but it was passing very far away, so that you could not even hear the thunder; only faint, long, forked lightning was continually flashing in the sky: it did not flash so much as it trembled and twitched like the wing of a dying bird. I got up, went over to the window, and stood there until morning.

The lightning did not stop for a moment; it was, as the peasants say, a *vorobinaya noch*.[1] I looked out at the silent sandy field, at the dark mass of Neskuchnyi Park, at the yellowish façades of the distant buildings, which also seemed to quiver at each pale flash. I kept looking—and could not tear myself away. This silent lightning, this restrained brilliance, it seemed, was responding to those silent and secret bursts which were flashing in me, too. It began to get light; the dawn came in vermilion patches. With the approach of the sun the lightning grew paler and died down: it quivered less and less often and finally disappeared, flooded out by the sobering, certain light of the rising day...

And the lightning in me disappeared too. I felt great fatigue and peace—but the image of Zinaida continued to hover, triumphantly, before my mind's eye. Only it itself—this image—seemed to have been assuaged: like a swan that has flown up from the marsh grass, it separated itself from the other unattractive figures around it, and I, falling asleep, clung to it in parting and trustful adoration...

O, intimate feelings, soft sounds, the goodness and calm of the heart that has been moved, the languishing joy of the first tender emotions of love—where are you, where are you?

VIII

The next morning when I went down to breakfast, Mother scolded me—less, however, than I had expected—and made me tell her how I had spent the evening before. I answered her in few words, leaving out many details and trying to give it all as innocent an appearance as possible.

"Still, they're not *comme il faut*," Mother remarked, "and there's no point in your tagging after them instead of studying and preparing for your examination."

Since I knew that Mother's concern over what I did would be limited to these few words, I didn't think I had to protest; but after breakfast my father took me by the arm, and, having gone out into

---

1   A night of continual summer lightning.

the garden with me, made me tell him everything I had seen at the Zasekins'.

My father had a strange influence on me—and our relations were strange. He hardly bothered about my up-bringing, but never insulted my feelings; he respected my freedom. He was even, if I may put it this way, courteous to me—only he did not let me get close to him. I loved him, I loved to look at him and admire him; he seemed to me the perfect man—and, my God, how passionately I would have become attached to him if I hadn't continually felt his rejecting hand! However, when he wanted to, he know how to arouse in me, almost instantaneously, by word, by gesture, unlimited confidence in himself. My heart would open up—I would chat away with him the way you would with an intelligent friend, with an indulgent tutor. And then he would just as suddenly leave me; his hand would again push me away—tenderly and gently, but push me away.

Sometimes he was in a gay mood—and then he was like a little boy, ready for horseplay and fun with me (he liked all violent bodily movement). Once—only once!—he caressed me with such tenderness I almost cried. But his gaiety, even, and his tenderness disappeared without a trace—and what had gone on between us gave me no hope for the future—as if it all had happened in a dream. Sometimes I would start studying his intelligent, handsome, shining face...my heart would give a shudder, and my whole being would yearn for him. As if he sensed what was going on in me, he would pat me on the cheek as he passed—and either go out, or get busy with something, suddenly all stiff, as only he knew how to, and I would quickly shrink into myself and grow cold, too. The rare fits of his affection for me were never provoked by my wordless but obvious supplication; they always came unexpectedly. Subsequently thinking about my father's character, I have come to the conclusion that he had no concern for me—or for family life; he liked something else and took pleasure in that completely. "Take what you can yourself, but don't yield to anyone. To belong to yourself—that's the whole trick in life," he told me once. Another time, in his presence, I, a young democrat, launched into a discussion of freedom (that day he was, as I used to call it, "good"; at such times you could talk to him about anything you wanted)…"Freedom," he repeated, "but do you know what can give man freedom?"

"What?"

"Will, his own will, and it gives power, too, which is better than freedom. Know how to desire—and you'll be free, and you'll be in command."

First of all and most of all, my father desired life…and he lived. Perhaps he had a foreboding that he would not enjoy "the trick" of life for long; he died at forty-two.

I told my father in detail about my visit to the Zasekins'. He listened to me half attentively, half absent-mindedly, sitting on a bench and drawing in the sand with the end of his riding crop. Now and then he chuckled, glanced at me in a rather bright and amused way—and egged me on with little questions and retorts. At first I didn't dare even mention Zinaida's name, but I could not hold back and began to extol her. My father kept right on chuckling. Then he became meditative, stretched, and got up.

I remembered that, as he was leaving the house, he had ordered his horse saddled. He was an excellent rider—and, long before Mr. Rarey, could tame the wildest horses.

"Am I going with you, Papa?" I asked him.

"No," he answered, and his face took on its usual, indifferently kind expression. "Go by yourself, if you want; but tell the coachman I'm not going."

He turned his back on me and went away quickly. I followed him with my eyes—he disappeared beyond the gate. I saw how his hat moved along the fence; he went in to the Zasekins'.

He stayed at their place somewhat less than an hour, but then immediately set out for town and returned home only toward evening.

After dinner, I myself went to the Zasekins'. I found the old princess alone in the living room. Having caught sight of me, she scratched her head under her little cap with the end of a knitting needle and suddenly asked me if I could copy out just one petition for her.

"I'd be glad to," I replied, and sat down on the edge of a chair.

"Only be careful, make the letters neat and big," the princess said, handing me a soiled sheet of paper. "And couldn't it be today, my dear?"

"I'll do it today, ma'am."

The door of the next room was opened just a crack—and Zinaida's face appeared in the opening—pale, pensive, with her hair thrown back carelessly. She looked at me with big cold eyes and quietly shut the door.

"Zina!—oh, Zina!" the old woman said. Zinaida did not respond. I took the old woman's petition home and sat over it all evening.

IX

My "passion" dates from that day. I remember I then felt something like what a man must feel who has taken a job: I had stopped being simply a young boy; I was a man in love. I said that my passion dates from that day; I could add that my sufferings, too, date from that same day. I pined away in Zinaida's absence: I couldn't concentrate on anything, nothing went well, and for whole days I thought about her intensely. I was pining away...but in her presence it was no easier. I was jealous, I acknowledged my own worthlessness, I stupidly sulked—and stupidly fawned on her; and still, an insuperable force drew me to her—and I stepped across the threshold of her room every time with an involuntary tremor of happiness. Zinaida quickly guessed that I had fallen in love with her, and, indeed, I never thought of hiding it. She was amused at my passion, made a fool of me, petted and tortured me. It is sweet to be the single source, the despotic and capricious cause of another's greatest joys and deepest grief—and in Zinaida's hands I was like soft wax. Besides, it was not only I who had fallen in love with her: all the men who visited her house doted on her, and she kept them all on a leash—at her feet. She was amused by exciting sometimes their hope, sometimes their apprehension, and by twisting them around her little finger as she fancied (she called this "knocking people together"), but they never even dreamed of resisting and willingly submitted to her. In all her essential being, with its great vitality and beauty, there was some especially fascinating mixture of slyness and carelessness, of artificiality and simplicity, of calmness and sportiveness; a subtle, facile charm emanated from all she did or said, from her every movement; and everything expressed her peculiar, playful power. Her face was constantly changing, playing, also; it would express, almost at one and the same time, mockery, thoughtfulness, passion. The most diverse feelings, light and flitting, like the shadows of clouds on a sunny, windy day, ran continually back and forth across her eyes and lips.

She needed each of her admirers. Belovzorov, whom she sometimes called "my wild animal" and sometimes simply "my own," would have willingly thrown himself into fire for her. Putting no stock in his own intellectual abilities and other qualities, he kept suggesting that she marry him, hinting that the rest were merely talking. Maidanov responded to the poetic strings of her heart: a rather cold man, like almost all authors, he strenuously assured her, and perhaps even himself, that he worshiped her, sang of her in never-ending verses, and read them to her with a sort of unnatural yet sincere enthusiasm. She both sympathized with him and lightly made fun of him. She trusted him little and, after having heard a lot of his outpourings, would make him read Pushkin, in order, as she put it, to clear the air. Lushin, a derisive, seemingly cynical doctor, knew her better than the others—and loved her more than any of them, although he criticized her behind her back and to her face. She respected him but did not give in to him—and sometimes, with a particular, gloating pleasure would make him feel that he, too, was in her hands. "I'm a flirt, I have no heart, I'm an actress by nature," she told him once in my presence. "Well, all right! So put out your hand, I'll stick a pin in it, and you'll be ashamed in front of this young man; it will hurt you, but still you, Mr. Upright Man, will laugh." Lushin flushed, turned away, bit his lip, but ended up by putting out his hand. She pricked him, and he indeed began to laugh…and she laughed, thrusting the pin in rather deep and peering into his eyes, which he was vainly turning from side to side…

I understood the relationship that existed between Zinaida and

Count Malevski least of all. He was good-looking, clever, and intelligent; but even to me, a sixteen-year-old boy, there seemed something shady, something false in him, and I was astounded that Zinaida did not notice it. Perhaps, indeed, she did and had no aversion to it. Improper upbringing, strange friendships and habits, the constant presence of her mother, poverty and disorder in the house—everything, beginning with the very freedom which the young girl enjoyed, with her consciousness of her superiority to the people around her, had developed a sort of half-contemptuous carelessness and easy-goingness. No matter what had happened—if Vonifati came in to announce there was no sugar, if some stupid piece of gossip came to light, if the guests started arguing—she would only shake her curls and say: "It's nothing!"—and think no more about it.

On the other hand, all my blood would boil when Malevski would go up to her, swaying slyly like a fox, lean elegantly on the back of her chair, and begin whispering in her ear with a self-satisfied and ingratiating smile. She would fold her arms, look at him intently, and smile too, and shake her head.

"How is it that you want to have Mr. Malevski here?" I asked her once.

"But he has such a pretty little moustache," she replied. "Besides, that's not in your line."

"You don't think I love him, do you?" she said to me another time. "No; I can't love people I have to look down on. I need a man who would tame me…But I hope I never run into such a man, God willing! I never want to fall into anyone's clutches, never!"

"Therefore, you'll never love anyone?"

"And you, now? Don't I love you?" she said, and struck my nose with the tip of her glove.

Yes, Zinaida made fun of me a great deal. In the course of three weeks I saw her every day—and what she didn't do to me! She came to our place rarely, and I didn't regret it: in our house she turned into a young lady, into a young princess—and I shunned her. I was afraid of giving myself away in front of Mother; she didn't look on Zinaida favorably at all and kept a hostile eye on us. I wasn't so afraid of my father: he seemed not to notice me and talked little to Zinaida, though when he did, it seemed especially clever and meaningful. I stopped studying and reading—I even stopped walking around the neighborhood and going riding. Like a beetle tethered by a leg, I spun continually around the adored little wing; I would, I think, have stayed there forever. But that was impossible, Mother grumbled at me, and sometimes Zinaida herself chased me away. Then I would lock myself in my room or go down to the very end of the garden, clamber up the ruins of a high, stone greenhouse, and, dangling my legs over the wall facing the road, would sit for hours and look and look, not seeing anything. Beside me, white butter flies fluttered lazily over dust-covered nettles; a pert sparrow landed nearby on a half-broken red brick and chirped irritably, incessantly turning around and spreading his tail; still suspicious crows cawed from time to time, sitting high, high up on the bare top of a birch; the sun and wind played quietly in among its sparse branches; the sound of the bells of the Donskoi Monastery came across the air intermittently, peaceful and sad. And I went on sitting, looking, listening—and became filled with some nameless sensation in which there was everything: sadness, and joy, and a premonition of the future, and desire, and the fear of life. But I didn't then understand any of this, and couldn't have put a name to any of the things that were fermenting in me—or I would have called them all by one name—the name of Zinaida.

And Zinaida kept on playing with me, like a cat with a mouse. Sometimes she would flirt with me—and I would get excited and melt; and sometimes she would suddenly push me away—and then I didn't dare get near her, didn't dare glance at her.

I remember she was very cold to me for several days in a row. I became completely timid—and apprehensively running over to the wing to their place, tried to keep near the old princess, despite the fact that she was shouting and scolding just at that time. The business with her debts was going badly, and she had already had two disputes with the district policeman.

Once I was walking in the garden past that special fence, and caught sight of Zinaida; leaning back on both arms, she was sitting on the grass, not moving. I was about to go away cautiously; but she suddenly raised her head and made a peremptory sign to me. I froze on the spot: I didn't understand her at first. She repeated the sign. I immediately jumped over the fence and joyfully ran toward her; but she stopped me with a glance and motioned me to the path two steps from her. In embarrassment, not knowing what to do, I knelt down on the edge of the path. She was so pale, such bitter sorrow, such grave fatigue showed in her every feature that my heart was wrung—and I involuntarily mumbled: "What's wrong?"

Zinaida stretched out her hand, picked a blade of grass, bit it, and threw it to one side.

"Do you love me very much?" she asked finally. "Do you?" I made no reply—indeed, what could have replied?

"You do," she said, looking at me as she used to. "It's true. The same eyes," she added very thoughtfully, and covered her face with her hands. "I'm sick of all," she whispered; "if only I could go to the end of the world. I can't bear this, can't cope with it…And What's ahead for me?…Oh, I'm miserable…my God, how miserable!"

"But why?" I asked timidly.

Zinaida didn't answer me but only shrugged her shoulders. I continued to kneel and look at her in bleak despondency. Her every word cut me to the quick. At that moment, it seemed, I would have willingly given up my life if only she would not grieve. I looked at her—and though not understanding why she was miserable, I vividly imagined how she suddenly, in a fit of irrepressible sorrow, had gone out into the garden and fallen on the ground as if shot. It was bright and green all around: the wind was rustling in the leaves of the trees, from time to time shaking a long branch of the raspberry bush over Zinaida's head. Pigeons were cooing somewhere, and bees were buzzing, flying low over the thin grass. Overhead the sky was a gentle blue—but I was so sad…

"Recite some poetry to me," Zinaida said in a low voice, and leaned on her elbow. "I like it when you recite poetry. You chant it, but that doesn't matter—it's because you're young. Recite 'On the Georgian Hills.' Only sit down first."

I sat down and recited "On the Georgian Hills."

"'It cannot help but be in love,'" Zinaida repeated. "That's what's good about poetry: it tells us about what doesn't exist and what's not only better than what does exist, but even more like the truth. It cannot help—but be in love'—and would like to, but cannot!" She fell silent again, and then suddenly shook herself and got up. "Let's go. Maidanov is with Mama; he brought me his poem, and I've left him. He's chagrined now, too…but what can you do! You'll find out sometime—only don't get angry with me!"

Zinaida hurriedly pressed my hand and ran on ahead. We went back to the wing. Maidanov started reading us his just-published "The Murderer," but I didn't listen to him. He shouted out his iambic tetrameters in a sing-song voice—the rhymes alternated and rang out like bells, hollowly and loudly. I kept looking at Zinaida and trying to understand the meaning of her last words.

> "Or, maybe, some clandestine rival
> Has won you unexpectedly?"

Maidanov suddenly exclaimed through his nose—and my eyes and Zinaida's met. She lowered hers and blushed slightly. I noticed the blush and grew cold from fright. I had been jealous about her before—but only in that moment did the thought that she had fallen in love flash through my head. "My God! She's fallen in love!"

X

My real torment set in from that moment. I racked my brains, pondered, changed my mind and, relentlessly, although as secretly as possible, kept my eye on Zinaida. A change had occurred in her—that was clear. She went out walking alone, and walked for a long time. Sometimes she didn't show up for her guests; for whole hours she would sit by herself in her room. This hadn't happened with her before. I had suddenly become—or it seemed to me I had become—extraordinarily astute. "Is it he, or isn't it?" I kept asking myself, my mind running anxiously from one to another of her admirers. Count Malevski (although I was ashamed to admit it for Zinaida's sake) secretly seemed to me more dangerous than the rest.

My keenness of observation saw no farther than the end of my nose, and my secrecy, probably, fooled no one. Doctor Lushin, at least, soon saw through me. Besides, he, too, had changed lately: he had grown thin; he laughed as often but somehow more hollowly, more maliciously, and more abruptly—an involuntary, neurotic irritability replaced his former light irony and affected cynicism.

"Why do you keep constantly hanging around here, young man?" he said to me once, left alone with me in the Zasekins' living room. (The young princess had not yet come back from a walk, and the shrill voice of the old princess resounded from the attic—she was having a row with her maid.) "You ought to be studying, doing your work, while you're young—but you—what do you do?"

"You can't know whether or not I work at home," I protested, not without haughtiness, but not without embarrassment either.

"What do you mean, work! That's not what's on your mind. Well, I won't argue. At your age it's the way things go. But your choice is hardly apt. Don't you really see what kind of house this is?"

"I don't understand you," I replied.

"Don't understand? So much the worse for you. I take it as my duty to warn you. Old bachelors like me can come here: what can happen to us? We're a hardened bunch, there's no way of getting at us; but you've still got tender skin. The air here is bad for you—believe me, you can get infected."

"How so?"

"Just like that. Are you really well right now? Are you really normal? Really, is what you feel—useful for you, good for you?"

"But what do I feel?" I said, though I admitted inside me that the doctor was right.

"Ah, young man, young man," the doctor went on with an expression as though there were something terribly shameful to me in those two words, "how can you be crafty? Because, still, thank God, what's in your heart is on your face. But why explain! I wouldn't be coming here myself, if" (the doctor clenched his teeth) "—if I weren't just such an odd ball. Only what surprises me is—how is it that you, with your intelligence, don't see what's going on around you?"

"But what is going on?" I asked, and became all attention.

The doctor looked at me with a sort of derisive pity.

"I'm a good one myself," he said, as if to himself; "a lot of need there is to tell him this. In short," he added, raising his voice, "I repeat: the atmosphere here is not suitable for you. You like it here—but you don't know the half of it! It smells nice in a greenhouse, too—but you can't live in it. Now, listen to me, take up Kaidanov again."

The old princess came in and started complaining to the doctor about a toothache. Then Zinaida appeared.

"Here, doctor," the old princess added, "give her a talking-to. She drinks ice water all day long. Is this good for her, with her weak chest?"

"Why do you do it?" Lushin asked.

"But what can happen?"

"What? You can catch a cold and die."

"Really? Is that so? Well, so what?—it would serve me right."

"That's so," the doctor muttered. The old princess left the room.

"That's so," Zinaida repeated. "Is life so enjoyable? Look around you…Well—is it good? Or do you think I don't understand this, don't feel it? It gives me pleasure—drinking ice water. And you can gravely assure me that such a life is worth not being risked for a moment's pleasure—I'm not talking about happiness."

"Yes, of course," Lushin remarked, "whim and independence— these two words completely sum you up. Your whole nature is in these two words."

Zinaida laughed nervously.

"You've missed the boat, my dear doctor. You observe badly— you're behind the times. Put your glasses on. I'm not interested in whims now. To make a fool of you, a fool myself—how enjoyable that is; and as for independence…Monsieur Voldemar," Zinaida suddenly added, and stamped her foot, "don't pull a long face. I can't stand when people feel sorry for me." She went out quickly.

"It's bad, bad for you, the atmosphere here, young man," Lushin told me again.

XI

The usual guests collected at the Zasekins' that same evening; I was among them.

The conversation started off on Maidanov's poem; Zinaida frankly praised it. "But, you know what?" she said to him. "If were poet, I'd choose different subjects. Maybe it's all silly, but sometimes get strange ideas, especially when I'm lying awake before dawn, when the sky begins to get pink and grey. For example, I'd—You won't laugh at me?"

"No! No!" we all shouted at once.

"I'd describe," she continued, folding her arms and turning her eyes aside, "a whole company of young girls, at night, in a big boat—on a quiet stream. The moon's shining, and they're all in white and in wreaths of white flowers, and they're singing—you know, something like a hymn."

"I understand, understand, go on," said Maidanov meaningfully and dreamily.

"Suddenly, there's an uproar, laughter, torches, tambourines on the shore. It's a crowd of Bacchantes running, and singing and shouting. And now it's your job to paint the picture, Mr. Poet…only I want the torches to be red and very smoky, and the Bacchantes' eyes to shine under their wreaths, but the wreaths must be dark. Also, don't forget the tiger skins and the goblets—and the gold, a lot of gold."

"And where's there supposed to be gold?" Maidanov asked, tossing his straight hair back and opening his nostrils wide.

"Where? On their shoulders, on their arms, on their legs, everywhere. They say that in olden times women wore gold rings on their ankles. The Bacchantes call the girls in the boat over to them. The girls have stopped singing their hymn—they can't go on—but they don't move. The river carries them to the shore. And suddenly one of them quietly stands up. This has to be described carefully: how she quietly stands up in the moonlight and how her friends are frightened…She has stepped over the side of the boat, the Bacchantes surround her; they flee into the night, into the darkness…Now you show clouds of smoke, and everything in confusion. You can hear only their screams, and her wreath is left on the shore."

Zinaida stopped talking. (Oh! She's fallen in love! crossed my mind again.)

"And that's all?" Maidanov asked.

"That's all," she replied.

"That can't be the subject of a whole epic," he remarked pompously, "but I'll use your idea for a little lyric."

"In the romantic style?" Malevski asked.

"Of course, in the romantic style, like Byron."

"But I think Hugo is better than Byron," the young count said casually; "more interesting."

"Hugo's a first-rate writer," Maidanov said, "and my friend Tonkosheyev, in his Spanish novel *El Trovador*—"

"Oh, is that the book with the upside-down question marks?" Zinaida interrupted.

"Yes, that's how the Spanish do it. I wanted to say that Tonkosheyev—"

"Well! You're arguing again about classicism and romanticism," Zinaida interrupted a second time. "Instead, let's play—"

"Forfeits?" Lushin cut in.

"No, forfeits is boring; similes." (Zinaida herself had invented this game: some object was named, everybody tried to compare it to something else, and the one who chose the best simile got the prize.) She went over to the window. The sun had just gone down; long, red clouds hung high in the sky.

"What are those clouds like?" Zinaida asked, and without waiting for our response, said: "I find them like those purple sails on Cleopatra's golden ship when she went to meet Antony. Remember, Maidanov, you told me about it not long ago?"

All of us, like Polonius in *Hamlet,* decided that the clouds reminded us exactly of those sails and that none of us could find a better simile.

"And how old was Antony then?" Zinaida asked.

"Most likely he was a young man," Malevski remarked. "Yes, young," Maidanov confirmed convincingly.

"Excuse me," Lushin exclaimed, "he was over forty."

"Over forty," Zinaida repeated, glancing at him quickly.

I soon went home. "She's fallen in love," my lips involuntarily whispered..."But with whom?"

XII

Days went by. Zinaida became more and more strange, more and more incomprehensible. Once I went into her room and saw her sitting in a wicker chair with her head bent down against the sharp edge of the table. She straightened up...her whole face was covered with tears.

"Oh! It's you!" she said with a cruel and ironic smile.

"Come on over here."

I went over to her: she put her hand on my head and, all of a sudden, having grabbed my hair, began twisting it.

"That hurts," I finally said.

"Oh! That hurts! But doesn't it hurt me? Doesn't it?" she repeated. "Oh!" she cried suddenly, seeing she had pulled out a little lock of hair. "What have I done? Poor Monsieur Voldemar."

She carefully smoothed out the plucked-out hair, wound it around her finger and rolled it into a little ring.

"I'll put your hair in my locket—and I'll wear it," she said; and her eyes were still all shiny with tears. "That, maybe, will comfort you a little...and now, good-bye."

I went back home and there ran into trouble. Mother and my father were having it out: she had reproached him for something, and he, as he usually did, coldly and politely said nothing—and soon left. I couldn't hear what Mother was talking about, and besides I didn't care; I remember only that, at the end of the conversation, she ordered me called into her study and with great displeasure talked of my frequent visits to the princess, who, according to her, was *une femme capable de tout.* I went over and kissed her hand—I always did this when I wanted to stop a conversation—and went to my room. Zinaida's tears had completely knocked me off balance; I had no idea where to start thinking, and was myself ready to cry: I still was a child, despite being sixteen.

I no longer thought about Malevski, although Belovzorov became more and more threatening every day and looked at the shifty count like a wolf at a ram; indeed, I didn't think about anything or anyone. I kept getting lost in reflection and always looked for lonely places. I especially liked the greenhouse ruins. I would climb up the high wall, sit down, and stay there such an unhappy, lonely, and sad young boy that I'd start feeling sorry for myself—and how gratifying these feelings of grief were for me, how I reveled in them!

Once, as I was sitting on the wall, looking into the distance and listening to the peal of the bells, something suddenly passed over me—not a breeze, not a shiver, but something like a puff, like sense of somebody's presence. I looked down. Below, on the road, in a light grey dress, Zinaida was hurrying along with a pink parasol on her shoulders. She caught sight of me, stopped, and, having raised the brim of her straw hat, looked up at me with her velvet eyes.

"What are you doing there, up so high?" she asked me with a rather strange smile. "Here," she went on, "you keep saying you love me—jump down to me here on the road, if you really do."

Zinaida had hardly finished saying this when I was already flying down as if someone had pushed me from behind. The wall was about fourteen feet high. I landed on my feet, but the jolt was so strong that I couldn't control myself; I fell and, for a moment, passed out. When I came to, not opening my eyes, I felt Zinaida beside me. "My sweet little boy," she said, bending over me, and her voice had a tone of anxious tenderness, "how could you do this, how could you obey... You know I love you...get up."

Her breast was heaving close to mine, her hands touched my head, and suddenly—what happened to me then?—her soft, pure lips began to cover my whole face with kisses...they touched my lips...But just then Zinaida must have guessed, by the expression on my face, that I had already come to, although I still had not opened my eyes—and, having stood up quickly, she said, "Now get up, you imp, you madman. What are you lying the dirt for?" I got up.

"Hand me my parasol," said Zinaida; "look where I threw it! And

don't stare at me like that...how stupid! You didn't get hurt? Just
stung by the nettles, I imagine. Don't look at me, I told you...Why,
he doesn't understand a thing, doesn't answer at all," she added, as if
to herself. "Go on home, Monsieur Voldemar, clean up—and don't
dare follow me or I'll get cross, and never again..."

She didn't finish what she was saying but walked off quickly and I
sat down the road. My legs wouldn't hold me. The nettles had stung
my hands, my back ached, and my head was spinning—but the feeling of bliss which I experienced then never occurred again in my
life. It lay like a sweet pain throughout my whole body and ended in
excited jumping up and down and shouting. Yes, indeed, I was still
a child.

XIII

I was so proud and cheerful that whole day, I kept on my face the
feeling of Zinaida's kisses so vividly—I remembered her every word
with such a shiver of delight—I so cherished my unexpected happiness—that I became terrified, I didn't even want to see her, the
one who was the cause of these new sensations. It seemed to me
that there was nothing more to ask of fate—that now it was time
"to collect myself, take a last deep breath, and die." However, on the
next day, setting out for the wing, I felt great embarrassment, which
I vainly tried to hide behind a mask of unpretentious familiarity, as
becoming in a man who wants to show that he knows how keep a
secret. Zinaida received me very simply, without to any excitement—
just shook her finger at me and asked if I didn't have some black-
and-blue spots. All my unpretentious familiarity and secretiveness
disappeared in a second, and along with them, my embarrassment.
Of course, I didn't expect anything special, but Zinaida's calmness
was like a bucket of cold water on me. I understood that in her eyes
I was a child—and I felt very miserable! Zinaida walked back and
forth in the room, smiling curtly each time she glanced at me—but
her thoughts were far away; I saw that clearly. "Maybe I should start
talking about yesterday myself," I thought; "ask her where she was

going in such a hurry, in order to find out once and for all…" but I gave it up as hopeless and sat down in a corner.

Belovzorov came in. I was glad to see him.

"I didn't find you a saddle horse, a gentle one," he started out in a gruff voice. "Freitag swears by one, but I'm not sure. I'm afraid."

"What are you afraid of," said Zinaida, "if I may ask?"

"What of? Why, you don't know how to ride. God knows what may happen! And what a crazy idea to have suddenly gotten into your head!"

"Well, that's my business, my dear Monsieur Wild-Animal. In that case, I'll ask Pyotr Vasilich. (My father was called Pyotr Vasilich. I was surprised that she dropped his name so freely and easily, as if she were sure of his readiness to do her a favor.)

"Really," Belovzorov retorted. "It's *him* you want to go riding with?"

"With him—or someone else—it makes no difference to you. Only not with you."

"Not with me," Belovzorov repeated. "As you wish. Why not? I'll get you a horse."

"Only be sure it's not an old cow. I give you advance notice I want to gallop."

"Gallop if you want. Who'll you be going with—Malevski, probably?"

"And why not with him, you warrior? Oh, calm down," she added, "and don't flash your eyes. I'll take you too. You know what Malevski means to me now—fie!" She shook her head.

"You say that to console me," Belovzorov muttered.

Zinaida screwed up her eyes. "That consoles you? Oh…oh…oh… you warrior!" she finally said, as if unable to find another word. "And you, Monsieur Voldemar, would you go with us?"

"I don't like—in a big group—" I muttered without looking up.

"You prefer tête-à-tête? Well, freedom for the free, and heaven for the blessed," she said with a sigh. "Go on, Belovzorov, get busy. I need a horse by tomorrow."

"Well and good, but where's the money coming from?" the old princess cut in.

Zinaida frowned. "I'm not asking you for any—Belovzorov trusts me."

"Trusts, trusts…" muttered the old princess, and suddenly shouted at the top of her voice, "Dunyashka!"

"Maman, I gave you the little bell," the young princess remarked.

"Dunyashka!" the old woman repeated.

Belovzorov said good-bye; I went out with him…Zinaida did not try to keep me.

XIV

The next morning I got up early, cut myself a stick, and set out beyond the gate. I'll go for a walk, I thought; shake off my grief. The day was beautiful, bright and not too hot. A lively, fresh wind blew across the land, whistling, dancing, yet all the while not disturbing anything. I wandered through the hills and forests for a long time. I did not feel happy. I had left the house meaning to give myself over despondency, but my youthfulness, the beautiful weather, the fresh air, the fun of quick walking, the voluptuousness of lying alone on the thick grass—all echoed in me. Remembrance of those unforgettable words, of those kisses, again crowded into my heart. I found it pleasant to think that Zinaida, at any rate, couldn't help but render justice to my resoluteness, my heroism. "For her the others are better than I," I thought, "all right! On the other hand, the others only say what they'll do but I did it…and what I'd still do for her!" My imagination started working. I began to picture how I would rescue her from the hands of enemies; how I, all covered with blood, would release her from a dungeon; how I would die at her feet. I remembered the picture hanging in our living room: Malech-Adele carrying off Mathilda—and right then got fascinated by the appearance of a big mottled woodpecker which was busily climbing up a thin birch trunk and nervously looking around from behind it to the right, to the left, like a musician from behind the neck of a double-bass.

After that I started singing "The Snow's Not White," and switched to the then well-known "I'll Be Waiting for You When the Playful Zephyr"; after that I began loudly to recite Ermak's apostrophe to the stars from Khomyakov's tragedy; I started to try to put together something in the sentimental vein—I even thought up the line which the whole poem had to end with: "O, Zinaida! Zinaida!" but nothing would come.

Meanwhile, it had become dinnertime. I went down into the valley; a narrow, sandy path wound through it and led into the town...I set out along this path...the dull beat of horses' hoofs resounded behind me. I looked back, involuntarily stood still, and took off my cap: I saw my father and Zinaida. They were riding side by side. Father was telling her something, bending his whole body toward her and leaning his hand on her horse's neck; he was smiling. Zinaida was listening to him without speaking, her eyes sternly lowered and her lips tightened. I first caught sight of them alone; only after a few moments did Belovzorov appear from around a curve in the valley, in his hussar uniform with a fur-trimmed cape, on a black horse all in a lather. The good horse shook his head, neighed, and pranced: the rider both held him back and dug in with his spurs. I stepped aside. Father picked up his reins and moved away from Zinaida. She slowly raised her eyes to look at him—and they both started galloping. Belovzorov dashed after them, rattling his saber. "He's as red as a lobster," I thought; "and she's—why is she so pale? Riding all morning—and pale?"

I began to walk twice as fast, and managed to get home just before dinner. Father, washed, freshened-up, and his clothes changed, was already sitting beside Mother's chair and reading to her, in his smooth and resounding voice, an article out of the *Journal des Débats*. Mother was listening to him without paying attention and, having seen me, asked where I had been all day, and added that she didn't like it when someone was gadding about God knows where— and God knows with whom. But I was out walking alone, I was about to answer; but I glanced at my father and for some reason kept silent.

XV

During the next five or six days I hardly saw Zinaida. They said she was sick, which nevertheless didn't prevent the usual visitors to the wing from, as they put it, reporting for duty—all except Maidanov, who immediately became despondent and bored as soon as he had no chance to feel enthusiastic. Belovzorov sat glumly in a corner, all buttoned up and red-faced. A sort of malicious smile continually wandered across Count Malevski's thin face; he had really fallen into disgrace with Zinaida and with a special effort was worming his way into the old princess's favor; he had taken the stagecoach with her to the governor-general's. This trip, incidentally, had turned out to be unsuccessful, and Malevski had even had an unpleasant experience: someone had reminded him of an occurrence with some transportation office—and he, in explanation, had had to admit that he had then been inexperienced. Lushin came about twice a day but stayed briefly. I was a little chary of him after our last conversation—and at the same time felt a real attraction to him. Once he went for a walk with me through Neskuchnyi Park and was very good-natured and polite; he told me the names and characteristics of various grasses and flowers; and suddenly—out of the blue, as the saying goes—exclaimed, striking his forehead: "And I, like a fool, thought she was a flirt! Obviously, self-sacrifice is sweet—for some."

"What do you mean by that?" I asked.

"I don't mean to tell *you* anything," Lushin retorted curtly.

Zinaida avoided me. My appearance, I couldn't help but notice, had a disagreeable effect on her. She involuntarily turned away from me…involuntarily—that was what was bitter, that was what grieved me, but there was nothing I could do, and I tried not to let her see me and to catch sight of her only from a distance, but I didn't always succeed. Something as incomprehensible was happening to her as had happened before: her face had become different, she herself had become completely different. The change that had occurred in her especially astounded me one warm, quiet evening. I was sitting on a low bench under a spreading elder bush; I loved this little place—you could see the window of Zinaida's room from it. I sat there; a little bird was moving about busily in the darkened foliage above my head; a grey cat, having stretched, carefully stole into the garden; and the first beetles droned sonorously in the air still limpid although no longer light. I was sitting and looking at the window, and waiting—would it open? Indeed, it opened, and Zinaida appeared. She had on a white dress, and she herself, her face, her shoulders, her hands were as white. She remained motionless a long time, and stared long and straight ahead from under knitted brows. I didn't know she could have such an expression. Then she clenched her hands together tightly, tightly, pressed them to her lips, to her forehead—and suddenly, spreading her fingers, pushed her hair back from her ears, tossed it, and, decisively nodding her head, slammed the window shut.

Three days later, she ran into me in the garden. I started to duck off to one side—but she stopped me.

"Give me your hand," she said to me with her old tenderness; "you and I haven't had a chat in a long time."

I glanced at her. Her eyes shone calmly, and her face was smiling as if through a haze.

"Are you still not well?" I asked her.

"No, it's all over now," she answered and picked a small red rose. "I'm little tired, but that will pass too."

"And you'll be just the same as before?" I asked.

Zinaida lifted the rose up to her face—and it seemed to me as if the reflection of the bright petals fell on her cheeks. "Have I changed?" she asked me.

"Yes, you have," I answered in a low voice.

"I was cold to you, I know," Zinaida began, "but you shouldn't have paid any attention to that. I couldn't help it. And, besides, what's the point of talking about it?"

"You don't want me to love you, that's what!" I exclaimed gloomily, in an unintentional outburst.

"No, love me—but not as you used to."

"How, then?"

"Let's be friends—that's how." Zinaida gave me the rose to smell. "Listen, you know I'm a lot older than you—I could be your aunt, really; well, not your aunt, but your older sister. And you—"

"To you I'm a child," I interrupted.

"Well, yes, a child, but a sweet, good, clever one, whom I love very much. You know what? From this day on I make you my page; and don't you forget that pages mustn't be separated from their ladies. Here's the sign of your new station," she added, putting the rose into the buttonhole of my jacket, "the sign of our favor to you."

"I used to get other favors from you," I muttered.

"Ah!" said Zinaida, and looked at me with a sidelong glance. "What a memory he has! Well! I'm ready now, too."

And, bending down to me, she imprinted on my forehead a pure, serene kiss.

I merely looked at her—and she turned away saying, "Follow me, my page," and went toward the wing. I set out after her, still perplexed. "Really," I thought, "is this meek, sober-minded girl the same Zinaida I used to know?" Even her walk seemed to me quieter, her whole figure more majestic and graceful.

But my God! With what new force did love flame up in me!

XVI

After dinner the guests again gathered in the wing, and the young princess came out to meet them. The whole group was present in full strength, as on that first, for me unforgettable, evening. Even Nirmatski had dragged himself in. Maidanov came before the others this time and brought some new poems. We started playing forfeits again but without the old, strange pranks, without the tomfoolery and the wit—the gypsy stuff had gone. Zinaida set a new tone for our gathering. I was sitting next to her, as was a page's right. She had, incidentally, proposed that the one whose forfeit fell out should tell his dream. But that didn't work. The dreams came out either uninteresting (Balovzorov dreamed that he fed his horse carp, and that it had a wooden head) or unnatural, made-up. Maidanov treated us to a whole story: there were burial vaults, and angels with lyres, and talking flowers, and sounds drifting in from afar...Zinaida didn't let him finish. "Since it's came to making things up," she said, "let every-body tell something really concocted." It was again Belovzorov's turn to speak first.

The young hussar became embarrassed. "I can't make up any-thing!" he exclaimed.

"What nonsense!" Zinaida retorted. "Imagine you're married, for example, and tell us how you'd spend the time with your wife. Would you lock her up?"

"I would."

"And stay with her yourself?"

"Absolutely."

"Wonderful. And if she got fed up with this and deceived you?"

"I'd kill her."

"But if she ran away?"

"I'd catch her and still kill her."

"Right. But now let's suppose I were your wife, what would you do then?"

Belovzorov was silent a moment. "I'd kill myself."

Zinaida laughed. "I see your song is short."

The second forfeit was Zinaida's. She looked up at the ceiling and became lost in thought. "Now, listen," she finally began, "to what I've made up. Imagine a splendid chamber, a summer night, and a wonderful ball. A young queen is giving this ball. Everywhere there's gold, marble, crystal, silk, lights, diamonds, flowers, incense, all the delights of luxury."

"You like luxury?" Lushin interrupted.

"Luxury is lovely," she retorted; "I like everything that's lovely."

"More than the beautiful?" he asked.

"That's somehow tricky—I don't understand. Don't pester me. And so, the ball is splendid. There are lots of guests, they're all young, beautiful, brave, and all head over heels in love with the Queen."

"No women among the guests?" asked Malevski.

"No...or wait a minute—there are."

"But unattractive?"

"Charming, but the men are all in love with the queen. She's tall and slender…she has a little gold diadem set in her black hair."

I looked at Zinaida—and at that moment she seemed to me so much above us all, and such a noble mind and such power seemed to emanate from her white forehead, from her motionless brows, that I thought: "You're that queen yourself."

"They're all crowding around her," Zinaida went on, "all showering her with the most flattering speeches."

"And she likes flattery?" Lushin asked.

"How unbearable you are—always interrupting. Who doesn't like flattery?"

"One last question," Malevski remarked. "Does the queen have a husband?"

"I didn't even think about that. No; why a husband?"

"Of course," Malevski agreed. "Why a husband?"

"*Silence!*" exclaimed Maidanov, who spoke French badly.

"*Merci,*" Zinaida said to him. "And so, the queen listens to these speeches, listens to the music, but doesn't look at a single one of the guests. Six windows are open from top to bottom, from the ceiling to the floor, and beyond them there's a dark sky with huge stars and a dark garden with huge trees. The queen looks out into the garden. There, among the trees, there is a fountain; it shines white in the darkness—tall, tall, like a ghost. Above the talk and the music the queen hears the tranquil splash of the water; she looks and thinks: All of you, gentlemen, are noble, clever, rich; you surround me; you value my every word; you all are ready to die at my feet; I possess you…But there by the fountain, by that splashing water, there stands and waits for me the one I love—the one who possesses me. He has no rich clothing, no precious stones, nobody knows him, but he is waiting for me and is certain I'm coming. And I am, and there's no power which can stop me once I want to go to him and be with him and get lost with him there in the garden's darkness amid the rustling of the trees, by the splashing of the fountain…"

Zinaida stopped.

"That…is made up?" Malevski cunningly asked.

Zinaida didn't even look at him.

"And what would we do, gentlemen," Lushin suddenly broke in, "if we were among those guests and knew about that lucky man at the fountain?"

"Wait, wait," Zinaida cut him off, "I'll tell you myself what each of you would do. You, Belovzorov, would challenge him to a duel. You, Maidanov, would write an epigram against him; actually, you wouldn't—you don't know how to write epigrams. You'll write a long iambic about him, in the style of Barbier and publish your work in the Telegraph. You, Nirmatski, would borrow from him no, you'd lend him money at interest. You, doctor..." She paused. "Now, I don't know what *you'd* do."

"As Her Majesty's doctor," Lushin replied, "I'd advise the queen not to give balls when she doesn't feel like having guests."

"Maybe you'd be right. And you, Count..."

"Me?" Malevski repeated with his malicious smile.

"And you'd treat him to a piece of poisoned candy."

Malevski's face became slightly distorted and for an instant assumed a Jewish expression, but he almost immediately burst out laughing.

"And as for you, Voldemar..." Zinaida went on. "But that's enough; let's play another game."

"Monsieur Voldemar, as the queen's page, would hold her train as she would be running into the garden," Malevski remarked venomously.

I flushed bright red; but Zinaida, nimbly putting her hands on my shoulders and getting up, said in a voice that trembled slightly: "I never gave Your Excellency the right of being impudent, and I therefore beg you—to leave." She pointed to the door.

"For pity's sake, Princess," Malevski mumbled, and blanched all over.

"The princess is right," exclaimed Belovzorov and he also stood up.

"I, honestly, didn't at all expect you to take it like that," Malevski went on. "In what I said, I think, there was nothing so...I had absolutely no intention of offending you. Forgive me."

Zinaida looked him up and down coldly and coldly smiled. "Why not; stay," she said with a casual gesture of her hands. "Monsieur Voldemar and I became angry for nothing. You enjoy being caustic. To your health."

"Forgive me," Malevski repeated once more, but I, remembering Zinaida's gesture, again thought that a real queen could not have shown an insolent man the door with greater dignity.

The game of forfeits didn't last long after this little scene; everybody was somewhat uneasy, not so much from the scene itself as from another, not entirely distinct, but depressing feeling. Nobody talked about it, but everyone recognized it both in himself and in his neighbor. Maidanov recited his poems to us, and Malevski showered praise on them with exaggerated fervor. "How much he now wants to appear in a good light," Lushin whispered to me. We soon broke up. A thoughtful mood suddenly fell on Zinaida; the old princess sent in word that she had a headache; Nirmatski began complaining about his rheumatism.

I couldn't fall asleep for a long time; Zinaida's story had impressed me. "Is there really an allusion in it?" I asked myself, "and to whom was she alluding, to what? And if there was something to allude to, how do you make up your mind to…No, no, impossible," I whispered, turning from one hot cheek to the other. But I remembered the expression on Zinaida's face during her story. I remembered the exclamation which had burst out of Lushin in Neskuchnyi Park, the sudden changes in her treatment of me—and got lost in the speculations. "Who is he?" These three words seemed to stand before my eyes, limned in the darkness. A low, ominous cloud seemed to be hanging over me; I felt its pressure, and waited for it to burst any minute. Lately I had become accustomed to a great deal, had seen a great deal at the Zasekins: their disorderliness, the tallow candle-ends, the broken knives and forks, sullen Vonifati, the shabby maids, the manners of the old princess herself—this whole strange life no longer surprised me. But what now vaguely disturbed me about Zinaida I could not get used to. "A little adventuress," my mother once said about her. A little adventuress—she, my idol, my deity! That label stung me—I tried to get away from it into the pillow. I was indignant…and at the same time, what wouldn't I have agreed to, what wouldn't I have given, just to have been that lucky man by the fountain!

The blood in me seethed and went wild. "Garden…fountain…" I thought. "I'll just go in the garden." I dressed hastily and slipped out of the house. The night was dark; the trees were just barely whispering; a soft chill descended from the sky, the scent of dill came from the kitchen garden. I skirted all the paths; the light sound of my steps made me both self-conscious and bold; I would stop, wait, and listen to how my heart was pounding— powerfully and fast. Finally I came up to the fence and leaned on a thin post. Suddenly—or was it my imagination?—a feminine figure flashed by a few paces from me. I held my breath. "What is it? Do I hear footsteps—or is it my heart pounding again? Who's there?" I babbled barely distinctly. What's that again? Suppressed laughter…or a rustling in the leaves—or a deep breath right by my ear? I was terrified. "Who's there?" I repeated still more quietly.

For a moment there was a rush of air; a fiery streak flashed in the sky, a star fell. "Zinaida?" I started to ask, but the sound died on my lips. And suddenly everything became profoundly silent all around, as often happens in the middle of the night. Even the crickets had stopped chirping in the trees—only a window somewhere rang shut. I stood there, stood there, and then went back to my room, to my cold bed. I felt a strange excitement: it seemed as if I had gone to a rendezvous—and remained alone, and passed by somebody else's happiness.

XVII

The next day I caught only a glimpse of Zinaida: she was going somewhere with the old princess in a cab. However, I did see Lushin, who, by the way, hardly bothered to say hello, and Malevski. The young count grinned and amicably started a conversation with me. Of all the visitors to the wing, he alone knew how to worm his way into our house, and he had caught Mother's fancy. Father didn't like him and treated him politely to the point of insult.

"Ah, monsieur le page," Malevski began, "I'm very glad to see you. What is your beautiful queen doing?"

His clean, handsome face was so repulsive to me at that moment, and he looked at me so scornfully, so waggishly, that I didn't answer him.

"You're still angry?" he went on. "That's silly. After all, it wasn't I who called you a page—and it is chiefly queens who have pages. But let me point out that you fulfill your duties badly."

"How so?"

"Pages must be inseparable from their mistresses; pages must know everything they do; they must keep an eye on them," he added, lowering his voice, "day—and night."

"What do you mean?"

"What do I mean? I express myself clearly, I think. Day—and night. By day, there's one thing and another; by day, it's light and there are lots of people about. But at night—then you have to watch out for trouble. I advise you not to sleep at night, and to keep an eye out, keep an eye out with all your might. Remember—in a garden, at night, by the fountain—that's where you have to keep watch. You'll thank me."

Malevski laughed and turned away from me. He probably attached no special importance to what he had told me; he had the reputation of a great hoaxer and was famous for his ability to fool people at masquerades, which was greatly helped by that almost unconscious mendacity with which his whole being was shot through. He just wanted to tease me; but his every word coursed like poison through my veins. The blood rushed to my head. "Ah! That's it!" I said to myself. "All right! That means I wasn't drawn to the garden for nothing! This must never happen!" I exclaimed aloud, and I beat my chest with my fist, although I had no idea *what* shouldn't happen. "Maybe Malevski himself will go to the garden," I wondered (maybe he had let the cat out of the bag; he had enough cheek to do that)—"or someone else" (the fence around our garden was very low, and it was no trouble to climb over it)—"but it will turn out badly for whoever crosses my path—I don't advise anyone to run into me! I'll show the whole world, and her, too, the traitress"

(I really called her traitress) "that I know how to get revenge!"

I returned to my room, got from my desk the English penknife I had bought recently, tested the sharpness of the blade and, frowning, with a cold and concentrated decisiveness shoved it in my pocket, as if it were neither strange nor the first time I was doing such things. The evil in my heart rose up and hardened; I didn't stop glowering or relax my lips until nightfall, and continually walked back and forth, with my hand in my pocket, squeezing the warmed knife and getting ready ahead of time for something terrible. These new, fantastic sensations so occupied and even delighted me that I actually thought very little about Zinaida. I kept imagining Aleko, the young gypsy—"Where are you going, handsome young man? Lie down..." And then: "You're all spattered with blood! Oh, what have you done?" "Nothing!" With what a fierce smile I repeated that "Nothing!"

Father was not at home, but Mother, who for some time had been in a state of almost continual, vague irritation, turned her attention to my morbid appearance and said to me at supper: "What are you pouting for, like a spoiled brat?" I just smiled at her condescendingly in reply and thought: "If only they knew!" It struck eleven; I went up to my room but did not undress. I was waiting for midnight; finally it, too, struck. "It's time!" I whispered through my teeth and, having buttoned my coat all the way up, having even turned up my sleeves, I set out for the garden.

I had picked out a place ahead of time to keep watch. At the bottom of the garden, where the fence dividing our property and the Zasekins' was set against a common wall, there grew a solitary fir; standing under its low thick branches, I could easily see, as much as the darkness of night allowed, what was going on around. Here meandered a little path, which had always seemed mysterious to me: like a snake it crawled under the fence, which in this spot carried traces of the feet that had climbed over, and led to a round arbor of solid acacia. I made my way to the fir, leaned against its trunk, and began my watch.

The night was as quiet as the one before; but there were fewer clouds in the sky—and the outlines of the bushes, even of the tall flowers, were more clearly visible. The first moments of waiting

were agonizing, almost terrible. I'd made up my mind to do anything. I was just wondering how I should do it. Should I thunder out:
"Where are you going? Stop! Confess or die!" Or should I simply
strike? Every round, every rustle and murmuring seemed to me significant, unusual. I got ready...I leaned forward...But half an hour
went by; an hour. My blood quieted down, cooled off; the idea that
I was doing all this for nothing, that I was even a bit ridiculous, that
Malevski had been making fun of me, began to creep into my mind.
I left my ambush and walked around the whole garden. As if on pur-
pose, there was not the slightest sound anywhere; everything was
at rest; even our dog was asleep, curled up into a little ball by the
gate. I climbed up onto the ruins of the greenhouse, saw before me
the distant field, remembered the meeting with Zinaida, and became
thoughtful.

I shuddered...I thought I heard the creak of a door opening, and
then the light crack of a broken twig. I got down from the ruins in
two jumps—and froze on the spot. Hurried, light but cautious footsteps could be clearly heard in the garden. They were coming toward
me. "It's he...it's he at last!" shot through my heart. I convulsively
pulled the knife out of my pocket, convulsively opened it, something
like red sparks started whirling before my eyes, my hair began to rise,
out of fear and fury. The footsteps were coming straight toward me. I
crouched down, I stretched out toward them. A man appeared...My
God, it was my father!

I recognized him at once—although he was all wrapped up in a
dark cloak and had pulled his hat down over his face. He went by
on tiptoe. He didn't notice me, although I wasn't concealed at all,
but I was so hunched up and shriveled that I think I was level with
the ground itself. Jealous, ready to murder, Othello suddenly turned
into a schoolboy...I was so frightened by my father's unexpected
appearance that I didn't even notice at first where he had come from
or where he disappeared to. Only when everything around had again
quieted down, I straightened up and started thinking: "Why is Father
walking through the garden at night?" Out of fear I had dropped my
knife in the grass—but I didn't even start looking for it: I was very
ashamed. I sobered up at once. Going home, however, I went over

to my bench under the elder bush and glanced at the little window of Zinaida's bed room. The small, somewhat curved panes of the window dimly shone dark blue in the pale light from the night sky. Suddenly their color started changing. Behind them—I saw it, saw it clearly—a whitish shade was carefully and quietly drawn down, down to the sill, and stayed like that, motionless.

"What was that?" I said aloud, almost involuntarily, when I found myself again in my own room. "A dream, a coincidence, or..." The suppositions which suddenly came into my head were so new and strange that I didn't dare even think about them.

XVIII

I got up in the morning with a headache. The excitement of the day before had gone. It was replaced by a depressing bewilderment and a sort of sadness I had never known before—as if something in me were dying.

"How is it that you look like a rabbit with half its brain taken out?" Lushin said to me as we met. During breakfast I kept glancing stealthily, first at my father and then at my mother. He was at ease, as usual; she, as usual, was covertly irritated. I waited to see if my father would start a friendly conversation with me, as he sometimes did. But he didn't even caress me with his ordinary, cold affection. "Shall I tell Zinaida everything?" I asked myself. "It won't make any difference—everything's over between us." I set out to see her, but not only did I tell her nothing—I didn't even get to talk to her, as I would have liked. The old princess's son, a cadet about twelve years old, had come from Petersburg for his vacation. Zinaida immediately handed her brother over to me. "Here," she said, "my dear Volodya (it was the first time she had called me that), is a friend for you. His name is Volodya, too. Please be nice to him; he's still a wilding, but his heart's in the right place. Show him Neskuchnyi, go walking with him, take him under your wing. You'll do this, won't you? You're so good, too!" She put her two hands tenderly on my shoulders—and I was completely lost. This boy's arrival turned me into a boy myself.

Without speaking, I looked at the cadet, who just as silently stared at me. Zinaida burst out laughing and pushed us together. "Go on, embrace each other, children!" We embraced.

"Would you like me to take you into the garden?" I asked the cadet.

"If you will, sir," he replied in a hoarse, strictly cadet voice. Zinaida laughed again. I managed to notice that such charming color had never appeared in her face before. The cadet and I set out. An old swing hung in our garden. I seated him on the thin board and began to push him. He sat still, in his new little uniform of heavy cloth with wide gold braid, and held onto the rope tightly. "Why don't you undo your collar?" I said to him. "It doesn't matter, sir; we're used to it," he said, and coughed. He looked like his sister: his eyes especially reminded me of her. I even liked doing him a favor, and at the same time aching grief quietly gnawed at my heart. "Now I'm like a child," I thought, "but yesterday…" I remembered where I had dropped the knife the day before and looked for it until I found it. The cadet asked for it, cut off a thick stalk of lovage, cut a pipe out of it, and started whistling. Othello whistled a bit, too.

But now he cried that evening, this same Othello, in Zinaida's arms when she, having found him in a corner of the garden, asked him why he was so sad. My tears gushed with such force that she grew frightened. "What's the matter with you? What's the matter with you, Volodya?" she repeated again and again and, seeing that I didn't respond and didn't stop crying, was about to kiss my wet cheek. But I turned away from her and whispered through my sobbing: "I know everything; why were you playing with me? What did you need my love for?"

"I'm guilty before you, Volodya," Zinaida said. "Ah, very guilty," she said, and clenched her hands. "How much evil, darkness, and sin there is in me! But I'm not playing with you now, I love you; you don't even suspect why—and how…But—what do you know?"

What could I tell her? She was standing before me and looking at me, and I belonged to her completely, from head to foot just as soon as she looked at me…A quarter of an hour later Zinaida and the cadet and I were chasing each other; I wasn't crying, I was laughing, although my swollen eyelids were shedding tears; Zinaida's ribbon was fastened around my neck instead of a tie, and I shouted from joy when I succeeded in catching her by her waist. She did with me anything she wanted to.

XIX

I would have a hard time if I were to have to tell in detail what happened to me during the week after my unsuccessful expedition. It was a strange, feverish time, a sort of chaos in which the most contradictory feelings, thoughts, suspicions, hopes, delights, and sufferings spun round like a whirlwind; I was afraid of looking inside myself—if, indeed, a boy just sixteen can—afraid of summing up anything at all; I simply hurried to get through the day until evening. But at night I slept...my child's light-heartedness helped me. I didn't want to know whether or not I was loved, and I didn't want to admit to myself that I wasn't. I avoided my father—but Zinaida I couldn't avoid. I was scorched as if by fire in her presence...but why should I have known what sort of fire it was in which I was burning and melting—it was supreme happiness for me sweetly to melt and burn. I indulged all my impressions and played tricks on myself, turned away from my memories, and shut my eyes to what I sensed lay ahead...This torment, probably, wouldn't have lasted long anyway...A thunderbolt stopped everything at once, and threw me onto a new path.

Once, coming home to dinner from a rather long walk, I learned to my surprise that I would dine alone; Father had gone out and Mother was unwell, didn't want to eat, and had locked herself in her bedroom. From the servants' faces I guessed that something unusual had happened. I didn't dare question them, but I had a friend, the young butler, Filipp, a passionate devotee of poetry and an artist on the guitar—I turned to him. From him I learned that a terrible scene had occurred between Father and Mother (and everything down to the last word had been heard in the maids' room; much of the quarrel was spoken in French—but the maid Masha had lived with

a seamstress from Paris for five years and understood everything).
My mother had accused my father of unfaithfulness, of intimacy
with the young lady next door; Father at first justified himself, then
flared up and in turn said something cruel "seemingly about her
age," which made Mother cry. Mother also reminded him about the
loan supposedly given the old princess and spoke about her very dis-
paragingly, and about the young lady, too, and at that point Father
threatened her. "And the whole trouble started," Filipp went on,
"from an anonymous letter; because, otherwise, there's no reason for
things like this to come out in the open."

"But was there really something?" I said with difficulty, while in
the meantime my hands and feet had grown cold and something was
trembling deep in my chest.

Filipp winked significantly. "There was. You can't hide these
things; no matter how careful your papa was this time, still you have
to, for example, get a carriage, or whatever—and you can't do without servants, either."

I sent Filipp out and fell on my bed. I didn't sob, didn't I give
myself up to despair; I didn't ask myself when and how all this had
happened; I wasn't surprised why I hadn't before, long ago, guessed
it; I didn't even reproach my father. What I had found out was
beyond my strength: this sudden discovery crushed me. Everything
was over. All my flowers had been plucked at once and lay around
me strewn and trampled.

XX

Mother announced the next day that she was going back to town.
In the morning Father went into her bedroom and stayed with her
alone for a long time. Nobody heard what he told her, but Mother
cried no more; she calmed down and asked for something to eat—
but she didn't come out, and didn't change her decision. I remember
I wandered around all day, but didn't go into the garden and didn't
once glance at the wing; but in the evening I was witness to an amazing event: my father escorted Count Malevski by the arm across the

hall into the vestibule and, in the valet's presence, coldly said to him: "A few days ago in a certain house Your Excellency was shown the door; I will not now go into details with you, but I have the honor to inform you that if you once more come to mine, I will throw you out the window. I don't like your handwriting." The count bowed, clenched his teeth, shrank into himself, and vanished.

Preparations started for the move to town, to the Arbat, where our house was. Father himself, probably, no longer wanted to stay in the country; but, clearly, he had succeeded in begging Mother not to make a fuss; everything was done calmly, without hurrying. Mother even sent a good-bye to the old princess and expressed her regret that, for reasons of ill health, she couldn't see her before leaving. I wandered around like a crazy man, and wished only for all this to end as quickly as possible. One thought would not leave my mind: how could she, a young girl—and a princess besides—take such a step, knowing that my father was not a free man, and having the opportunity of marrying even, say, Belovzorov! What did she hope for? How was it that she wasn't afraid of ruining her whole future? Indeed, I thought, that's love, that's passion, that's devotion; and I recalled Lushin's words: Self-sacrifice is sweet—for some. Somehow I happened to catch sight of a pale spot in one of the windows of the wing. "Is that really Zinaida's face?" I wondered. Indeed, it was her face. I couldn't bear it. I couldn't leave her without having said a last good bye. I caught a convenient moment and set out for the wing.

In the living room the old princess received me with her usual slovenly-casual greeting.

"How is it, my friend, that your people are running all about so early?" she said, stuffing snuff into both nostrils. I looked at her and felt relieved. The word *loan* which Filipp had said tortured me. She suspected nothing, at least it seemed so to me then. Zinaida appeared from the next room, in a black dress, pale, her hair loose; she silently took me by the hand and led me out.

"I heard your voice," she began, "and immediately came in. And was it so easy for you to desert us, wicked boy?"

"I came to say good-bye to you, Princess," I answered, "probably forever. You have, perhaps, heard—we're leaving."

Zinaida looked at me intently.

"Yes, I heard. Thank you for coming. I had thought I wouldn't see you. Think kindly of me. I sometimes tormented you, but nevertheless I'm not what you imagine."

She turned away and leaned against the window.

"Really, I'm not. I know you have a bad opinion of me."

"I?"

"Yes, you…you."

"I?" I repeated sorrowfully, and my heart trembled as before under the influence of her irresistible, inexpressible charm. "I? Believe me, Zinaida Aleksandrovna, no matter what you do, no matter how you torment me—I will love and adore you to the end of my days.

She quickly turned around toward me and, spreading her arms wide, embraced my head and kissed me hard and passionately. God knows for whom that long, farewell kiss was meant, but I greedily tasted its sweetness—I knew that it would never be repeated. "Good-bye, good-bye," I said again and again.

She tore herself away and went out. I, too, left. I'm not able to convey the feeling with which I went away. I don't want it ever to come again, but I would consider myself unfortunate if I had never experienced it.

We moved to town. I didn't soon put the past behind me, didn't soon get down to work. My wound healed slowly; but I actually bore my father no ill will. On the contrary, he had somehow grown more in my eyes—let psychologists explain that contradiction, if they can. Once I was going down the avenue and, to my indescribable joy, ran into Lushin. I liked him for his straightforward and unhypocritical manners, and, besides, he was dear to me for those memories which he awoke in me. I rushed toward him.

"Aha!" he said and frowned. "It's you, young man! Let me look at you. You're still green, but your eyes don't have that old trashy look. You look the way a man does, not a lap dog. That's good. Well, what're you up to? Working?"

I sighed. I didn't want to lie—and I was ashamed to tell the truth.

"Well, never mind," Lushin went on; "don't be shy. The main thing is to live normally and not give in to distractions. Or else, what's the point? Wherever the waves take you, it's all no good; a man must stand on his own two feet—even on a rock. I have a cough now, and Belovzorov—did you hear?"

"No. What?"

"Disappeared without a trace. They say he went to the Caucasus. A lesson for you, young man. And all because they don't know how to part in time, to break the ties. Now you, I think, came out safely. But look out, don't get caught again. Good-bye."

"I won't," I thought. "I'll never see her again"; but I was fated to see Zinaida once more.

XXI

My father went out riding every day; he had a fine chestnut-roan English horse with a long thin neck and long legs, tireless and vicious; its name was Electric. Nobody could ride it except my father. Once he came to me in a good mood, which he hadn't been in for a long time; he was planning on going out and had already put on his spurs. I started begging him to take me along.

"Let's play leapfrog instead," Father answered me, "for you on your old nag can't keep up with me."

"I can; I'll put spurs on, too."

"Well, all right."

We set out. I had a little shaggy black horse, sturdy-legged and rather fast; true, he had to canter as fast as he could when Electric went at a full trot, but all the same I didn't lag behind. I never saw a rider like my father; he sat so handsomely, so casually and adroitly that it seemed the horse itself under him sensed it and wanted to show him off. We rode down all the avenues, went to Devichie Field, jumped several fences (at first I was afraid to jump, but my father scorned timid people, and I stopped being afraid), crossed the Moscow River twice, and I thought we were already headed home—all the more because Father himself remarked that my horse was tired—when suddenly he wheeled away from me toward the Krymskii Ford and galloped along the shore. I set off after him. Coming up to a high pile of old logs, he agilely jumped down from Electric, ordered me to get off, and, having handed me his horse's bridle, told me to wait for him here, by the logs, and he himself turned into a little alley and disappeared. I started walking back and forth along the shore, leading the horses and struggling with Electric who, as we were walking along, kept pulling his head up continually, shaking it, snorting, neighing; and, when I would stop, alternately pawing the ground with his hoof, nipping my nag in the neck with a squeal—in short, behaving like a spoiled thoroughbred. Father didn't come back. An unpleasant dampness drifted in from the river; a light drizzle softly set in and covered with tiny dark spots the dumb grey logs around which I was wandering, and with which I was really fed up. I was getting bored stiff, and still Father hadn't come. Some policeman on duty, a Finn, also all grey and with a huge shako in the shape of a pot on his head and with a halberd (What was a policeman on duty doing, I wondered, on the bank of the Moscow River!) came up to me and, turning his old-womanish, wrinkled face toward me, said: "What're you doing here with horses, young man? Let me have 'em, I'll hold 'em."

I didn't answer him; he asked me for some tobacco. To get rid of him (besides, my impatience was torturing me), I took several steps in the direction my father had gone; then I went down the little alley to the end, turned the corner, and stopped. On the street about forty paces from me in front of the open window of a little wooden house my father was standing with his back to me; he was leaning his chest on the window sill, and, in the little house, half hidden by a curtain, a woman in a dark dress was sitting and talking to my father. This woman was Zinaida.

I was dumbfounded. This, I admit, I hadn't expected. My first impulse was to run. "Father will look around," I thought, "and I'm done for." But a strange sensation, a sensation stronger than curiosity, stronger even than jealousy, stronger than fear—stopped me. I started watching; I tried to overhear. My father seemed to be insisting on something. Zinaida wouldn't agree. Even now I see her face— sad, serious, lovely, and with an ineffable imprint of devotion, grief, love, and a certain despair—I can't find another word. She spoke in monosyllables, didn't raise her eyes, and merely smiled—meekly but obstinately. By just this smile I recognized my old Zinaida. Father shrugged his shoulders and adjusted his hat, which with him was always a sign of impatience…then I heard: *Vous devez vous séparer de cette…*Zinaida straightened up and extended her hand…Suddenly something amazing happened before my eyes: Father all of a sudden raised the whip with which he had been knocking the dust off the skirt of his coat—and there was the sound of a sharp blow on this arm bare to the elbow. I almost screamed, and Zinaida shuddered, silently looked at my father, and, having slowly raised her arm to her lips, kissed the red welt on it. Father hurled the whip away and, hastily running up the steps of the little porch, stormed into the house. Zinaida turned around—and, her hands stretched out, her head thrown back, also moved away from the window.

With a sinking feeling of fright, with a sort of bewildered horror in my heart, I fled back—and, having run to the end of the little alley, almost letting go of Electric, returned to the river bank. I couldn't think. I knew that my cold and restrained father was sometimes seized by fits of rage, and still I couldn't understand at all what it was I had seen. But I sensed then that as long as I lived I could never forget that gesture, that look, that smile of Zinaida's, that her image—that new image suddenly placed before me—was forever stamped on my memory. I stared vacantly at the river and didn't notice that tears were pouring down my face. She's being beaten, I thought… beaten…beaten…

"Well, what are you doing? Give me my horse!" I heard my father's voice behind me.

I handed him the bridle mechanically. He jumped on Electric… the chilled horse reared on his hind legs and leaped forward three yards. But Father soon curbed him: he dug his spurs into his sides and struck him on the neck with his fist "Ah, I've no whip," he muttered.

I remembered the recent whine and whack of that very whip— and shuddered.

"What did you do with it?" I asked my father after a minute.

Father didn't answer me and galloped on ahead. I caught up with him. I absolutely had to see his face.

"Did you miss me?" he said through his teeth.

"Some. Where did you drop your whip?" I asked again.

Father glanced at me. "I didn't drop it," he said; "I threw it away." He became thoughtful and lowered his head...and I then saw for the first and almost last time how much tenderness and pity his stern features could show.

He galloped on again, and I couldn't catch up to him; I got home a quarter of an hour after him.

"So that's love," I said to myself again, that night while sitting at my desk that was already beginning to be covered with books and notebooks. "That's passion. There's no rebellion, it seems; you have to put up with whatever strikes...even the most beloved hand! And clearly you can, if you're in love. But I, somehow...I somehow imagined..."

The last month had made me much older—and my love, with all its excitements and suffering, seemed to me something so little, and childish and meager before that other, unknown something which I could hardly surmise, and which frightened me, like an unfamiliar, handsome, but ominous face which you in vain try to make out in the dusk...

That same night I dreamed a strange and terrible dream. I dreamed that I was going into a low, dark room...My father was standing with a whip in his hand and stamping his feet; Zinaida was crouched in a corner—and there was a red mark, not on her arm but on her forehead...And behind them both there arose Belovzorov, all covered with blood—he opened his pale lips and angrily threatened Father.

Two months later I entered the university, and six months after that my father died (of a stroke) in Petersburg, where he had just moved with my mother and me. A few days before his death he received a letter from Moscow, which upset him extremely...He went to ask Mother for something and, they say, he even cried—he, my father! On the very morning of the day he had his stroke, he started a letter to me in French: "My son," he wrote me, "beware of a woman's love—beware of this happiness, of this poison..." Mother, after his death, sent a rather substantial sum of money to Moscow.

XXII

Some four years went by. I had just left the university and still didn't know very well where to begin, which door to knock on; for the time being I was just loafing. One evening I ran into Maidanov in the theater. He had managed to get married and get a job—but I found him unchanged. He just as senselessly got all excited and just as suddenly got depressed.

"You know," he told me, among other things, "Madame Dolskaia's here."

"What Madame Dolskaia?"

"Have you forgotten? The former Princess Zasekina, whom we all were in love with, even you. Remember, in the dacha, next to Neskuchnyi?"

"She's married to Dolski?"

"Yes."

"And she's here, in the theater?"

"No, in Petersburg. She arrived the other day; she's getting ready to go abroad."

"What kind of man is her husband?" I asked.

"A fine fellow, with a fortune. A colleague of mine, in Moscow. You understand, after all that happened…it must all be well-known to you" (Maidanov smiled sententiously) "—it wasn't easy for her to find herself a match; there were consequences…but with her intelligence anything's possible. Go see her; she'd be very glad. She's grown even prettier."

Maidanov gave me Zinaida's address. She was staying at the Hotel Demut. Old memories stirred me…I promised myself to call on my former "passion" the very next day. But something came up: a week went by, another, and when I finally got to the Hotel Demut and asked for Madame Dolskaia, I found out that she had died four days before—practically without warning, in childbirth.

Something seemed to have struck me in the heart. The thought that I could have seen her, and didn't—and never will—this bitter thought stung me with all the force of an irrefutable reproach. "Dead!" I repeated, stupidly staring at the doorman. I quietly got out

onto the street and went away, not knowing where. The whole past
arose at once before me. And that's what it had come to, that's what it
had been headed for, rushing and all excited, this young, passionate,
brilliant life! This was what I was thinking: I pictured to myself those
dear features, those eyes, those curls—in a tight box, in the damp,
underground darkness—here, not far from me, still alive, and, perhaps a few steps from my father…I thought all this, I strained my
imagination— and meanwhile

> I heard the news of death out of indifferent lips
> And heeded it indifferently…

rang in my heart. O youth! youth! You have no cares, you seem to
possess all the treasures of the universe, even grief pleases you, even
sorrow becomes you, you are self-confident and bold; you say: I alone
am alive—look, but for you, too, the days run on and vanish without
trace or number, and everything in you vanishes, like wax in the sunlight, like snow…And perhaps the whole secret of your charm does
not lie in the possibility of doing everything, but in the possibility
of thinking that you will do everything—lies exactly in your setting
against the wind a strength which you wouldn't have known how to
use for anything else; lies in each of us seriously considering himself
a spendthrift, seriously supposing that he has the right to say: Oh,
what I would have done if I hadn't needlessly wasted my time!

Here I, too—what did I hope for, what was I waiting for, what rich
future did I foresee, when I had hardly escorted, with only a sigh,
with only a sense of despondency, the momentarily risen ghost of
my first love?

And what came of all that I hoped for? Even now, when evening
shadows have begun to fall across my life, what has remained fresher
and dearer to me than the memories of that quickly gone, spring
morning thunderstorm?

But I slander myself falsely. Even then in that light-hearted, youthful time, I wasn't deaf to a sad voice appealing to me, to a triumphant
voice, flying to me from beyond the grave. I remember, a few days
after that day when I found out about Zinaida's death, I myself, by

my own irresistible inclination, was present at the death of a poor old woman who lived in our house. Covered with rags, on hard boards, with a bag under her head, she died hard and painfully. Her whole life had gone in a bitter struggle with daily want, she had not known joy, had not tasted the cup of happiness—wouldn't she be glad of death, of its freedom and peace? But, instead, as long as her chest still painfully heaved under the ice-cold hand lying on it, as long as the last strength hadn't left her, the old woman kept crossing herself and whispering: "Lord, forgive me my sins…" and the expression of fear and of horror of dying disappeared only with the last spark of consciousness. And I remember that there, by this poor old woman's deathbed, I became terrified for Zinaida, and I wanted to pray for her, for my father—and for myself.

PREFACE TO *SPRING TORRENTS*

Passing through Frankfurt on his first trip out of Russia in 1838, Turgenev was asked by a Jewish girl in a confectioner's shop to save her brother. Turgenev fell in love with the girl; the decision to leave and continue to Berlin was especially difficult for him.

Later, he became deeply attached to Pauline Viardot, who possessed him without ever being possessed by him, a fact Turgenev admitted to the well-known Russian poet, Fet, during Fet's visit to Turgenev at the Viardots' country place in France. Angrily and desperately, Turgenev confessed that the woman had him in her power. According to Fet's interpretation, Turgenev delighted in his own submission. Viardot's taste, elegance, and musical talent literally enchanted Turgenev. He stayed with her or near her almost all his life, although shortly after the episode of the admission to Fet, he broke with her temporarily, partly in anger with himself for being so captivated and partly in annoyance at her for having become involved in an affair with another man.

These two loves, the one pure, the other passionate, are the autobiographical starting points of *Spring Torrents,* one of the most moving love stories ever written. Turgenev's work on it extended through the spring and summer of 1871, covering the period of the Paris Commune of March 18 to May 28, 1871. But, though Turgenev's daughter was in Paris and Turgenev's interest in the uprising was keen, the only reference in the story to the important political events is the comparison of first love to revolution through dramatization of the great change both bring, and to the vital enthusiasm with which they await whatever may come.

Turgenev himself was not completely pleased with the story, for as he said, it had "absolutely no social or political or contemporary allusions." In fact, of course, it does: besides the reference just mentioned, the caricature of the German officers and businessmen, the attack on the German theater, actually angered the Germans. Pietsch, the artist and writer, wrote Turgenev a letter of sharp protest, and Russians interpreted the story as an expression of Turgenev's disgust with the Germans for the Franco-Prussian War. Besides this, the warm sympathy and the fiercely sexual passions described in the story made it extraordinarily popular. Turgenev had finished it by the end of 1871, and it was printed in the January 1872 issue of *The Messenger of Europe*. It was so popular, so successful, that the issue of the magazine had a second printing. The greatest praise came from Flaubert, who, in a letter in August 1873, said that it was an exquisite love story and that Turgenev not only knew all about life but knew how to write about it, how to put it into words. *"Quel homme que mon ami Tourgueneff! Quel homme!"*

Spring Torrents

The laughter-filled years,
The happiest days—
Like the torrents of spring
They've all rushed away!
From an old song.

Sometime after one o'clock at night he returned to his study. He sent out the servant who had lit the candles and, dropping into an armchair by the fire, covered his face with both hands.

He had never before felt such fatigue—physical and spiritual. He had spent the whole evening with agreeable ladies and well-educated men. Some of the ladies were beautiful, practically all the men were marked by intelligence and ability; he himself had talked very successfully and even brilliantly. And, even so, that *taedium vitae,* that "disgust with life" which the old Romans had talked about, had never before overwhelmed him with such irresistible force, never before so oppressed him. Had he been somewhat younger, he would have started crying from depression, from boredom, from irritation. A caustic and scalding bitterness, like the bitterness of wormwood, filled his whole being. Something importunately repellent, unpleasantly painful pressed in on him from all sides, like a dark autumn night; and he did not know how to get free of that darkness, of that bitterness. There was no use in counting on sleep; he knew that he would not fall asleep.

He started thinking—slowly, dully, and spitefully.

He thought of the vanity, the uselessness, the cheap

meretriciousness of everything human. All the ages of man passed
gradually before his mind's eye (he himself had turned fifty-two just
recently), and not one received his mercy. Everywhere there was the
same eternal milling of the wind, the same pointless lashing of the
waves, the same half well-intentioned, half deliberate deluding of
oneself—anything to keep the child happy. And then suddenly, like
a bolt from the blue, old age takes you unawares—and along with
it, the ever-increasing, corroding, and undermining fear of death.
And then plop! you've fallen into the deep! It's still all right if life
works out like this. But sometimes, perhaps, before the end there
start creeping up, like rust on iron, feebleness, sufferings. The sea
of life seemed to him covered, not with wild and stormy waves, as
poets describe it—no. He imagined this sea imperturbably smooth,
still, and limpid right to the dark, dark bottom. He himself is sitting
in a little, shaky boat—and there, on that dark, slimy bottom, one
can just barely make out hideous monsters, like enormous fish; all
life's ailments, illnesses, sorrows, madness, poverty, blindness...He
looks—and, there, one of the monsters is moving out of the darkness, is rising up higher and higher, is becoming more and more
distinct, more and more repulsively distinct...Another minute—and
the boat under him will be over turned! But, there, the thing seems
to be fading again, it's receding, going down to the bottom—and it
lies there, just barely moving its tail...But the day of reckoning will
come, and this thing will overturn the boat.

He shook his head, jumped up from the chair, walked back and
forth in the room a couple of times, sat down at his desk, and, pulling out one drawer after another, started going through his papers,
through old letters, mostly from women. He himself did not know
why he was doing this; he was not looking for anything—he simply
wanted, by doing something, to get rid of the thoughts that were
tormenting him. Having opened several letters at random (in one
of them there was a dried-out flower tied with a faded ribbon), he
merely shrugged his shoulders and, glancing at the fire, threw them
aside, probably intending to burn up all this useless trash. Hurriedly
sticking his hands first into one drawer and then another, he suddenly opened his eyes wide and, having pulled out a small octagonal

antique box, slowly raised its lid. In the box, under a double layer of yellowed cotton, was a little garnet cross.

For several moments he stared at this little cross in bewilderment—and suddenly gave a faint cry. His features expressed half regret, half delight. Such a look comes on a man's face when he happens suddenly to run into someone whom he long ago lost sight of, whom he once was very fond of, and who now unexpectedly appears before his eyes, still the same—and completely changed by the years.

He got up and, going back to the fireplace, sat down again in the armchair, and again covered his face with his hands. "Why today? Why precisely today?" he thought, and he remembered many things that had happened long ago.

This is what he remembered...

But first one must be told his name, patronymic, and surname. He was called Sanin, Dmitri Pavlovich. This is what he remembered.

I

It happened in the summer of 1840. Sanin had turned twenty-two, and was in Frankfurt on his way back to Russia from Italy. He was a man whose fortune was small, but he was independent, and almost without family ties. It turned out that he had, following the death of a distant relative, several thousand rubles—and he had decided to spend them abroad before entering the service, before finally putting on that government yoke without which a comfortable existence was, for him, inconceivable. Sanin had carried out his intention exactly and had managed so skillfully that on the day of his arrival in Frankfurt he had just as much money as he needed to get back to Petersburg. In 1840 there were very few railroads in existence; tourists traveled by public stage coach. Sanin reserved a seat in the *Beiwagen,* but the coach did not leave until after ten at night. There was a good deal of time left. Fortunately, the weather was wonderful, and Sanin, having dined in the White Swan, a well-known hotel of that time, set out to wander around town. He went in to take a look at Dannecker's "Ariadne," which he did not like very much; visited

the house of Goethe, of whose works, by the way, he had read only
Werther—and that in a French translation; he took a walk along the
shore of the Main, and was somewhat bored, as any decent traveler
should be; and finally, at six o'clock in the evening, worn-out, with
dust-covered feet, found himself in one of the most insignificant
streets of Frankfurt.

For a long time afterwards he could not forget this street. On one
of its few houses he caught sight of a sign: "Italian Confectionery,
Giovanni Roselli" it announced to passers-by. Sanin went in to have
a glass of lemonade, but there wasn't a soul in the first room. Behind
a plain counter, on the shelves of a painted cupboard, reminding one
of a pharmacy, stood several bottles with gold labels and the same
number of glass jars with rusk, chocolate cookies, and fruit drops.
On a tall wicker chair by the window a grey cat was blinking and
purring, moving its paws up and down; and, glowing brightly in the
slanting rays of the evening sun, a big ball of red wool lay on the floor
beside an overturned fretwork basket. There was a vague noise in the
next room. Sanin stood there a moment—and, having waited for the
little bell on the door to stop ringing, he raised his voice and called:
"Is nobody here?" Just at that moment the door from the next room
opened, and Sanin could not help but be amazed.

II

A girl of about nineteen, her dark curls hanging loosely over her bare
shoulders, her bare arms stretched out in front of her, ran impetu-
ously into the shop and, having caught sight of Sanin, immediately
rushed to him, grabbed his arm and started pulling him after her,
saying again and again in a gasping voice: "Hurry, hurry, in here, save
him!" Not from any unwillingness to obey, but simply from being
overwhelmed by surprise, Sanin did not follow the girl at once—he
seemed to have become rooted to the spot: in his whole life he had
never seen such a beautiful girl. She turned around to him and said,
"But come, come!" with such despair in her voice, in her eyes, in the
gesture of her clenched hand, which she convulsively put up against

her pale cheek, that he immediately lunged through the open door behind her.

In the room into which he had run, following the girl, on an old-fashioned horsehair couch lay a boy of about fourteen, all white—white with a yellowish tinge, like wax or like ancient marble—strikingly like the girl, evidently her brother. His eyes were closed; the shadow of his thick, black hair fell like a blotch on his stony forehead, on his thin, motionless eyebrows; his clenched teeth showed between his blue lips. He seemed not to be breathing; one hand had dropped down to the floor, the other he had flung back up over his head. The boy was dressed, and his coat was buttoned; a necktie was tight about his neck.

The girl rushed to him with a loud wail.

"He's dead, he's dead!" she cried. "Just now he was sitting here talking to me—and suddenly he fell and was motionless…My God! can't anything be done to help? And Mama's out! Pantaleone, Pantaleone, what about the doctor?" she added suddenly in Italian. "Did you go for the doctor?"

"Signorina, I didn't, I sent Louise," said a hoarse voice behind the door, and into the room, hobbling on his bandy legs, came a little old man in a lavender frock coat with black buttons, a high white tie, nankeen breeches, and dark blue wool stockings. His tiny little face was completely hidden by a huge mass of iron grey hair. Rising up sharply on all sides and falling back in tousled locks, it made the old man look like a tufted chicken—a resemblance all the more striking because, under the dark grey mass, one could only just make out a pointed nose and round yellow eyes.

"Louise will run over quicker, and I can't run," the little old man continued in Italian, lifting, one after another, his flat, gouty feet shod in high button-up boots. "But, here, I've brought some water."

He was squeezing the neck of the bottle with his dry, crooked fingers.

"But meanwhile Emilio will die!" cried the girl, and reached out toward Sanin. "Oh sir, *oh mein Herr!* Can't you possibly help?"

"He has to be bled—it's a stroke," remarked the little old man called Pantaleone.

Although Sanin had not the least knowledge of medicine, he knew one thing for sure: fourteen-year-old boys do not have strokes.

"It's a fainting spell, not a stroke," he said, turning to Pantaleone. "Have you brushes?"

The old man raised his face.

"What?" "Brushes, brushes," Sanin repeated in German and in French. "Brushes," he added, making the gesture of cleaning his clothes.

The old man finally understood him.

"Ah, brushes! *Spazette!* Of course we have!"

"Let me have them; we'll take off his coat, and start rubbing him down."

"Very good...*Benone!* But shouldn't you pour some water on his head?"

"No—later; now hurry up, and get the brushes quickly."

Pantaleone put the bottle on the floor and ran out, and immediately came back with two brushes, one a clothesbrush and the other a hairbrush.

A curly poodle was accompanying him and, earnestly wagging his tail, was looking inquisitively at the old man, at the girl, and even at Sanin—as if wanting to know what all this commotion meant.

Sanin deftly took off the boy's coat, unbuttoned his collar, rolled up the sleeves of his shirt, and, having equipped himself with a brush, started rubbing his chest and arms as hard as he could. Pantaleone just as zealously rubbed with the hairbrush over the boy's boots and trousers. The girl fell on her knees beside the couch and, having seized his head in both hands, fixed her eyes, without winking an eyelash, on her brother's face.

Sanin himself kept rubbing, and kept looking at her furtively. My Lord! What a beautiful girl!

III

Her nose was a bit large, but of a beautiful aquiline shape; a little down just barely set off her upper lip; the color of her face, however, smooth and lusterless, was exactly like ivory or like milky amber; she had a wavy gloss to her hair, like Allorio's Judith in the Palazzo Pitti; and especially her eyes, dark grey with a black rim around the pupils, were magnificent, triumphant eyes—even now when fright and sadness had dulled their sheen…Sanin involuntarily thought of the marvelous land from which he was returning…Indeed, even in Italy he had not run into anything like this! The girl was breathing unevenly and slowly; it seemed that, with each breath, she was waiting to see whether her brother would start breathing.

Sanin kept on rubbing the boy, but he was looking not only at the girl. Pantaleone's eccentric figure also drew his attention. The old man had become weak all over and was puffing and panting; he kept jumping up and down at each stroke of the brush and groaning shrilly; and his huge mane of hair, wet with perspiration, swung heavily from side to side like the roots of a great plant eroded by water.

"At least take off his boots," Sanin started to tell him.

The poodle, probably excited by the unusualness of everything going on, suddenly sank down onto its front paws and began to bark.

"*Tartaglia! Canaglia!*" the old man hissed at it.

But at that moment the girl's face was transformed. Her brows rose, her eyes became still bigger and shone with delight…

Sanin looked around. Color had broken out on the young man's face; his eyelids moved…his nostrils quivered. He inhaled air through his still clenched teeth, he sighed…

"Emilio!" cried the girl. "*Emilio mio!*"

The big black eyes slowly opened. They still stared vacantly, but they were smiling—weakly; the same weak smile crossed the pale lips. Then he moved the arm that was hanging down—and, with an effort, swung it up onto his chest.

"*Emilio!*" the girl repeated, and got up. The expression on her face was so intense and striking that, it seemed, she would either burst into tears or break out in laughter.

"Emilio! What's going on? Emilio!" came from behind the door, and a neatly dressed lady with silver-grey hair and a dark face came quickly into the room. An elderly man was following her; a maid's head appeared for an instant behind his shoulders.

The girl ran to meet them.

"He's saved, Mama, he's alive!" she cried, convulsively embracing the lady who had entered.

"But what's going on?" she repeated. "I was just coming back—and I suddenly ran into the doctor and Louise..."

The girl started telling what had happened, and the doctor went over to the patient, who was coming round more and more, and all the while continuing to smile; he seemed to be beginning to be ashamed of the alarm he had caused.

"I see you rubbed him with brushes," the doctor said, turning to Sanin and Pantaleone, "and a good thing that was. A very good idea—and now we'll see if there's anything else." He felt the young man's pulse. "Hm! Say 'ah!'"

The lady bent down to him solicitously. He smiled still more openly, raised his eyes to her, and blushed.

It struck Sanin that he was not needed; he went out into the shop. But before he could even touch the handle of the street door, the girl had again appeared in front of him and stopped him.

"You're going?" she began, looking straight at him warmly. "I won't keep you, but you absolutely have to come back this evening, we're so indebted to you—you probably saved my brother—we want to thank you—Mama wants to. You have to tell us who you are, you have to rejoice with us..."

"But I'm leaving for Berlin today," Sanin began hesitantly.

"You still can," the girl replied vivaciously. "Come have a cup of chocolate with us in an hour. You promise?...But I have to go back to him. You'll come?"

What was there for Sanin to do?

"I will," he answered.

The beautiful girl quickly pressed his hand, darted off—and he found himself on the street.

IV

When, an hour and a half later, Sanin returned to the Roselli

confectionery, he was greeted like one of the family. Emilio was sitting on the same couch on which he had been rubbed down; the
doctor had prescribed some medicine for him and recommended
"extreme caution in emotional excitement"—since the patient was
of a nervous temperament and had a tendency toward heart trouble.
He had even had fainting spells before, but no attack had ever been
so long or so strong. However, the doctor announced, all danger
was past. Emilio was dressed, as a convalescent ought to be, in a
loose dressing gown; his mother had wound a blue woolen kerchief
around his neck; but he had a cheerful, almost carefree, expression,
and, indeed, everything around him seemed carefree. In front of the
couch, on a round table covered with a clean cloth, stood a huge
china coffee-pot filled with fragrant chocolate and surrounded by
cups, carafes of syrup, ladyfingers and rolls, and even flowers; six
thin wax candles were burning in two old silver candelabra; soft and
inviting, a Voltaire chair stood on one side of the couch—and in that
chair they seated Sanin.

All the inhabitants of the shop whom he had happened to meet
that day were on hand, including the poodle Tartaglia and the cat.
Everyone seemed unspeakably happy; the poodle was even sneezing from pleasure; only the cat kept mincing, as always, and closing
its eyes. They made Sanin explain who he was, and where he came
from, and what his name was. When he said that he was Russian,
both ladies were somewhat taken aback and even gasped—and at
once declared, with one accord, that he spoke German excellently,
but if it was easier for him to speak French, he could use that language, too, for they both could understand it and speak it well. Sanin
immediately availed himself of the suggestion. "Sanin! Sanin!" The
ladies had not in the least expected that a Russian name could be
pronounced so easily. His first name, "Dmitri," they liked that very
much, too. The older lady remarked that in her youth she had heard
a beautiful opera, "Demetrio e Polibio"—but that "Dimitri" was
much better than "Demetrio." Sanin talked away like this for about
an hour. The ladies, for their part, let him in on all the details of their
own lives. The mother, the lady with grey hair, talked most of all.
Sanin found out from her that her name was Leonora Roselli, that

she had been left a widow by her husband, Giovanni Battista Roselli, who had settled in Frankfurt as a confectioner twenty-five years ago, that Giovanni Battista had come from a family in Vicenza and was a very good man, though somewhat irascible and overbearing, and a republican besides! As she said this, Signora Roselli pointed to his portrait, done in oils and hanging over the couch. One had to presume that the artist—"also a republican," as Signora Roselli remarked with a sigh—had not quite managed to catch the likeness, for in the portrait the late Giovanni Battista seemed a somewhat gloomy and austere brigand—rather like Rinaldo Rinaldini!

Signora Roselli herself was a native "of the old and beautiful city of Parma, where there is the marvelous dome painted by the immortal Correggio!" But from her long stay in Germany she had become almost completely Germanized. Then she added, shaking her head sadly, that all she had left was *this* daughter and *this* son (she pointed to each in turn); the daughter was called Gemma and the son Emilio, they were both very good and obedient children, especially Emilio... ("I'm not obedient?" the daughter put in; "Oh, you're a republican, too!" the mother replied); and that, of course, things were going worse now than when her husband—who had been a great master in the confectioner's trade—was alive *("Un grand'uomo!"* Pantaleone chimed in with a stern look); but that, still, thank God, they could make out!

V

Gemma listened to her mother, and sometimes laughed softly, sometimes sighed, sometimes patted her shoulder, sometimes shook her finger at her, or sometimes looked at Sanin. Finally she got up, put her arms around her mother, and kissed her neck—in the hollow of her throat, which made her mother laugh a good deal, and even squeal.

Pantaleone, also, was introduced to Sanin. It turned out that he had once been an opera singer, a baritone, but had long ago dropped his theatrical activities and in the Roselli family was something between a friend of the family and a servant. Despite his long stay in Germany, he spoke German very badly and could only swear in it, mercilessly mangling even the swear words. "Ferroflucto spiccebubbio!"[1] he called almost every German. Italian he spoke perfectly—for his family was from Sinigaglia, where one hears *"lingua toscana in bocca romana."* Emilio, quite obviously, was taking it easy and giving himself up to the pleasant sensations of one who has just avoided danger or who is convalescing; and, besides, it was quite clear that his family spoiled him. He thanked Sanin shyly, and set to work harder on the syrup and the sweets. Sanin was forced to drink two big cups of excellent chocolate and to eat an extraordinary number of ladyfingers: he would just get one down when Gemma would already be offering him another—and it was impossible to refuse! He soon felt at home; the time flew by with unbelievable swiftness.

There was a lot he had to tell them about—about Russia in general, about Russia's climate, about Russian society, about the Russian peasant—and especially about the Cossacks; about the War of '12, Peter the Great, the Kremlin, and about Russian songs and church bells. Both ladies had an extremely vague idea of our vast and faraway native land; Signora Roselli, or, as she was more often called, Frau Lenore, even astounded Sanin by asking: Does there still exist in Petersburg the famous ice-palace, built in the last century, about which she had recently read such an interesting article in one of her late husband's books, *Bellezze delle arti?* And in reply to Sanin's exclamation: "Do you really believe that there never is any summer in Russia?" Frau Lenore protested that until then she had thought of Russia like this: eternal snow, everyone going around in fur coats, and everyone a soldier—but amazing hospitality and all the peasants very obedient. Sanin tried to give her and her daughter some more nearly accurate information.

When the conversation turned to Russian music, they immediately begged him to sing a Russian aria and pointed to a tiny piano in the room with black keys instead of white, and white instead of black. He at once did as he was asked and, accompanying himself with two fingers of his right hand and three (the thumb, middle, and little

---

1   For *verfluchte Spitzbube.*

finger) of his left, he sang in a thin nasal tenor, first "Sarafan" and then "Along a Cobbled Street." The ladies praised his voice and the music, but were still more delighted with the softness and richness of Russian and requested a translation of the text. Sanin did as they wished, but since the words of "Sarafan" and, especially, of "Along a Cobbled Street (*sur une rue pavée une jeune fitte allait à l'eau* was how he rendered the meaning of the original) could not inspire his listeners with a high regard for Russian poetry, he first recited, then translated, and then sang Pushkin's "I Recall a Marvelous Moment" set to music by Glinka, the minor bars of which he slightly garbled. The ladies were ecstatic—Frau Lenore even found a remarkable similarity between the sounds of Russian and Italian: "Mgnovenie"—"o, vieni"; "so mnoi"—"siam noi"; and so forth.[2] Even the names Pushkin (she pronounced it Pussekin) and Glinka sounded like her native tongue to her. Sanin, in his turn, asked the ladies to sing something; they, too, were not awkward or formal about it. Frau Lenore sat down at the piano and with Gemma sang several little duets and *stornelle*. The mother had once had a nice contralto; the daughter's voice was rather weak, but pleasant.

VI

But it was not Gemma's voice, it was the girl herself that Sanin was admiring. He was sitting somewhat behind her and to one side, and was thinking to himself that no palm tree—even in the poems of Benediktov, a fashionable poet at that time—could rival the elegant grace of her figure. When, on the little tender notes, she raised her eyes up, it seemed to him that there was no heaven which would not open wide at such a look. Even old Pantaleone who, leaning his shoulder against the door jamb, his chin and mouth tucked into his broad cravat, was listening with an air of importance, with the expression of a connoisseur—even he was admiring the face of the beautiful girl and marveling at it—though, one would have thought, he should have become used to it! Having finished her duets with her

---

2   "Moment"—"oh, come"; "with me"—"it's we."

daughter, Frau Lenore made the remark that Emilio had an excellent voice, pure silver, but that he had now reached the age when the voice changes (he really did talk in a kind of continually cracking bass), and that therefore he was not allowed to sing; but that now Pantaleone might, in honor of their guest, bring back the old days.

Pantaleone immediately assumed a dissatisfied expression, frowned, ruffled his hair, and announced that he had given all this up long ago, although he could really do well when he was young—that in general he belonged to that great age when there were real, classical singers—no comparison to the squeakers they had now!—and a real school of singing. Once he, Pantaleone Cippatola of Varese, had been given a laurel wreath at Modena, and on that occasion they had even let out several white doves in the theater; and, by the way, a certain Russian Prince Tarbusski—*il principe Tarbusski*—with whom he had been extremely friendly, as they sat at dinner was always inviting him to Russia, promising him mountains of gold, mountains! But he had not wanted to leave Italy, the country of Dante—*il paese del Dante!*—Later, of course, there were—unfortunate circumstances, he himself had been careless—Here the old man broke off, sighed deeply once or twice, looked down—and again started talking about the classical age of singing, about the great tenor Garcia, for whom he nourished a reverential, boundless respect.

"That was a man!" he exclaimed. "The great Garcia—*il gran Garcia*—never stooped to singing falsetto as these little tenors—*tenoracci*—do now: always with the chest, the chest, *voce di petto, si!*" The old man rapped his little dried-up fist hard on his *jabot*. "And what an actor! A volcano, *signori miei*, a volcano, *un Vesuvio!* I had the honor and good fortune of singing with him in an opera *dell'illustrissimo maestro* Rossini—in *Otello!* Garcia was Otello, I was Iago, and when he uttered this phrase..."

Here Pantaleone struck a pose and started singing in a trembling and husky but still deeply moving voice:

"L'i...ra daver...so daver...so il fato
Io più no...no...no...non temerò!

"The theater was shaking, *signori miei!* but I, too, didn't hang back, I went on right after him:

"L'i...ra daver...so daver...so il fato
Temèr più non dovro!

And then suddenly, like lightning, like a tiger, he replied: *Morro!...
ma vendicato...*

"Or then again, when he was singing...when he was singing the famous aria from *Matrimonio segreto: Pria che spunti...*Here he, *il gran Garcia,* after the words *I cavalli di galoppo* made, at the words *Senza posa cassiera*—listen how great it is, *comè stupendo!* Here he made..." The old man started to make a sort of unusual flourish—faltered on the tenth note, coughed, and, waving his hand in disgust, turned away, and muttered: "Why do you torture me?" Gemma immediately jumped up from her chair and, loudly applauding, shouting "Bravo! Bravo!" ran over to the poor retired Iago and with both hands affectionately patted him on his shoulders. Only Emilio laughed pitilessly. *Cet âge est sans pitié*—that age has no pity, Lafontaine once said.

Sanin tried to comfort the aged singer and started talking to him in Italian (he had picked up a little during his last trip)—started talking about *paese del Dante, dove il si suona.* This phrase, along with *Lasciate ogni speranza,* was the young tourist's entire Italian poetic baggage, but Pantaleone did not yield to his flattery. Tucking his chin more deeply than ever into his cravat and sullenly bulging his eyes, he again resembled a bird, but an angry one—a raven, maybe, or a kite. At that point Emilio, blushing slightly for an instant, as spoiled children usually do, turned to his sister and said to her that if she wanted to entertain their guest she could not do better than to read him one of the little comedies of Malz, which she read so well. Gemma laughed, slapped her brother on the hand, and exclaimed that he "was always thinking up such things!" She went straight to her own room, however, and, having come back with a small book in her hand, sat down at the table in front of the lamp, looked around, raised her finger, as if to say, Silence!—a completely Italian gesture—and started reading.

VII

Malz was a Frankfurt literary figure of the Thirties who, in his very short and light comedies, written in the local dialect, drew with amusing and sharp, although not profound, humor the local, Frankfurt types. Gemma, it turned out, did indeed read superbly—just like an actress. She set off each character and brilliantly maintained his characteristics, using that mimicry she had inherited along with her Italian blood. She spared neither her soft voice nor her beautiful face; whenever she had to portray some old woman who had become a dotard, or some stupid burgomaster, she made the most amusing faces, screwed up her eyes, wrinkled her nose, talked with a guttural burr, whined...During the reading she herself did not laugh, but when her listeners (excepting, it is true, Pantaleone: he had immediately gone away in indignation as soon as there was mention of *quel ferroflucto Tedesco*)—when her listeners interrupted her by a burst of sudden genuine laughter, she, having put the book on her lap, would laugh ringingly herself with her head thrown back—and her black curls would jump in soft ringlets on her neck and shaking shoulders. The laughter would stop and she would immediately pick up the book and, again assuming the expression that went with the role, start reading seriously. Sanin could not admire her sufficiently; he was especially amazed by what miracle such an ideally beautiful face suddenly took on such a comic, sometimes almost banal, expression. Gemma read the young girls' parts, the so-called *jeunes premières,* less satisfactorily; she was not very good in the love scenes especially; she herself sensed that, and therefore read them with a light tone of ridicule—as if she did not believe all these rapturous vows and noble protestations, which the author himself, however, refrained from, as much as he could.

Sanin did not notice how the evening flew by, and remembered the journey ahead of him only when the clock struck ten. He jumped up from his chair as if he had been stung.

"What's the matter?" Frau Lenore asked.

"Why, I was supposed to leave for Berlin today—and I've already reserved a seat in the coach!"

"But when does the coach leave?"

"At ten-thirty."

"Well, now you can't make it," Gemma remarked. "Stay...I'll read a little more."

"Did you pay the whole fare, or just leave a deposit?" Frau Lenore inquired.

"The whole fare!" Sanin wailed with a mournful look.

Gemma looked at him, half closed her eyes, and burst out laughing; but her mother scolded her.

"The young man's spent his money for nothing, and you're laughing!"

"It doesn't matter," replied Gemma. "This won't ruin him, and we'll try to console him. Do you want some lemonade?"

Sanin drank a glass of lemonade. Gemma again began to read Malz, and again everything was going just fine.

The clock struck twelve. Sanin started to say good-bye.

"Now that you have to stay in Frankfurt a few days," Gemma said to him, "where do you have to hurry to? It wouldn't be any gayer in another town." She was silent a moment. "Really, it wouldn't," she added and smiled. Sanin answered nothing, and thought that owing to the emptiness of his purse he would, willy-nilly, have to stay in Frankfurt until an answer came from a certain Berlin friend to whom he intended to turn for money.

"Stay, stay," said Frau Lenore, too. "We'll introduce you to Gemma's fiancé, Herr Karl Klüber. He couldn't come today because he's very busy in his store. You probably saw it: the biggest store for yard goods and silks on the *Zeile*. Well, he's the manager there. But he'll be very glad to call and introduce himself to you."

This news—God knows why—somewhat took Sanin aback. "That fiancé's a lucky man!" flashed through his mind. He looked at Gemma—and he thought he caught a mocking expression in her eyes. He began bowing and saying good-bye.

"Until tomorrow? It is tomorrow, isn't it?" said Frau Lenore.

"Until tomorrow!" said Gemma, not in an interrogative but in an affirmative tone, as if it could not be otherwise.

"Until tomorrow!" echoed Sanin.

Emilio, Pantaleone, and the poodle Tartaglia walked with him to the street corner. Pantaleone could not hold back from expressing his displeasure at Gemma's reading.

"She ought to be ashamed of herself! Making faces, whining— *una caricatura!* She ought to be doing Merope or Clytemnestra— something great, tragic, and she does a take-off on some disgusting German woman! Even I can do that...Merts, kerts, smerts," he added in a hoarse voice, thrusting his face forward and spreading his fingers. Tartaglia barked at him, and Emilio burst into a loud laugh. The old man turned back sharply.

Sanin returned to the White Swan hotel (he had left his things there in the lobby) in a rather troubled state of mind. All those German-French-Italian conversations were still ringing in his ears.

"She's engaged!" he whispered, lying in bed in the little hotel room assigned him. "And what a beautiful girl! But why did I stay?"

However, the next day he sent a letter to his Berlin friend.

VIII

He had just barely gotten dressed when the waiter announced the arrival of two gentlemen. One of them turned out to be Emilio; the other, a tall and attractive young man with a very fine-looking face, was Herr Karl Klüber, the fiancé of the beautiful Gemma.

It is safe to assume that at that time in all of Frankfurt there was not another store with such a courteous, presentable, dignified, obliging manager as Herr Klüber. The impeccability of his dress was on the same high level as the dignity of his bearing and the elegance—a little stiff, it is true, and reserved, in the English style (he had spent two years in England)—but nevertheless, the captivating elegance of his manners! From the first glance it was clear that this handsome, somewhat stern, excellently brought-up, and superbly clean young man was accustomed to obeying superiors and ordering inferiors, and that behind the counter of his store he must have unfailingly inspired respect in his customers themselves! There could not be the slightest doubt of his supernatural honesty: one had only to look at his stiffly starched collar! His voice, also, was what one would have expected: rich and self-confidently full, but not too loud, with even a certain gentleness of timbre. Such a voice is particularly good for giving orders to the clerks under you: "Please show the piece of crimson Lyons velvet!" or "Bring this lady a chair!"

Herr Klüber began by introducing himself, bending at the waist so nobly, moving his feet so pleasantly, and touching one heel against the other so respectfully that anyone would certainly have felt: "Both this man's underwear and his spiritual qualities are of first quality!" The trim of his exposed right hand (in his left, clothed in a suede glove, he held a hat polished to a mirror sheen, in which lay his other glove)—the trim of this right hand, which he modestly but firmly extended to Sanin, exceeded all belief: each nail was perfection in itself! Then he explained, in the most refined German, that he wished to pay his respects and his gratitude to the gentleman from abroad who had rendered such an important service to his future relative, the brother of his fiancée. As he said this, he moved his left hand, holding the hat, in the direction of Emilio, who seemed embarrassed and, having turned to the window, put his finger in his mouth. Herr Klüber added that he would consider himself fortunate if, for his part, he might be able to do something pleasant for the gentleman from abroad. Sanin answered, not without some difficulty, also in German, that he was very glad…that his service was un important… and begged his guests to sit down. Herr Klüber thanked him—and, instantly spreading the tails of his dress coat, lowered himself onto a chair—but he lowered himself so delicately and sat on it so precariously that it was impossible not to realize: "That man sat down out of politeness—and will jump up again any minute!" And actually, he did jump up right away and, discreetly shifting from one foot to another once or twice, as if dancing, announced that, unfortunately, he could not stay longer, for he was in a hurry to get to his store— business comes first!—but that since tomorrow was Sunday, he had, with the consent of Frau Lenore and Fraulein Gemma, arranged a pleasure trip to Soden, to which he had the honor of inviting tie gentleman from abroad—and that he cherished the hope that he would not refuse to grace it by his presence. Sanin did not refuse to grace it—and Herr Klüber bowed a second time and went out, pleasantly flashing his trousers of a most delicate pea-green color and just as pleasantly squeaking with the soles of his brand new boots.

IX

Emilio, who continued to stand facing the window even after Sanin's invitation to be seated, swung around to the left just as soon as his future relative had gone, and, making a childish face and blushing, asked Sanin if he could stay a little longer. "I'm a lot better today," he added, "but the doctor forbade my working."

"Stay!" Sanin exclaimed at once. "You're not in my way at all." Like every true Russian, he was glad to seize the first excuse for not having to do something himself.

Emilio thanked him—and in the shortest time had completely fitted himself in both with Sanin and his room; he was looking over his things, and asking questions about almost every one of them: where did he buy it, and what was it worth? He helped him shave, and as he did so commented that Sanin was wrong not to let his moustache grow; told him, finally, a lot of little things about his own mother, his sister, Pantaleone, even about the poodle Tartaglia, about their whole way of life. Every semblance of timidity in Emilio disappeared; he suddenly felt extraordinarily attracted to Sanin—and not at all because he had saved his life the day before, but because he was such a nice man! He immediately entrusted all his secrets to Sanin. He particularly heatedly insisted on the fact that his mama absolutely wanted to make him a merchant, but he *knew*, knew for sure, that he was born an artist, a musician, a singer; that the theater was his real calling; that even Pantaleone was encouraging him. But Herr Klüber was supporting Mama, on whom he had great influence; the very idea of making him a shopkeeper was personally Herr Klüber's, according to whose understanding nothing in the world can be compared to being a merchant! To sell cloth and velvet and swindle the public, to charge them *Narren—oder Russen-Preise* (fool's—or Russians' prices)—that's his ideal![3]

"Well, so! Now we have to go to our place!" he exclaimed as soon as Sanin had finished getting ready and had written the letter to Berlin.

"It's too early yet," remarked Sanin.

"That doesn't mean anything," said Emilio, playing up to him. "Let's go! We'll drop by the post-office, and from there go to our place. Gemma will be so glad to see you! You'll have lunch with us. You can put in a good word to Mama for me, about my career."

"Well, let's go," said Sanin, and they set out.

X

Gemma was indeed delighted to see him, and Frau Lenore greeted him very warmly: it was clear that he had made a good impression on both of them the day before. Emilio ran off to see about the lunch, having first whispered in Sanin's ear: "Don't forget!"

"I won't," replied Sanin.

Frau Lenore was not feeling quite well: she was suffering from migraine, and, half-lying in an armchair, was trying not to move. Gemma had on a loose yellow smock with a black leather belt around her waist; she, too, looked tired and was somewhat pale; darkish circles shadowed her eyes, but their brilliance was no less for that, and her paleness added something mysterious and endearing to the classically severe features of her face. The exquisite beauty of her hands struck Sanin especially that day; when she fixed or put up her dark, shiny curls with them, he could not take his eyes off her fingers, supple and long and set apart from each other as on Raphael's Fornarina.

Outdoors it was very hot; after lunch Sanin was about to leave, but

---

3   In former times—and, perhaps, it has continued even now—when, beginning with May, many Russians appeared in Frankfurt, the prices were raised in all the stores and came to be called *Russen,* or—alas!—*Narren-Preise. (Author's note.)*

they pointed out to him that on such a day it was best not to move around—and he agreed; he stayed. In the back room where he was sitting with his hostesses, coolness reigned; the windows looked out on a little garden overgrown with acacia. A great number of bees, wasps, and bumblebees were buzzing constantly and greedily in their thick branches covered with gold blossoms; this incessant noise pierced through the half-closed shutters and the drawn blinds into the room: it told of the sultry heat that filled the outside air—and the coolness of the closed and comfortable house became that much sweeter.

Sanin talked a good deal, as he had the day before, but not about Russia and not about Russian life. Wanting to please his young friend, who had been sent off to Herr Klüber's right after lunch, to practice bookkeeping, he began talking about the comparative advantages and disadvantages of art and of trade. He was not surprised that Frau Lenore took the side of trade—he expected that; but Gemma, too, shared her opinion.

"If you're an artist—and especially a singer," she asserted, bringing her hand down forcefully, "you absolutely must be in the first rank! Second is no good at all; and who knows if you can reach first rank?" Pantaleone, who was also taking part in the conversation (as a long-time servant and an old man, he was allowed even to sit on a chair in his masters' presence; the Italians in general are not strict about etiquette)—Pantaleone, of course, was completely for art. To tell the truth, his reasons were rather weak: he mostly talked about how it was above all essential to have *un certo estro d'inspirazione*—a certain fit of inspiration! Frau Lenore remarked to him that he, of course, had had this *estro*—yet that…

"I had enemies," Pantaleone commented gloomily. "But how do you[4] know that Emilio won't have enemies, even if this *estro* is discovered in him?"

"Well, so make him a tradesman," said Pantaleone with annoyance, "but Giovann' Battista wouldn't have done it, though he was a confectioner himself!"

"Giovann' Battista, my husband, was a sensible man—and if he

---

4   In Russian, *ty*—"thou." The distinction cannot be easily translated into English.

was carried away when he was young…"

But the old man did not want to hear any more, and left the room, having said once more, reproachfully:

"Ah! Giovann' Battista!…"

Gemma exclaimed that if Emilio felt patriotic and wanted to devote all his energies to the liberation of Italy—why, of course, for such a noble and sacred cause a secure future might, indeed, be sacrificed—but not for the theater! At this point Frau Lenore became upset and started imploring her daughter at least not to confuse her brother, and be content that she herself was such a desperate republican! Having said this, Frau Lenore began to groan and complain about her head, which was "ready to burst." (Frau Lenore, out of respect for their guest, was talking to her daughter in French.)

Gemma immediately started taking care of her, blew gently on her forehead, having first moistened it with Eau de Cologne, softly kissed her cheeks, put some pillows under her head, forbade her to talk—and again kissed her. Then, turning to Sanin, she began telling him in a half-joking, half-serious tone what a wonderful mother she had, and what a beautiful woman she had been! "What am I saying: had been? She's charming even now. Look, look, what eyes she has!"

Gemma instantly took a white handkerchief out of her pocket, covered her mother's face with it, and, slowly lowering the upper edge, gradually uncovered Frau Lenore's fore head, eyebrows, and eyes; she stopped a moment and asked her to open them. Her mother obeyed, Gemma cried out in delight (Frau Lenore's eyes were really very beautiful), and, having quickly slid the handkerchief over the lower, less regular part of her mother's face, started kissing her again. Frau Lenore laughed and turned slightly away, and with feigned effort pushed her daughter back. She, too, pretended she was struggling with her mother and pressed up to her—not like a cat, not in the French manner, but with that Italian grace in which the presence of power is always felt.

Finally, Frau Lenore declared that she was tired…Then Gemma immediately advised her to take a little nap, right there, in the chair; "and the Russian gentleman—*le monsieur russe*—and I will be as quiet, as quiet…as little mice…*comme des petites souris.*" Frau Lenore smiled in response to her, shut her eyes, and, having sighed a little, dozed off. Gemma quickly dropped down onto a footstool beside her and did not move; once in a while she would raise the finger of one hand to her lips—she was holding a pillow under her mother's head with the other hand—and barely say "Shh!" glancing sidelong at Sanin, whenever he made the slightest movement. In the end he also became completely still and sat motionless, like a man in a trance. With all deepest feeling, he delighted in the picture presented him by this half-dark room—where here and there fresh, magnificent roses placed in green, antique glasses glowed like bright dots—and by this sleeping woman with the unassumingly folded hands and the good, tired face framed by the snowy whiteness of the pillow, and by this young, sharply watchful, and also good, intelligent, pure, and ineffably beautiful creature with such black, deep, shadow-filled, but still so shining, eyes…What was this? A dream? A fairy tale? And how did *he* come to be here?

The little bell tinkled over the outside door. A young peasant in a fur cap and a red vest came into the confectioner's shop. Since early morning not a single customer had even looked in. "That's the kind of business we do!" said Frau Lenore to Sanin with a sigh during lunch. She continued dozing; Gemma was afraid to take her hand away from under the pillow and whispered to Sanin: "Go in and take care of the customer for me!" Sanin immediately went out into the shop on tiptoe. The young boy wanted a quarter-pound of peppermints.

"What do I ask for them?" Sanin whispered through the door to Gemma.

"Six kreutzers!" she answered in the same sort of whisper. Sanin weighed out a quarter of a pound, found a piece of paper, made a cone out of it, poured the mints into it, spilled them, poured them in again, again spilled them, finally gave them to the boy, and took the money. The boy stared at him in amazement, twirling his cap on his stomach, and in the next room Gemma, her hand over her mouth, was dying of laughter. This customer had barely gone out when another showed up, and then a third…."Well, obviously, I'm lucky!" Sanin thought. The second one asked for a glass of almond drink; the third, for a half-pound of candy. Sanin served them, clinking the spoons with abandon, pushing the saucers around, and boldly sticking his fingers into drawers and jars. On totaling up, it turned out that he had charged too little for the almond drink and had taken two kreutzers too much for the candy. Gemma did not stop laughing surreptitiously, and even Sanin himself had a sense of an unusual gaiety. He felt as if he could stand behind the counter like that for ages, selling candy and almond drinks while that dear creature watched him from behind the door with friendly, mocking eyes; and the summer sun, cutting its way through the thick foliage of the chestnuts growing in front of the windows, filled the whole room with the greenish gold of its midday rays, its midday shadows, and the heart was basking in the sweet languor of idleness, of unconcern, and of youth—of first youth!

The fourth visitor asked for a cup of coffee: he had to turn to Pantaleone (Emilio still had not returned from Herr Küber's store). Sanin again sat down beside Gemma. Frau Lenore continued to doze, to her daughter's great satisfaction.

"Mama's migraine always goes away when she sleeps," she observed.

Sanin started talking—in a whisper, of course, as before—about his "selling"; completely seriously, he asked about the price of various confectioner's goods; Gemma gave him these prices just as seriously, and all the while they were both inwardly laughing together, as if admitting that they were acting out the most amusing comedy. Suddenly, outside, a street organ struck up an aria from the *Freischütz: Durch die Felder, durch die Auen...* Trembling and whistling, the whining sounds whimpered in the still air. Gemma shuddered..."He'll wake up Mama!" Sanin immediately ran out to the street, shoved several kreutzers into the organ-grinder's hand, and made him stop playing and go away. When he came back, Gemma thanked him with a slight nod of her head and, smiling reflectively, herself started singing, just barely audibly, the beautiful Weber tune with which Max expresses all the wonder of first love. Then she asked Sanin whether he knew the *Freischütz*, if he liked Weber, and added that, though she was an Italian herself, she liked music like that most of all. From Weber the conversation passed to poetry and romanticism, to Hoffmann, who was then still read by everybody...

Frau Lenore was still dozing and even just barely snoring, and the sun's rays, falling through the shutters in narrow streaks, were constantly shifting, unnoticed, and traveling across the floor, the furniture, Gemma's dress, the leaves and petals of the flowers.

XII

It turned out that Gemma was not too fond of Hoffmann, and even found him...boring! The fantastic, foggy, northern element of his stories was hardly accessible to her bright, southern nature. "It's all fairy tales, it's all written for children!" she asserted, not without disdain. She also vaguely sensed the lack of poetry in Hoffmann. But there was one story whose title she had forgotten, which she liked very much. Strictly speaking, she liked only the beginning of the story: either she had not read the ending, or she had forgotten that too. It was about a certain young man who somewhere—maybe even in a confectioner's shop—meets a girl of extraordinary beauty, a Greek girl; she is accompanied by a mysterious and strange, evil old man. The young man falls in love with the girl at first sight; she looks at him so pitifully, as if she were begging him to liberate her. He goes away for a moment and, on returning to the shop, finds neither the girl nor the old man; he sets out to find her, continually keeps stumbling on their fresh trail, chases after them—and can never get to them in any way, any place, any time. The beautiful girl disappears for him forever and ever, but he is not able to forget her imploring look, and he is tormented by the idea that perhaps his life's happiness has slipped through his hands.

Hoffmann hardly ends his tale like that, but that was the way she had put it together, that was the way it had remained in Gemma's memory.

"It seems to me," she said, "that such meetings and such partings take place in this world more often than we think."

Sanin was silent, and a little later he began to talk about Herr

Klüber. It was the first time he had mentioned him; he had not once thought about him until that moment.

Gemma, in turn, was silent and lost in thought, lightly biting the nail of her index finger and staring to one side. Then she praised her fiancé, referred to the next day's outing he had arranged, and, glancing quickly at Sanin, fell silent again.

Sanin did not know what to talk about.

Emilio ran in noisily and woke up Frau Lenore...Sanin was relieved that he had come.

Frau Lenore got up from the armchair. Pantaleone appeared and announced that dinner was ready. The family friend, ex-singer, and servant also served as cook.

XIII

Sanin stayed on after dinner, too. They did not let him go, still on the same excuse of the terrible heat; and when the heat had gone, they suggested going out into the garden to drink coffee in the shade of the acacias. Sanin agreed. He felt very good. Great delights are hidden in the monotonous, placid, and even flow of life—and he gave himself over to them with enjoyment, asking nothing special of the day and not thinking of the morrow nor remembering the day before. What was just the closeness of such a girl as Gemma worth to him? He would be parting from her soon, probably forever; but while the same boat, as in Uhland's love-poem, carried them along life's calm currents—rejoice, enjoy yourself, traveler! And to the happy traveler everything seemed pleasant and sweet.

Frau Lenore proposed that he play *tresette* with her and Pantaleone, and taught him this simple Italian card game; she won a few kreutzers from him and he was very pleased. At Emilio's request, Pantaleone made the poodle Tartaglia do all its tricks—and Tartaglia jumped over a stick, "spoke," that is barked, sneezed, shut the door with his nose, fetched his master's worn-out slipper, and, finally, with an old shako on his head, played Marshal Bernadotte being subjected to the harsh reproaches of the Emperor Napoleon for his treachery.

Pantaleone, of course, played Napoleon—and played him very real-
istically: he folded his arms on his chest, pulled his tricorner down
over his eyes, and spoke coarsely and sharply in French—but, my
Lord, *what* French! Tartaglia sat in front of his sovereign all hunched
up, his tail between his legs, blinking confusedly and squinting under
the vizor of the shako set crookedly on his head; from time to time,
when Napoleon raised his voice, Bernadotte rose up on his hind legs.
"Fuori, traditore!" Napoleon finally shouted, having forgotten, in his
excess of irritation, that he ought to have kept his French character
to the end—and Bernadotte rushed headlong under the couch, but
immediately jumped back out with a joyful bark, as if indicating by
this that the performance was over. All the spectators laughed—
Sanin most of all.

Gemma had an especially endearing, unceasing, soft laugh with
little, extremely amusing shrieks…Sanin was dissolved by this
laugh—he could have smothered her with kisses for these shrieks!

At last night fell. It was time for him to go home. Having said
good-bye to everyone several times, having told everyone several
times: "Until tomorrow!" (he even kissed Emilio), Sanin set out
for the hotel and took with him the image of a young girl, sometimes laughing, sometimes thoughtful, sometimes calm and even
indifferent, but always attractive! Her eyes, at times wide open and
bright and joyful as the day, at times half-covered by their lashes and
deep and dark as night, were virtually in front of him, strangely and
sweetly penetrating all other images and fancies.

He did not once think about Herr Klüber, about the reasons why
he had stayed in Frankfurt—in short, about everything that had
worried him the day before.

XIV

A few words, however, must be said about Sanin himself. In the first
place, he was really not at all bad-looking. Tall, of slender stature;
with pleasant, slightly vague features, tender little bluish eyes, golden
hair, white skin, and rosy cheeks—but, most important, that artlessly

gay, trusting, candid, at first seemingly rather foolish expression by which in olden times one could immediately recognize the children of the best families, sons who took after their fathers, fine young noblemen born and bred in our open semi-steppe regions; a hesitant way of walking, a lisping voice, a child's smile as soon as you barely glanced at him, and, finally, freshness, healthiness—and softness, softness, softness—there you have the whole of Sanin. And, in the second place, he was not stupid and had learned a few things. He had retained his freshness, despite his trip abroad: the feelings of anxiety which disturbed the better part of the young people in those days were little known to him.

Recently, after a vain search for "new men," our literature has begun to be filled with young man who have decided to be fresh at any cost—as fresh as Flensburg oysters imported into Petersburg. Sanin was not like them. If it is a question of comparison, he rather reminded one of a young, bushy, recently grafted apple tree in our black-earth orchards—or, better still, a sleek, smooth, thick-legged, tender three-year-old on one of our former "gentleman's" stud farms, who had just begun to be schooled on a lunge. Those who ran across Sanin subsequently, when life in its course had broken him and his youthful, unnatural plumpness had long since left him, saw him as a completely different man.

The next day Sanin was still lying in bed when Emilio, in holiday best and with a cane in his hand and his hair very slicked down, burst into his room and announced that Herr Klüber would arrive any minute now in his carriage, that wonderful weather was promised, that they had everything ready, but that Mama wasn't going because she again had a headache. He started trying to hurry Sanin up, swearing to him there wasn't a minute to lose. And indeed, Herr Klüber found Sanin still getting dressed. He knocked on the door, came in, bowed, bent deeply at the waist, expressed his readiness to wait any length of time, and sat down, gracefully resting his hat on his knee. The handsome manager had dressed to the hilt and perfumed himself all over: each of his movements was accompanied by a strong rush of a very delicate aroma. He had arrived in a roomy, open carriage, a so-called landau, drawn by two large and strong, though not handsome, horses. A quarter of an hour later, Sanin, Klüber, and Emilio in this carriage rolled triumphantly up to the front door of the confectioner's shop. Signora Roselli absolutely declined to take part in the outing; Gemma wanted to stay with her mother, but was, as they say, chased out.

"I don't need anyone," her mother insisted; "I'm going to sleep. I'd send Pantaleone with you, but there'd be nobody to mind the shop."

"May we take Tartaglia?" asked Emilio.

"Yes, of course."

Tartaglia immediately, with joyful efforts, scrambled up onto the box and sat down, licking his chops: clearly, he was used to this. Gemma put on a big straw hat with brown ribbons; the hat turned down in front, shielding almost her whole face from the sun. The shadow ended just above the lips: they glowed virginally and softly, like the petals of a hundred-leaved rose, and her teeth shone through her parted lips innocently, as with children. Gemma sat down on the rear seat, beside Sanin; Klüber and Emilio sat opposite. Frau Lenore's pale face appeared in the window. Gemma waved her handkerchief to her—and the horses were off.

XV

Soden is a little town about a half-hour from Frankfurt. It lies in a lovely district in the foothills of the Taunus Mountains and is famous among us in Russia for its waters, supposedly healthy for people with weak chests. The people of Frankfurt go there chiefly for amusement, since Soden has a beautiful park and various *Wirtschaften* where one can drink beer and coffee in the shade of tall lindens and maples. The road from Frankfurt to Soden goes along the right bank of the Main and is lined with fruit trees. As the carriage was rolling quietly along the excellent highway, Sanin was furtively watching how Gemma treated her fiancé: this was the first time he had seen them together. *She* was composed and natural—but a little more reserved and more serious than usual; *he* looked like a condescending schoolteacher who had allowed both himself and those under him a modest and decorous pleasure. Sanin did not notice in him any special attentiveness to Gemma, what the French call *empressement*. It was clear that Herr Klüber considered the business settled and therefore saw no reason to make a special effort or to be concerned. But his condescension did not leave him for a moment! Even during the long walk before dinner through the wooded hills and valleys beyond Soden, even while enjoying the beauties of nature, he treated it, nature itself, with the same condescension, pierced from time to time by his regular headclerk's harshness. So, for example, he commented about one little stream that it flowed through the hollow too straight, instead of making several picturesque turns; he also did not approve of the behavior of a certain bird, a finch, which did not vary its strains enough!

Gemma was not bored and even, evidently, was pleased, but Sanin did not recognize the old Gemma in her: it was not that a shadow had come over her—her beauty had never been more radiant—but her soul had turned inward, had sunk with in her. Having opened her parasol and not unbuttoned her gloves, she walked along sedately, without hurrying—as well-brought- up young ladies walk—and talked little. Emilio also felt a kind of constraint, as Sanin had for quite a while. He, by the way, was somewhat ill at ease because of the fact that the conversation was continually in German. Only Tartaglia was not dejected! Barking madly, he dashed off after all the blackbirds he saw, jumped over ruts, tree stumps and holes in the ground; rushed into the water with a splash and eagerly lapped it, shook himself, yelped—and again flew off like an arrow, his red tongue flung back almost to his shoulder! Herr Klüber, for his part, did everything which he thought necessary for the party's amusement; he invited everyone to sit down in the shade of a spreading oak, and, having taken out of his side pocket a little book with the title *Knallerbsen— oder du sollst und wirst lachen!* (Firecrackers—or You Must and Shall Laugh!), started reading amusing jokes, with which this little book was filled. He read about twelve of the things, but provoked little mirth; only Sanin smiled out of politeness, and Herr Klüber himself, after each joke, let out a brief, business-like, but still condescending laugh. Toward noon, the whole group returned to Soden, to the best restaurant there.

Arrangements for dinner had to be made. Herr Klüber proposed that this dinner take place in the arbor, enclosed on all sides— *im Gartensalon;* but at this point Gemma suddenly balked and announced she would dine only in the open air, in the garden, at one of the little tables set out in front of the restaurant; that she was tired of always being face to face with the same people and that she wanted to see others. Groups of newly arrived guests were already sitting at several of the tables.

While Herr Klüber, condescendingly indulging "the whim of his fiancée," was off talking to the headwaiter, Gemma stood motionless, her eyes lowered and her lips drawn; she felt that Sanin was staring at her constantly and somehow questioningly—and this, apparently, made her angry. Herr Klüber finally came back, announced that dinner would be ready in half an hour, and suggested that until then they play skittles, adding that this was very good for the appetite, he-he-he! He played skittles expertly; when throwing the ball he struck amazingly dashing poses, foppishly flexed his muscles, foppishly swung and shook his leg. He was an athlete in his own way— and superbly built. His hands were so white and beautiful, and he wiped them with such a very gorgeous, gold-striped Indian foulard!

It came time for dinner—and the whole group sat down at the little table.

XVI

Who does not know what a German dinner is? Watery soup with knobby dumplings and cinnamon, well-cooked beef dry as a cork with white fat on it, clammy potatoes, plump beets and chopped horseradish, a dark blue eel with capers and vinegar, roast meat with preserves, and the inevitable *Mehlspeise,* something like a pudding with a tart red sauce; but then, also, excellent wine and beer! The Soden restaurateur treated his guests to just such a dinner. The dinner, however, went fine. True, there was no particular animation, not even when Herr Klüber drank a toast to "what we love!" *(Was wir lieben!)* Everything was very proper and decorous. Coffee was served after dinner, weak, rusty-colored, really German coffee. Herr Klüber, as a true cavalier, asked Gemma's permission to light a cigar…But at this point there suddenly happened something unforeseen and, indeed, unpleasant—and even improper!

Several officers of the Mainz garrison had sat down at one of the nearby tables. By their glances and whispering it was easy to guess that Gemma's beauty had struck them; one of them, who had probably been in Frankfurt, kept continually staring at her as at a familiar face: evidently he knew who she was. He suddenly got up and with his glass in his hand—the officers were somewhat under the weather, and the whole tablecloth in front of them was covered with bottles—approached the table at which Gemma was sitting. He was a very young, tow-haired man with a rather pleasant, even likable face, but the wine he had drunk distorted it: his cheeks were twitching, his bloodshot eyes wandered and had taken on a daring expression. His friends at first tried to hold him back, but then they let him go; whether or not it was the confectioner's daughter—why not see what would happen?

Slightly swaying on his feet, the officer stopped in front of Gemma and in an artificially shrill voice, in which, despite himself, the struggle that was going on inside him showed through, said: "I drink to the health of the most beautiful coffee-house girl in all of Frankfurt, in all the world" (he downed his glass in one swallow), "and in return I take this flower picked by her divine little fingers!" He picked up from the table the rose which had been lying in front of Gemma's place. She was at first astounded, frightened, and became terribly pale; then her fright changed to indignation, she suddenly blushed to the roots of her hair, and her eyes, fixed directly on the man who had insulted her, simultaneously darkened and flashed, filled with gloom and burned with the fire of irrepressible anger. This look probably embarrassed the officer; he muttered something indistinct, bowed— and went back to his friends. They greeted him with laughter and light applause.

Herr Klüber suddenly got up from his chair and, straightening up fully and putting on his hat, said with dignity but not too loudly: "It is unheard-of! Unheard-of insolence!" *(Unerhört! Unerhörte Frechheit!)*—and immediately calling the waiter over in a stern voice, asked for the check at once. And as if that weren't enough, he ordered the carriage harnessed and added that respectable people could not possibly come here, for they were subjected to insults! At these words, Gemma, who had continued to sit in her place without stirring, her chest rising and falling violently—Gemma turned her eyes to Herr Klüber and stared at him just as intently, with exactly the same look as she had at the officer. Emilio was simply trembling from rage.

"Get up, *mein Fräulein*," Herr Klüber said with the same severity; "it isn't proper for you to stay. We'll settle the account there, in the restaurant!"

Gemma got up silently; he offered her his arm, she gave him hers, and he went toward the restaurant majestically, with a gait which, like his bearing, became more and more majestic and haughty the farther away he got from the place where they had dined. Poor Emilio trailed after them.

But while Herr Klüber was settling things with the waiter, to whom he, as a form of penalty, did not give even one kreutzer as a tip, Sanin went quickly up to the table at which the officers were sitting, and, turning to the one who had insulted Gemma (he was at that moment letting each of his comrades in turn smell her rose), said clearly, in French:

"What you have just done, sir, is unworthy of an honorable man, unworthy of the uniform you are wearing—and I have come to tell you that you are a bad-mannered, impudent fellow!"

The young man jumped to his feet, but another officer, a little older, stopped him with a gesture, made him sit down, and, turning to Sanin, asked him, also in French: "Are you a relative, a brother, or the fiancé of that young lady?"

"I am a complete stranger to her," exclaimed Sanin; "I am a Russian, but I cannot look at such insolence indifferently; Here, however, is my card and my address: the officer can look me up."

Having said this, Sanin threw his visiting card on the table and at
the same time deftly picked up Gemma's rose which one of the officers sitting at the table had dropped on his plate. The young man was
again about to jump up from his chair, but his friend again stopped
him, saying: "Dönhof, be quiet!" *(Dönhof, sei still!).* Then he himself
got up, and, saluting, said to Sanin, not without a certain shade of
respect in his voice and gestures, that tomorrow morning an officer
from their regiment would have the honor of calling on him at his
apartment. Sanin responded with a little bow, and quickly returned
to his friends.

Herr Klüber pretended not to have noticed at all either Sanin's
absence or his conversation with the officers; he was hurrying up the
coachman harnessing the horses and was very angry at his slowness.
Gemma, also, said nothing to Sanin, did not even glance at him: one
could see by her knitted brows, her pale and compressed lips, by her
very stillness, that she felt very disturbed. Only Emilio obviously
wanted to talk to Sanin, wanted to ask him all about it: he had seen
how Sanin went up to the officers, and that he gave them something
white—a piece of paper, a note, a card...The poor boy's heart was
pounding, his cheeks were inflamed, he was ready to throw himself
on Sanin's neck, ready to cry or to go with him at once and beat up all
those foul officers! However, he controlled himself and was content
to follow carefully each movement of his noble Russian friend.

The coachman, finally, had harnessed the horses; the whole
group seated itself in the carriage. Emilio climbed up on the box
right behind Tartaglia; he had more room there, and besides, Klüber,
whom he could not look at calmly, would not be sticking up in front
of him.

Herr Klüber kept talking away the whole trip—and kept talking
alone; nobody, nobody contradicted him, and nobody agreed
with him. He particularly insisted on the fact, that they had been
wrong in not listening to him when he had suggested dining in the
enclosed arbor. There would have been no unpleasantness! Then he
pronounced several sharp and even liberal judgments about how the
government was unforgivably indulging its officers, not watching
over their discipline and not showing enough respect for the civilian

element of society *(das bürgerliche Element in der Societät!)*—and how in time this would give rise to discontent, from which it is but a short step to revolution, a sad example of which (here he sighed sympathetically but sternly)—a sad example of which is France! At this point, however, he added that he personally had much respect for authority and never—never!—would be a revolutionary, but that he could not help but express his...disapproval at the sight of such licentiousness! He then added a few more general comments on morality and immorality, on decorum and the sense of dignity!

During all this discourse, Gemma, who had not seemed completely satisfied with Herr Klüber even during their walk before dinner (because of which she had kept somewhat aloof from Sanin and seemed to have been embarrassed by his presence)—Gemma clearly was becoming ashamed of her fiancé. At the end of the ride she was positively suffering, and although, as before, she said nothing to Sanin, she suddenly cast him an imploring look. On his part, he felt much more pity for her than indignation at Herr Klüber; he was even secretly, half-consciously delighted with everything that had happened in the course of that day, although he could expect a challenge the following morning.

This painful *partie de plaisir* finally ended. Helping Gemma alight from the carriage in front of the confectioner's shop, Sanin, without saying a word, handed her the rose he had taken back. She flushed all over, pressed his hand, and instantly hid the rose. He did not want to go into the house, although the evening was just beginning. She herself did not invite him. Besides, Pantaleone, who had come out onto the porch, announced that Frau Lenore was resting. Emilio said good-bye to Sanin bashfully; he seemed to be really shy of him: actually he was filled with wonder for him. Klüber took Sanin to his hotel room and primly took leave of him. The thoroughly organized German, for all his self-confidence, was ill-at-ease. Indeed, everybody was.

However, for Sanin this feeling, the feeling of awkwardness, soon disappeared. It was replaced by an undefined, but pleasant, even rapturous mood. He walked back and forth in his room, did not want to think about anything, whistled, and was very pleased with himself...

XVII

"I'll wait for the officer until ten o'clock" he thought to himself the following morning as he was getting dressed, "and then let him look for me!" But the Germans get up early: it had not yet struck nine when the waiter announced to Sanin that Second Lieutenant (*der Herr Seconde Leutnant*) von Richter wanted to see him. Sanin quickly pulled on his frock coat and ordered him shown in. Herr Richter turned out to be, contrary to Sanin's expectations, a very young man, almost a boy. He tried to give an air of importance to his beardless face—but he could not do it: he could not even conceal his embarrassment, and as he sat down on a chair, almost fell, tripping over his sword. Stuttering and sputtering, he informed Sanin in execrable French that he had come with a commission from his friend, Baron von Dönhof; that his commission was to demand from Herr von Zanin an apology for certain insulting expressions used by him the day before; and that in case Herr von Zanin refused it, Baron von Dönhof would seek satisfaction. Sanin replied that he had no intention of apologizing and was ready to give satisfaction. Then Herr von Richter, still stammering, asked with whom, at what time, and in what place would he have to make the necessary negotiations? Sanin replied that he could come back to his room in two hours and that in the meantime he, Sanin, would try to find a second. ("Damn it, who'll I ask to be second?" he in the meanwhile thought to himself.) Herr von Richter got up and began taking his leave, but stopped on the threshold, as if he had felt a pang of conscience, and, turning to Sanin, said that his friend, Baron von Dönhof, did not deny... to a certain degree...of his own guilt in yesterday's occurrence— and therefore would be satisfied with mild apologies—*des exghizes lèchéres*. Sanin replied to this that he did not intend to make any apologies, strong or mild, since he did not consider himself at fault.

"In that case," replied Herr von Richter and flushed even more, "it will be necessary to exchange friendly shots—*des goups de bisdolet à l'amiaple!*"

"That I don't understand in the least," said Sanin. "We're supposed to shoot in the air, is that it?"

"Oh, no, no, not so," mumbled the lieutenant, completely embarrassed, "but I'd supposed that since this is something between two gentlemen...I'll talk to your second," he cut himself off and left.

Sanin sank down onto a chair, as soon as the other had gone out, and stared at the floor. "What is all this?" he thought. "How did life suddenly take such a turn? The whole past, the whole future is suddenly rubbed out, is gone—and there's nothing left but the fact that here I am in Frankfurt fighting somebody about something." He recalled only his crazy aunt who used to dance and sing all the time:

O lieutenant!
Darling boy!
Sweetest love! Come dance with me, my joy!

And he burst out laughing and sang, as she had: "O lieutenant! Come dance with me, my joy!"

"However, I must act; there's no time to lose!" he exclaimed aloud, and he jumped up and saw Pantaleone standing in front of him with a note in his hand.

"I knocked several times, but you didn't answer; I thought you were out," said the old man, and gave him the note. "From Signorina Gemma."

Sanin took the note—as they say, mechanically—opened it, and read it. Gemma wrote him that she was very worried about a certain matter well-known to him and wanted to see him at once.

"The signorina is very worried," Pantaleone began, who apparently knew what was in the note; "she told me to see what you were doing and bring you to her."

Sanin glanced at the old Italian, and fell to thinking. A sudden idea flashed through his mind. In the first instant it seemed impossibly strange to him.

"However—why not?" he asked himself.

"Signor Pantaleone!" he said aloud.

The old man started, tucked his chin into his cravat, and stared at Sanin.

"Do you know," Sanin went on, "what happened yesterday?"

Pantaleone bit his lips and shook his enormous tuft of hair. "I do."
(Emilio had told him everything just as soon as he had gotten in.)
"Ah! You know! Well, now. Just a moment ago an officer left here.
That impudent fellow is challenging me to a duel. I've accepted his
challenge. But I haven't got a second. Do *you* want to be my second?"

Pantaleone shuddered and raised his eyebrows so high they disappeared under his hair that was hanging down.

"You absolutely must fight?" he said finally in Italian; until that
moment he had been speaking French.

"Absolutely. To do anything else would be to shame myself forever."

"Hm. If I don't agree to be your second, you'll look for another?"

"I will...absolutely."

Pantaleone dropped his eyes.

"But may I ask you, Signor de Tsanini, won't your duel cast a certain unseemly shadow on the reputation of a certain person?"

"I don't think so; but, whether it does or not, there's nothing else
to be done."

"Hm." Pantaleone withdrew into his cravat completely. "Well, and
that *ferroflucto Kluberio*—what about him?" he suddenly exclaimed
and lifted up his face.

"Him? He has nothing to do with it."

"*Che!*[5] Pantaleone shrugged his shoulders contemptuously. "I
must at least thank you," he said at last in an unsteady voice, "that
even in my present humble state you were able to recognize me as an
honorable man—*un galant'uomo!* In so doing, you show yourself to
be a real *un galant'uomo.* But I have to think your suggestion over."

"Time won't let you, dear Signer Ci—Cippa—"

"—tola," the old man finished. "I ask for just an hour to think it
over. The daughter of my benefactors is involved here. And therefore
I must, I'm obliged—to think it over. In an hour, in three-quarters of
an hour, you will know my decision."

All right, I'll wait."

"And now...what answer will I give Signorina Gemma?"

Sanin took a sheet of paper and wrote on it: "Rest assured, my dear
friend, that in three hours I will come to see you, and everything will

---

5   An Italian exclamation much like the English "Well!" *(Author's note.)*

be explained. I sincerely thank you for your concern," and handed this little sheet to Pantaleone.

The old man carefully put it in his side pocket, and, repeating once more "In an hour!" started toward the door, but spun suddenly around, rushed up to Sanin, grabbed his hand, and, pressing it to his *jabot*, his eyes raised toward the heavens, exclaimed: "Noble youth! Great heart! *(Nobil giovanotto! Gran cuore!)* let a feeble old man *(un vecchiotto!)* shake your courageous right hand! *(la vostra valorosa destra!)*" Then he jumped back a little, shook both his arms in the air and went out.

Sanin looked after him…picked up a newspaper, and started reading. But his eyes ran over the lines pointlessly; he understood nothing.

XVIII

An hour later the waiter came into Sanin's room again and handed him an old, stained visiting card on which there was the following: Pantaleone Cippatola, from Varese, Court Singer *(cantante di camera)* to his Royal Highness the Duke of Modena. Right after the waiter, Pantaleone himself appeared. He had changed his clothes from head to foot. He had on black dress coat, somewhat rusty, and a white piqué vest on which a little pinchbeck chain curled fancifully; a heavy carnelian seal hung low on his narrow black trousers. In his right hand he held a black hat of rabbit's fur; in his left, two thick chamois gloves; he had tied his cravat still wider and higher than usual, and in his starched *jabot* had stuck a pin with a stone, a so-called "cat's eye" *(œil de chat)*. On the index finger of his right hand there was a splendid ring showing two hands clasped together and a burning heart between them. The old man's whole person gave off a stale smell, a smell of camphor and musk; the worried solemnity of his bearing would have astounded the most indifferent spectator. Sanin rose to meet him.

"I'm your second," said Pantaleone in French and bowed with his whole body, turning his toes out, as dancers do. I've come for instructions. Do you want to fight to the death?"

"Why to the death, my dear Signor Cippatola? I won't take back the words I said yesterday for anything in the world, but I'm not a bloodsucker! Just wait now, my opponent's second will be here any minute. I'll go into the next room—and you and he can arrange everything. Believe me, for the rest of my life I'll never forget your kindness, and I thank you from my heart."

"Honor comes first!" replied Pantaleone, and he sat down in an armchair without waiting for Sanin to ask him. "If that *ferroflucto spiccebubbio*" he began, passing from French to Italian, "if that clerk Kluberio didn't understand his own responsibility or grow scared—so much the worse for him! A cheap and petty man—*basta!* As concerns the conditions of the duel, I'm your second and your interests are sacred to me! When I was living in Padua, there was a regiment of White Dragoons there, and I knew many of the officers very well! I know their whole code very well. And I often used to chat with your *principe* Tarbuski about these problems...The other second is supposed to come soon?"

"I'm expecting him any minute—why, there he is, coming along himself," Sanin added, glancing at the street.

Pantaleone got up, looked at his watch, adjusted his topknot, and hurriedly stuck into his shoe a tape that was hanging down from under his trousers. The young lieutenant came in, still just as flushed and embarrassed.

Sanin introduced the seconds to each other.

"Monsieur Richter, *souslieutenant!*—Monsieur Cippatola, *artiste!*" The lieutenant was somewhat surprised at the sight of the old man... Oh, what would he have said if someone had whispered to him at that moment that the *artiste* who had been introduced to him was also engaged in the culinary art! But Pantaleone's expression indicated that taking part in arranging a duel was, for him, the most ordinary thing to do: probably he was helped in this by memories of his theatrical career—and he was playing the role of second exactly like a role in a play. Both he and the lieutenant were silent for a moment.

"Well? Let's get down to it!" Pantaleone spoke first, playing with his carnelian seal.

"Let's," replied the lieutenant, "but...the presence of one of the antagonists..."

"Ill leave you at once, gentlemen," exclaimed Sanin, bowed, went into the bedroom—and locked the door behind him.

He threw himself onto the bed and started thinking about Gemma, but the conversation of the seconds came to him through the closed door. It was in French; both were mangling it unmercifully, each in his own way. Pantaleone again brought up the dragoons in Padua and *principe* Tarbusski; the lieutenant, his *exghizes lèchéres* and *goups à l'amiaple*. But the old man would not hear a word about any *exghizes!* To Sanin's horror, he suddenly launched into a lecture to his interlocutor about a certain young and pure girl whose little finger alone was worth more than all the officers in the world... *(oune zeune damigella innoucenta, qu'a ella sola sans soun péti doa vale piu que toutt le zouffissié del mondo!)* and said heatedly several times: "It's shameful! it's shameful!" *(E ouna onta, ouna onta!)* The lieutenant at first did not protest, but after a while an angry tremble could be heard in the young man's voice and he remarked that he had not come to listen to moral maxims...

"At your age it's always good to listen to true and fair words!" exclaimed Pantaleone.

The discussion between the two seconds became stormy several times; it went on for over an hour and ended, finally, with the following conditions: "Baron von Dönhof and Herr de Sanin will duel tomorrow morning at ten o'clock in a small woods near Hanau, at a distance of twenty paces; each has the right of firing twice on signal given by the seconds; the pistols to be with hair-triggers and their barrels to be unrifled." Herr von Richter left and Pantaleone triumphantly opened the bedroom door and, having communicated the result of the meeting, again exclaimed, "*Bravo, Russo! Bravo, giovanotto!* You'll be the winner!"

Several minutes later they both set out for the Roselli confectioner's shop. Sanin had made Pantaleone swear be forehand to keep the business of the duel the deepest secret. In response the old man only raised his finger and, squinting, whispered twice quickly: "*Segredezza!* (Secrecy!)" He had become obviously younger, and even moved more freely. All these events, unusual, although also unpleasant, vividly put him back in that time when he, too, had made and accepted challenges—only on the stage, to be sure. Baritones, as everyone knows, very much ride the high horse in their roles.

XIX

Emilio ran out to meet Sanin—he had been waiting over an hour for him to arrive—and hurriedly whispered in his ear that his mother knew nothing about yesterday's unpleasantness and that there was no point in even hinting to her about it; and that he was being sent off again to the store, but rather than go there, he was going to hide somewhere! Having told all this in the course of a few seconds, he suddenly pressed against Sanin's shoulder, impulsively kissed it, and ran off down the street. Gemma met Sanin in the shop; she wanted to say something—and she could not. Her lips were slightly quivering, and her eyes were narrowed and turned aside. He hastened to calm her with the assurance that the whole matter was settled—there was nothing to it.

"Nobody was at your place today?" she asked.

"One person was—he and I talked things out and we—we came to a most satisfactory decision."

Gemma turned back behind the counter.

"She doesn't believe me!" he thought; however, he went into the next room and there found Frau Lenore.

Her migraine was gone, but she was in a melancholy mood. She smiled cheerfully at him, but at the same time warned him that he would find it boring with her today, since she wasn't in a condition to entertain him. He sat down beside her and noticed that her eyelids were red and swollen.

"What's the matter, Frau Lenore? Have you been crying?"

"Shhh…" she whispered, and nodded her head in the direction of the room where her daughter was. "Don't say that…out loud."

"But what were you crying about?"

"Ah, Monsieur Sanin, I don't know myself!"

"Somebody's grieved you?"

"Oh no! I just suddenly feel very down. I remembered Giovann'
Battista...my young days...And then how quickly it all passed. I'm
getting old, my dear—and I just can't get used to it. I think I'm still
the same myself, as before, but old age—here it is...here it is!" Little
tears came to Frau Lenore's eyes. "I can see you're looking at me and
wondering. But you'll get old, too, my dear, and you'll find out how
bitter it is!"

Sanin began trying to comfort her, reminded her of her children,
in whom her own youth was resurrected, tried even to tease her a
little, asserting that she was just looking for compliments. But she,
not joking, asked him to stop, and he then for the first time could
understand that there is nothing possible with which to comfort and
disperse such despondency, the despondency of the consciousness
of old age; one must wait for it to go away by itself. He suggested that
they play *tresette*—and he could not have thought of anything better.
She agreed immediately and seemed to cheer up somewhat.

Sanin played with her until dinner, and after dinner Pantaleone
also took part in the game. His topknot had never fallen so low over
his forehead, his chin had never retreated so far into his cravat! His
every movement expressed such concentrated solemnity that, looking at him, the thought involuntarily arose: what is the secret that
this man is keeping with such firmness?

But—*segredezza! segredezza!*

All day long he had tried in every way to show Sanin the greatest
respect; at table, solemnly and decisively, passing up the ladies, he
served him first; during the card game he let him get extra cards and
did not dare fine him; he kept announcing, apropos of nothing, that
the Russians were the most magnanimous, courageous, and resolute
people in the world!

"Ah, you old ham!" thought Sanin to himself.

And he was not so amazed at the unexpected frame of mind of
Signora Roselli as he was at the way her daughter treated him. She
was not really avoiding him—on the contrary, she was continually
sitting down not far from him, listening to what he said, looking at
him; but she determinedly did not want to enter into a conversation

with him, and just as soon as he would start talking to her, she would quietly get up from her place and go away for a few moments. Then she would come back again, and again sit down somewhere in a corner—sit still, as if deep in thought and perplexed—above all, perplexed. Frau Lenore herself finally noticed the unusualness of her behavior and asked her once or twice what was the matter.

"Nothing," replied Gemma; "you know I'm often like this."

"That's true," her mother agreed.

Thus passed the whole of that long day, neither animatedly nor dully—neither gaily nor boringly. Had Gemma behaved differently, Sanin—who knows?—might not have resisted the temptation to show off a bit, or might simply given himself over to a feeling of sadness before a probable parting, perhaps eternal. But since he did not once get into conversation with Gemma, he had to content himself with picking out minor chords on the piano for a quarter of an hour before evening coffee.

Emilio came home late and, to avoid questions about Herr Klüber, went off to bed almost right away. It came Sanin's turn to leave.

He began saying good-bye to Gemma. For some reason he remembered Lenski's parting with Olga in *Onegin*. He pressed her hand hard and tried to look into her eyes, but she turned slightly away and freed her fingers.

XX

The stars were already shining when he came out onto the porch. And how many there were scattered all over, how many stars—big, little, yellow, red, dark blue, white! They all shone and swarmed, their rays crossing and sparkling. There was no moon, but even without it each object was clearly visible in the shadowless twilight dusk. Sanin walked down to the end of the street. He did not want to go straight home; he felt the need of taking a walk in the pure air. He turned back—and had just come up to the house in which the Roselli's shop was, when one of the windows facing the street suddenly shook and opened; in its black rectangle (there was no light in the room) a woman's figure appeared and he heard himself being called;

"Monsieur Dmitri!"

He immediately rushed to the window—Gemma!

She put her elbows on the window sill and leaned out.

"Monsieur Dmitri," she began in a cautious tone of voice, "all day long I've wanted to give you one thing, but I didn't dare; and now, seeing you again unexpectedly, I thought that, obviously, it was fated…"

Gemma involuntarily stopped on this word. She could not go on: something extraordinary happened at that very moment.

Suddenly, in the midst of complete stillness, under a completely cloudless sky, such a burst of wind came up that the earth itself, it seemed, was shaking under one's feet, the faint light of the stars started quivering and shimmering, the air itself started whirling around. A whirlwind, not cold but warm, almost suffocating, struck the trees, the roof of the house, its walls, the street; it instantaneously tore off Sanin's hat, twined up and ruffled Gemma's black curls. Sanin's head came on a level with the window sill; he involuntarily pressed against it—and Gemma seized his shoulders with both hands, pressed her bosom against his head. The noise, ringing and roaring, lasted about a minute…Like a flock of huge birds, the whirlwind swirled past… Again the deep stillness fell over everything.

Sanin looked up and saw above him such a marvelous, frightened, excited face, such enormous, terrified, magnificent eyes—saw such a beautiful girl that his heart stopped beating, he pressed his lips to the thin lock of hair that had fallen on his chest, and could say only:

"O Gemma!"

"What was that? Lightning?" she asked, opening her eyes wider and not taking her bare arms from his shoulders.

"Gemma!" repeated Sanin.

She sighed, looked around behind her in the room—and quickly taking the already withered rose out of her bodice, tossed it to Sanin.

"I wanted to give you this flower…"

He recognized the rose which he had won back the day before.

But the little window had already slammed shut, and nothing could be seen, nothing showed white, behind its dark glass. Sanin

arrived home without his hat...He did not even notice that he had
lost it.

XXI

It was just before dawn when he fell asleep. And no wonder! Under
the force of that instantaneous summer whirl wind, he felt, almost
as instantly, not that Gemma was beautiful or that he liked her—he
knew that before—but that he had just about...fallen in love with
her! Love came over him instantaneously, like that whirlwind. And
now there was that stupid duel! Mournful forebodings began to torment him. Well, supposing he isn't killed...What can come of his
love for a girl who is someone else's fiancée? Even supposing that
this "other" man is no rival to him, that Gemma herself could fall
in love with him, or already has...What of that? What then? Such a
beautiful girl...

He paced the room, sat down at the table, took a piece of paper,
dashed off a few lines on it—and immediately crossed them out. He
would recall Gemma's wonderful face in the dark window, under the
starlight, her hair all scattered by the warm whirlwind; he remembered her marble arms, like the arms of Olympian goddesses, felt
their living weight on his shoulders...Then he picked up the rose
that had been tossed to him—and it seemed to him that its half-with-
ered petals gave off a different and more lovely aroma than the usual
aroma of roses...

And if suddenly he were killed or maimed?...

He did not go to bed, but fell asleep, fully dressed, on the sofa.

Someone was shaking his shoulder...

He opened his eyes and saw Pantaleone.

"Sleeping like Alexander the Great on the eve of the Battle of
Babylon!" the old man exclaimed.

"What time is it?" asked Sanin.

"A quarter of seven; it's a two-hour ride to Hanau, and we must be there first. The Russians always get ahead of their enemies! I've hired the best carriage in Frankfurt!"

Sanin began to wash up.

"And where are the pistols?"

"The *ferroflucto Tedesco* is bringing the pistols. And a doctor, too." Pantaleone was obviously trying to keep up his spirits, as he had the day before; but when he had sat down in the carriage with Sanin, when the coachman had cracked his whip and the horses had started galloping off, there was a sudden change in the former singer and friend of the Padua dragoons. He became uneasy, even frightened. It was as if something inside him had given way, like a badly built little wall.

"But what are we doing, good Lord, *santissima Madonna!*" he exclaimed in an unexpectedly squeaky voice and clutched at his head. "What am I doing, old fool that I am, madman, *frenetico?*"

Sanin was surprised and laughed and, putting his arm lightly around Pantaleone's waist, reminded him of the French saying: *Le vin est tiré—il faut le boire* (or, to phrase it a bit differently: You can't back out now that you've begun).

"Yes, yes," the old man answered, "we'll drain this cup together—but still I'm crazy! I'm crazy! Everything was so peaceful, so good… and suddenly: ta-ta-ta, tra-ta-ta!"

"Like *tutti* in the orchestra," commented Sanin with a forced smile. "But it's not your fault."

"I know it's not! Of course! Still it's all—such an unbridled act. *Diavolo! Diavolo!*" Pantaleone repeated, shaking his top knot and sighing.

And the carriage kept rolling on and on.

The morning was lovely. The streets of Frankfurt, just beginning to come alive, seemed so clean and comfortable; the windows of the houses shone iridescently, like tinfoil; and the carriage had just passed through the gates when from above, from the light blue, still pale sky the loud peals of the larks came scattering down. Suddenly at a turn in the highway, a familiar figure appeared from behind a tall poplar, took a few steps, and stopped. Sanin looked closely. My God! Emilio!

"But does he know anything about it?" he said, turning to Pantaleone.

"I tell you I'm crazy!" the poor Italian cried in despair, almost shouting. "This ill-fated boy pestered me all night—and finally, this morning I told him everything!"

"There's your *segredezza* for you!" thought Sanin.

The carriage came up to Emilio; Sanin ordered the driver to halt the horses and called the "ill-fated boy" over to him. Emilio, all pale, as pale as on the day of his attack, came over hesitantly. He could hardly stand up.

"What are you doing here?" Sanin asked him sharply. "Why aren't you at home?"

"Please—please let me come with you," Emilio muttered in a trembling voice, and clasped his hands together. His teeth were chattering as in fever. "I won't get in your way—only take me!"

"If you feel even the slightest attachment or respect for me," said Sanin, "you will go home right away, or else to Herr Klüber's store, and not say a word to anyone, and await my return!"

"Your return," moaned Emilio, and his voice quavered and broke off; "but if you're—"

"Emilio!" Sanin cut him off and indicated the coachman with his eyes, "pull yourself together! Emilio, please, go home! Listen to me, my friend, and do what I say! You say you love me. So, I beg you!"

He put out his hand to him. Emilio swung forward, sobbed, pressed it to his lips, and, jumping off the road, ran back toward Frankfurt across the fields.

"A noble heart, too," Pantaleone mumbled, but Sanin looked at him sullenly. The old man shrank into a corner of the carriage. He admitted his fault; on top of that, with every passing moment he was becoming more and more surprised: had *he* really become a second, had *he* gotten the horses and made all the arrangements and left his peaceful abode at six o'clock in the morning? Besides, his legs had started paining him and aching.

Sanin felt it necessary to pluck up his courage—and he landed on the right thing, found the right word:

"Where's your old spirit, worthy Signer Cippatola? Where's *il antico valor?*"

Signer Cippatola straightened up and frowned.

"*Il antico valor?*" he said in a bass voice. "*Non è ancora spento* (It's not all gone yet)— *il antico valor!!*"

He assumed a dignified air, started talking about his own career, about opera, about the great tenor Garcia—and arrived in Hanau on top of the world. Come to think of it, there's nothing in the world stronger—and weaker than a word!

XXII

The little wood in which the bloody battle was supposed to occur was a quarter of a mile from Hanau. Sanin and Pantaleone arrived first, as he had predicted, told the coachman to wait on the edge of the woods, and went into the shade of the rather thick and dense trees. They had to wait about an hour.

The waiting did not seem especially painful to Sanin; he kept walking back and forth along the path, listened to the birds singing, watched the dragonflies darting past, and, like the majority of Russians on similar occasions, tried not to think. Only once did deep reflection come over him: he had stumbled on a young linden broken off, quite likely, by yesterday's storm. It was definitely dying...all its leaves were dying. "What's this? A portent?" flashed through his mind, but he immediately started whistling, jumped right over the linden itself, and walked on down the path. Pantaleone was grumbling, cursing the Germans, groaning, rubbing his back or his knees. He was even yawning from nervousness, which gave his shriveled little face a very ridiculous expression. Sanin almost burst out laughing, looking at him.

At last the rumble of wheels was heard on the soft road. "It's they!" said Pantaleone, and pricked up his ears and straightened up, not without a momentary nervous shudder which, however, he hurried to cover up with the exclamation, "Brrr!" and the comment that it was rather chilly this morning. A heavy dew soaked the grass and the leaves, but the heat of the day was already beginning to pierce into the woods itself.

Both officers soon appeared under its vaults; they were accompanied by a stocky little man with a phlegmatic, almost sleepy face—an army doctor. In one hand he was carrying a clay pitcher of water—just in case; a bag with surgical instruments and bandages was hanging from his left shoulder. It was clear that he was completely accustomed to such excursions; they constituted one of his sources of income: each duel brought him in eight gold pieces—four from each of the warring parties. Herr von Richter was carrying the box with pistols; Herr von Dönhof was twirling in his hand—probably to appear "chic"—a little riding crop.

"Pantaleone!" Sanin whispered to the old man, "if...if I'm killed—anything can happen—take the piece of paper out of my side pocket—there's a flower wrapped up in it—and give it to Signorina Gemma. You hear? Do you promise?"

The old man glanced at him sorrowfully, and nodded his head affirmatively...But God only knows whether or not he understood what Sanin asked him to do.

The antagonists and seconds bowed to each other, as is customary; only the doctor did not even raise an eyebrow and sat down, yawning, on the grass: I've got nothing to do, he seemed to say, with expressions of chivalrous courtesy. Herr von Richter suggested that Herr "Tshibadola" select the place; Herr "Tshibadola" replied, dully moving his tongue (the "little wall" inside him had again fallen down): "You go ahead, my dear sir; I'll watch..."

And Herr von Richter started going ahead. He found right there in the woods a lovely little glade all covered with flowers; measured off the paces, marked the two end-points with hastily sharpened sticks, got the pistols out of the box, and, squatting on his heels, rammed in the bullets; in short, he was as busy and working as hard as he could, continually wiping off his perspiring face with a little white handkerchief. Pantaleone, who accompanied him, looked rather like a man completely chilled. During all these preparations, both antagonists stood some distance apart, reminding one of two chastised schoolboys sulking at their teachers.

The decisive moment came…

Each one took his pistol up…

But at this point Herr von Richter remarked to Pantaleone that he, as the older of the seconds, ought, according to the rules of dueling, before calling out the fatal One! two! three!, turn to the antagonists with a final word of advice and the recommendation that they be reconciled; that although this recommendation never had any affect and generally was nothing but a mere formality, still, by observing this formality Herr Cippatola would absolve himself of a certain amount of responsibility; that, indeed, such an *allocutio* was the immediate responsibility of the so-called "impartial witness" *(unparteisicher Zeuge)*—but since they had no such witness, he, Herr von Richter, gladly yielded this privilege to his respected colleague. Pantaleone, who had managed to duck behind a bush in order not to see the offending officer at all, at first understood nothing of all that Herr Richter said, especially because it had been said through the nose; but he suddenly gave a start, stepped forward deftly, and, convulsively beating his hands on his chest, cried out in a husky voice in his own mixed dialect: *"A la-la-la…Che bestialità! Deux zeun' ommes comme ça que si battono—perché? Che diavolo? Andate a casa!"*

"I do not consent to a reconciliation," Sanin said quickly.

"Nor do I," his opponent said after him.

"So then," von Richter turned to Pantaleone, who was hopelessly lost, "cry out: one, two, three!"

Pantaleone immediately ducked into the bushes again—and from there started shouting out, cowering, squinting his eyes, and turning his head away, at the top of his voice:

"Uno…due…tre!"

Sanin shot first—and missed. His bullet sounded against a tree. Baron von Dönhof fired immediately after him—deliberately to one side, into the air.

A tense silence fell…Nobody moved. Pantaleone groaned feebly.

"Do we continue?" asked Dönhof.

"Why did you shoot into the air?" asked Sanin.

"That's not your business."

"Will you shoot into the air the second time also?" Sanin asked.

"Perhaps: I don't know."

"Please, please, gentlemen..." von Richter began, "duelists don't have the right to talk to each other. This is quite out of order."

"I refuse my shot," said Sanin and threw his pistol on the ground.

"I, too, have no intention of continuing the duel!" exclaimed Dönhof, and he also threw his pistol down. "And besides, I'm now ready to admit that I was wrong the day before yesterday."

He hesitated a moment where he stood—and then indecisively held out his hand. Sanin quickly went over to him and shook it. Both young men looked at each other smilingly—and then both of them flushed.

"*Bravi! bravi!*" Pantaleone suddenly yelled like a madman, and, clapping, away, came tumbling out from behind the bushes; and the doctor, who had been sitting at one side on a felled tree, got up at once, poured the water out of the pitcher, and set off, swaying lazily, toward the edge of the woods.

"Honor is satisfied—and the duel is over!" von Richter announced.

"*Fuori!* (Odds even!)" barked Pantaleone once more, from old habit.

Having exchanged bows with the officers and seated himself in the carriage, Sanin really felt all over, if not pleasure, at least a certain release, as after a successful operation; but another feeling, also, stirred inside him—a feeling something like shame. The duel in which he had just played his part seemed to him something spurious, an agreed-upon conventionality, a usual thing officers or students do. He remembered the phlegmatic doctor, remembered how he had smiled—that is, wrinkled up his nose—when he had seen him leaving the woods almost arm-in-arm with Baron Dönhof. And then when Pantaleone had paid this same doctor the four gold pieces owed him...Ah! Something was wrong!

Indeed, Sanin felt somewhat ashamed and conscience-stricken... although, on the other hand, what could he have done? How could he have let the young officer's insolence pass, the way Herr Klüber had? He had stood up for Gemma, he had defended her...Very well; but still his heart was heavy, and he was ashamed, and even sorry.

On the other hand, Pantaleone was simply triumphant! He was suddenly seized with pride. A victorious general returning from the field of a battle he has just won, does not look around with greater self-satisfaction. Sanin's conduct during the duel filled him with delight. He called him a hero—and would not even listen to Sanin's admonitions and even his requests. He compared him to a statue of marble or bronze to the statue of the Commander in *Don Juan!* About himself, he admitted that he had felt a certain perturbation. "But you know I'm an actor," he commented; "I have a nervous nature, but you—you're the child of snows and granite cliffs."

Sanin had no idea how to quiet down the actor, who was getting out of control.

Almost at the same spot on the road where two hours back they had run into Emilio, he again jumped from behind the tree and with a shout of delight, waving his cap over his head and jumping up and down, rushed straight for the carriage, almost fell under the wheel, and, not waiting for the horses to stop, opened the doors and climbed in—and bore his eyes into Sanin.

"You're alive, you're not wounded!" he kept repeating. "Forgive me—I didn't do what you said, I didn't go back to Frankfurt…I couldn't! I waited for you here…Tell me, what was it like? You—killed him?"

With difficulty Sanin calmed Emilio and made him sit down.

At great length, and with obvious pleasure, Pantaleone told him all the details of the duel and, of course, did not fail to mention again the statue of bronze, the statue of the Commander. He even got up from his seat and, spreading his legs to keep his balance, folded his arms on his chest, and looking scornfully back over his shoulder, personally portrayed Sanin the Commander! Emilio listened in awe, from time to time interrupting the story with an exclamation, or quickly getting up and very quickly kissing his heroic friend.

The wheels of the carriage clattered on the paved streets of

Frankfurt and finally stopped in front of the hotel where Sanin was living.

Escorted by his two companions, he climbed up the stairs to the second floor—when suddenly a woman came out of the dark little corridor with very quick steps: her face was covered with a veil; she stopped in front of Sanin, swayed a little, gasped slightly, and immediately ran down and out onto the street and disappeared, to the waiter's great amazement, who announced that "this lady was waiting over an hour for the return of the gentleman from abroad." No matter how momentary her appearance had been, Sanin had recognized her as Gemma. He had recognized her eyes under the heavy silk of her brown veil.

"Did Fräulein Gemma know…" he said in a displeased tone of voice, in German, turning to Emilio and Pantaleone, who were following on his heels.

Emilio blushed and became all confused.

"I had to tell her everything," he mumbled. "She was guessing—and I just couldn't…But now it doesn't matter," he went on animatedly, "it's all ended so wonderfully, and she's seen you well and unhurt!"

Sanin turned away.

"What old gossips you are, both of you!" he said with annoyance, and he went into his room and sat down.

"Don't be angry, please," begged Emilio.

"All right, I won't." (Sanin really was not angry—and, after all, he could hardly have wished that Gemma should have found out *nothing*.) "All right…that's enough hugging me. Go on, now. I want to be alone. I'm going to go to sleep. I'm tired."

"An excellent idea!" exclaimed Pantaleone. "You need rest! You've fully earned it, noble *signore!* Let's go, Emilio! On tiptoe! On tiptoe! Shhhh!"

Though he had said that he wanted to sleep, Sanin wanted only to get rid of his friends; but, left alone, he really felt a great tiredness all through his body. He had hardly shut his eyes all the night before; and, throwing himself on his bed, he immediately fell into a deep sleep.

XXIII

He slept heavily for several hours. Then he began to dream that he was again fighting a duel, that the opponent facing him was Herr Klüber, and a parrot was sitting in the fir tree, and that parrot was Pantaleone, who kept repeating, tapping his beak: One-one-one! One-one-one!

One…one…one!—he heard it only too clearly; he opened his eyes, raised his head…Someone was knocking on his door.

"Come in!" cried Sanin.

The waiter appeared and announced that a certain lady very much wanted to see him.

"Gemma!" flashed through his mind, but the lady turned out to be her mother—Frau Lenore.

As soon as she came in, she sat down on a chair and began to cry.

"What's the matter, my good, dear Signora Roselli?" began Sanin, having sat down beside her and gently touched her arm. "What's happened? Do calm down, please."

"Ah, Herr Dmitri, I'm very…very unhappy!"

"You're unhappy?"

"Ah, very! And how could I have expected it? Suddenly, like a bolt out of a clear sky…"

She was breathing with difficulty.

"But what is it? Explain! Do you want a glass of water?"

"No, thank you very much." Frau Lenore wiped her eyes with her handkerchief and started crying again even harder. "You see, I know everything! Everything!"

"What do you mean—everything?"

"Everything that happened today! And I…know the reason, too! You behaved like an honorable man, but what an unhappy coincidence! There was a reason I didn't like that ride to Soden—there was a reason!" (On the day of the trip, Frau Lenore had said nothing of the kind, but now she thought she had then had a presentiment of "everything.") "And so I've come to you as to a noble man, as to a friend, although I saw you for the first time just five days ago…But you know I'm a widow, all alone…My daughter…"

Tears choked Frau Lenore's voice. Sanin did not know what to think.

"Your daughter?" he repeated.

"My daughter Gemma," burst from Frau Lenore, almost with a moan, from behind the handkerchief wet with tears, "told me today that she doesn't want to marry Herr Klüber and that I have to refuse him!"

Sanin even stepped back a little; he had not expected this.

"I'm not even talking about the fact," Frau Lenore went on, "that it's a disgrace, that it's never before happened in the whole world that a bride-to-be has turned down her groom, but the fact that it's ruin for us, Herr Dmitri!" Frau Lenore carefully rolled her handkerchief up tightly into a tiny little ball, as if she wanted to squeeze all her grief into it "We can't live off what the store brings in any more, Herr Dmitri! and Herr Klüber's very rich and will be still richer. And refuse him for what? Because he didn't stand up for his bride? Agreed, it wasn't very good on his part, but you know he's a civilian, he didn't go to the university, and, as a solid tradesman, had to look down on the thoughtless prank of some unknown little officer. And what was the insult, Herr Dmitri?"

"Please, Frau Lenore, you seem to be blaming me…"

"I'm not blaming you at all, not at all! You're something else completely; like all Russians, you're a military man…"

"Excuse me, I'm not at all…"

"You're a foreigner, a tourist, and I'm grateful to you," continued Frau Lenore without listening to Sanin. She kept sighing, throwing up her hands in dismay, unfolding her handkerchief again and blowing her nose. Merely by the way her grief expressed itself one could see that she had not been born under a northern sky.

"And how's Herr Klüber going to do business in the store if he's going to be fighting with his customers? It's absolutely absurd! And now I have to refuse him. But what are we going to live on? Before, we were the only ones who made sweet cough syrup and pistachio nougat, and customers kept coming; but now everybody makes sweet cough syrup! Think about it now: as it is, they're going to be talking about your duel all over town…how could you hide it? And

suddenly the wedding is off! Why, it's a *Skandal, a Skandal!* Gemma's
a beautiful girl; she loves me very much, but she's a stubborn republican, doesn't care a bit for other people's opinions. Only you can
persuade her!"

Sanin was even more astonished than before.

"Me, Frau Lenore?"

"Yes, only you...Only you. That's why I came here: I couldn't think
of anything else! You're such an educated, such a good man! You
stood up for her. She'll trust you! She *has* to trust you—why, you
risked your own life! You'll show her, but I can't do a thing more!
You'll show her that she's going to ruin herself and all of us. You
saved my son—now save my daughter, too! God Himself sent you
here...I'm ready to beg you on my knees..."

And Frau Lenore half rose from her chair, as if getting ready to fall
at Sanin's feet. He held her back.

"Frau Lenore! For God's sake! What are you doing?"

She convulsively grasped his hands.

"Do you promise?"

"Frau Lenore, think now, why should I..."

"You promise? You don't want me to die here right now in front
of you, do you?"

Sanin was lost completely. This was the first time in his life that he
had to deal with burning Italian blood.

"I'll do anything you want!" he exclaimed. "I'll talk to Fräulein
Gemma..."

Frau Lenore cried out with delight.

"Only, really, I don't know what the result may be..."

"Ah, don't refuse, don't refuse!" said Frau Lenore in a pleading
voice; "you've already agreed! The result, I'm sure, will be fine. In any
case, *I* can't do anything more! She won't listen to *me!*"

"She's told you definitely of her unwillingness to marry Herr
Klüber?" Sanin asked after a brief silence.

"She almost chopped my head off! She's just like her father, like
Giovann' Battista! Headstrong!"

"Headstrong? She?" Sanin repeated slowly.

"Yes...yes...but she's an angel too. She's listen to you. You'll come,

come soon? O my dear Russian friend!" Frau Lenore impulsively got up from her chair and just as impulsively embraced Sanin's head as he sat in front of her. "Accept a mother's blessing—and let me have some water!"

Sanin brought Signora Roselli a glass of water, gave her his word of honor that he would come immediately, escorted her downstairs to the street—and, having returned to his room, threw up his hands and his eyes grew wide.

"There," he thought, "*now* life's really spinning! In fact, it's started spinning so that my head is in a whirl." He did not try to look within himself, to understand what was going on there; real commotion—*basta!* "What a day!" his lips involuntarily whispered. "Headstrong—her mother says...And I have to advise her—*her!* Advise her what?"

Sanin's head was definitely spinning—and over this whole whirl of various feelings, impressions, and unfinished thoughts there constantly hovered the image of Gemma, that image which had so unforgettably etched itself in his memory on that warm, electrically turbulent night, in that dark window, under the light of the swarming stars!

XXIV

Sanin went to the Roselli's house hesitantly. His heart was pounding hard; he distinctly felt and even heard how it was knocking against his ribs. What would he tell Gemma, how would he start talking to her? He went into the house, not through the shop, but by the back entrance. He met Frau Lenore in the little vestibule. She was both delighted to see him and afraid.

"I was waiting, waiting for you," she said in a whisper, squeezing his hand with each of hers in turn. "Go into the garden; she's there. And don't forget: I'm counting on you!"

Sanin headed for the garden.

Gemma was sitting on a bench by the path and was picking the ripest cherries out of a large basket filled with them, and putting them on a plate. The sun was low in the sky—it was already after six—and in the wide, slanting rays with which it flooded Signora Roselli's little garden there was more crimson than gold. Every so often, barely audibly and seemingly unhurriedly, the leaves whispered among themselves, the tardy bees buzzed intermittently, flying from flower to neighboring flower, and somewhere a turtledove cooed monotonously and unceasingly.

Gemma had on that same round hat which she had worn to Soden. She glanced at Sanin from under its turned-down brim and bent over the basket again. Sanin came up to her, involuntarily shortening each step, and...and...And could find nothing to say to her except to ask why she was sorting the cherries.

Gemma, without hurrying, answered.

"These—the riper," she said, finally, "will go for jam, and these for pie filling. You know those round pies with sugar that we sell." Having said this, Gemma bent her head still lower, and her right hand, with two cherries in her fingers, hung in mid-air between the basket and the plate.

"May I sit beside you?" Sanin asked.

"You may." Gemma moved a little on the bench. Sanin sat down. "How do I begin?" he thought. But Gemma got him out of his difficulty.

"You fought a duel today," she started in animatedly, and turned her whole beautiful, bashfully blushing face to him—and what deep gratitude shone in her eyes! "And you're so calm? Does that mean danger doesn't exist for you?"

"Heavens! I wasn't in any danger. Everything came off very well and harmlessly."

Gemma wagged her finger right and left in front of her eyes... That's also an Italian gesture. "No, no! Don't say that! You won't fool me! Pantaleone has told me everything!"

"What a man to believe! Was he comparing me to the statue of the Commander?"

"His way of putting things may be silly, but neither his feeling is, nor what you did today. And it's all because of me—for me. I'll never forget it."

"I assure you, Fräulein Gemma…"

"I'll never forget it," she repeated with hesitation, once again looking intently at him and then turning away.

He could now see her delicate, pure profile, and it seemed to him that he had never seen anything like it—and never experienced anything like what he was experiencing at that moment. His heart was on fire.

"But my promise!" flashed through his mind.

"Fräulein Gemma…" he began after a momentary hesitation.

"What?"

She did not turn toward him; she kept on sorting the cherries, carefully picking them up by their stems with the ends of her fingers and conscientiously picking out the leaves. But with what trusting affection did that one word ring: "What?"

"Your mother didn't tell you anything about…"

"About?"

"About me?"

Gemma suddenly threw the cherries she had picked up back into the basket.

"She was talking to you?" she asked in turn.

"Yes."

"What did she say to you?"

"She told me that you…that you had suddenly decided to change…your previous plans."

Gemma's head again bent down. It completely disappeared under her hat; only her neck could be seen, supple and tender, like the stalk of a large flower.

"What plans?"

"Your plans…in connection with…the future arrangement of your life."

"That is…You're talking about…Herr Klüber?"

"Yes."

"Mama told you that I don't want to be Herr Klüber's wife?"

"Yes."

Gemma moved on the bench. The basket tilted, fell down…several cherries rolled down onto the path. A minute went by…another…

"Why did she tell you that?" he heard her say. Sanin, as before, saw only Gemma's neck. Her bosom was rising and falling more quickly than before.

"Why? Your mother thought that, since you and I had, one might say, become friends in a short time and you've come to have a certain confidence in me, well, that I was in a position to give you some useful advice—and that you'd listen to me."

Gemma's hands slid softly into her lap...She began adjusting the folds of her dress.

"What advice are you going to give me, Monsieur Dmitri?" she asked after a brief pause.

Sanin noticed that Gemma's fingers were trembling in her lap... She was adjusting the folds of her dress merely to hide the trembling. He gently put his hand on these pale, quivering fingers.

"Gemma," he said, "why don't you look at me?"

She instantly pushed her hat back to hang between her shoulders and fastened her eyes on him, eyes as trusting and grateful as before. She waited for him to speak...But the expression on her face confused him and seemed to blind him. The warm brilliance of the evening sun bathed her young head in light—and the expression of that head was brighter and more striking than the brilliance of the sun itself.

"I'll listen to you, Monsieur Dmitri," she began, barely smiling and barely raising her eyebrows, "but what advice are you going to give me?"

"What advice?" Sanin repeated. "Well, you see, your mother thinks that to refuse Herr Klüber just because he didn't show much courage the day before yesterday..."

"Just because?" said Gemma, bent down, picked up the basket, and put it beside her on the bench.

"That...in general...to refuse him, on your part, is unwise; that this is a step of which all the consequences must be carefully weighed; that, finally, your whole business situation lays certain obligations on each member of your family—"

"That's all Mania's opinion," Gemma interrupted, "that's what she says. I know that, but what's your opinion?"

"Mine?" Sanin was silent a moment. He felt that something had caught in his throat and was choking him. "I also think," he began with an effort.

Gemma sat up straight.

"Also? You—also?"

"Yes…That is…" Sanin could not, absolutely could not add another word.

"All right," said Gemma. "If, as a friend, you advise me to change my decision…that is, not to change my former decision, I'll think it over." Without noticing what she was doing herself, she began putting cherries from the plate back into the basket…"Mama hopes I'll listen to you…Well? Maybe I really will…"

"But, please, Fräulein Gemma, I'd first like to know what reasons induced you…"

"I'll listen to you," repeated Gemma, but her brows frowned more and more, her cheeks grew paler and paler, she kept biting her lower lip. "You did so much for me that I'm obliged to do what you want, obliged to carry out your wishes. I'll tell Mama…I'll think about it. Incidentally, look, here she comes."

Indeed, Frau Lenore appeared on the threshold of the doorway leading from the house into the garden. Impatience was consuming her: she could not sit still. According to her calculations, Sanin should have finished his talk with Gemma long ago, although, in fact, his chat with her had not lasted even a quarter of an hour.

"No, no, no, for God's sake, don't say a word to her for the time being," said Sanin hastily, almost in fright. "Wait a little…I'll tell you, I'll write you…and don't you decide a thing until then…wait!"

He pressed Gemma's hand, jumped up from the bench—and to Frau Lenore's great surprise, darted past her, doffing his hat, said something inaudible, and disappeared.

She went over to her daughter.

"Tell me, please, Gemma…"

Gemma suddenly got up and embraced her.

"Mama darling, can you wait a little bit, just a little bit, until tomorrow? Can you? And not a word until tomorrow, either?…Ah!…"

She dissolved in sudden, bright tears, to herself completely unexpected. This astonished Frau Lenore all the more because the expression on Gemma's face was anything but sad—on the contrary, it was joyful.

"What's the matter?" she asked. "You never cry—and now suddenly..."

"Nothing, Mama, never mind! You just wait a little! You and I both have to wait. Don't ask any questions until tomorrow—and let's sort the cherries before the sun's gone."

"But you'll be sensible?"

"Oh, I'm very sensible!" Gemma nodded significantly. She began tying small bunches of cherries together, holding them up high in front of her reddening face. She did not wipe away her tears: they had dried up of themselves.

XXV

Sanin went back to his hotel almost at a run. He felt, he knew that only there, only alone with himself, would it finally become clear what was the matter with him, what was happening to him. And, indeed, he had hardly managed to get into his room, to sit down in front of his desk, when, leaning on it with both elbows and pressing his palms against his face, he mournfully and hollowly exclaimed: "I love her, love her madly!"—and glowed all over inside, like a coal from which the layer of dead ash has just been blown off. A moment later...and already he could not understand how he could have been sitting beside her—beside her!—and talking to her, and not feeling how he worshiped the hem of her dress; how he was ready, as young people say, to "die at her feet." The last meeting in the garden had decided everything. Now, as he thought of her, he no longer thought of her with her wind-tossed curls in the light of the stars; he saw her sitting on a little bench, saw how she threw back her hat with a sudden gesture, and looked at him so trust-ingly...and a shudder and the thirst of love coursed through all his veins. He remembered the rose which he had been carrying in his pocket for three days now: he pulled it out—and pressed it to his lips with such feverish force that he involuntarily frowned from pain. Now he no longer deliberated about anything, did not imagine, count on, or foresee anything; he had cut himself off from his entire past, he had leaped forward; from the cheerless shore of his bachelor life he had fallen straight into this gay, boiling, mighty current—and little did he care, and little did he want to know, where it would take him, or whether it would dash him against the rocks! This was now not the gentle streams of a Uhland love poem, which had lulled him not long ago...These were powerful, irrepressible waves! They were flying and leaping onward—and he with them!

He took a sheet of paper and, without a correction, practically with one sweep of the pen, wrote the following:

Gemma dear,

You know what advice I took upon myself to give you; you know what your mother wants and what she asked me to do, but what you don't know and what I now must tell you—is that I love you, love you with all the passion of a heart that has fallen in love for the first time! This flame blazed up suddenly in me, but with such force that I can't find words to describe it!! When your mother came to me and asked me, it was still smoldering in me, or else I, as an honest man, would certainly have refused to carry out her request...The very confession which I'm now making to you is the confession of an honest man. You must know with whom you're dealing—there must be no misunderstandings between us. You see I can't give you any advice....I love you, love you, love you—and there's nothing else either in my mind or in my heart!!

Dm. Sanin

Having folded the note and sealed it, Sanin was just about to call the waiter and send it by him. "No! That's awkward. By Emilio? But to go to the store, find him there among the other clerks—that's awkward, too. Besides, it's already dark outside—and he's probably already left the store." Thinking like that, Sanin nevertheless put on his hat and went out to the street; he turned one corner, another—and, to his indescribable delight, caught sight of Emilio in front of him. With a bag under his arm, a roll of paper in his hand, the young enthusiast was hurrying home.

"They mean it when they say every lover has his lucky star," thought Sanin, and he called Emilio over.

Emilio turned around and rushed toward him.

Sanin gave him no chance to be ecstatic, handed him the note, told him how and to whom to give it. Emilio listened carefully.

"So nobody sees?" he asked, putting on a knowing and mysterious look: "We understand what it's all about!" he seemed to say.

"Yes, my friend," said Sanin, and became somewhat embarrassed, but he patted Emilio's cheek…"And if there's an answer…You'll bring me an answer, won't you? I'll be at home."

"Don't worry about that!" Emilio whispered gaily, ran off, and as he ran nodded his head once more.

Sanin went back to his place and, without lighting a candle, threw himself on the sofa, put his hands up behind his head, and gave himself over to the recently admitted feelings of love—feelings which there is no point in describing: he who has experienced them knows their torments and sweetness; he who has not, cannot have them explained to him.

The door burst open—Emilio's head appeared.

"I've brought it," he said in a whisper; "here it is, the answer!"

He held a folded piece of paper up over his head.

Sanin jumped up from the sofa and snatched it from Emilio's hands. His passion had grown too strong: he was not now concerned about keeping things secret, about observing decorum—even in front of this boy, her brother. He would have been ashamed of himself in front of him, he would have forced himself to be restrained—if only he could have!

He went over to the window, and by the light of the street lamp that stood in front of the house, read the following lines:

I beg you, I implore you—*don't come to see us the whole of tomorrow, don't appear.* This is necessary for me, absolutely necessary—and then everything will be decided. I know you won't refuse me, because…

Gemma

Sanin read the note through twice—oh, how deeply sweet and beautiful her handwriting seemed to him! He thought a moment, and, turning to Emilio, who, to show what a modest young man he was, was standing with his face to the wall and picking a little hole in it with his fingernail, called his name aloud.

Emilio immediately ran up to him.

"What would you like?"

"Listen, my friend—"

"Monsieur Dmitri," Emilio interrupted in a sad voice, "why is it you don't say *thou* to me?"

Sanin laughed.

"Well, all right. Listen, my friend" (Emilio gave a little jump from joy), "listen: *there*—you know what I mean— *there* you say that everything will be carried out exactly" (Emilio bit his lips and nodded his head solemnly) "—and you yourself…what are you doing tomorrow?"

"Me? What am I doing? What do you want me to?"

"If you can, come early in the morning, as early as you can, and we'll take a walk through the outskirts of Frankfurt until evening… Do you want to?"

Emilio gave another little jump.

"Heavens, what could be better? To take a walk with you—that's simply wonderful! I'll certainly come!"

"And if they don't let you off?"

"They will!"

"Listen…Don't say *there* that I asked you for the whole day."

"Why should I? I'll just go anyway! What's wrong with that!"

Emilio kissed Sanin hard and ran off.

And Sanin walked back and forth in his room for a long time—and went to bed late. He gave himself over to those same sweet and awe-inspiring feelings, to that same delightful breathlessness before a new life. Sanin was very pleased that he had had the idea of inviting

Emilio for the next day; his face looked just like his sister's. "He'll
remind me of her," Sanin thought. But he was, above all, amazed
at how he could be different yesterday from what he was today. It
seemed to him that he had loved Gemma "eternally"—and loved her
exactly l as he loved her today.

XXVI

The next day at eight in the morning, Emilio, with Tartaglia on a
leash, made his appearance at Sanin's place. If he had been the child
of German parents, he could not have been more on time. At home
he had told a lie: he had said he was going to take a walk with Sanin
until breakfast and then go to the store. While Sanin was dressing,
Emilio started talking to him, rather hesitantly, to be sure, about
Gemma, about her falling-out with Herr Klüber, but Sanin was
sternly silent in reply; and Emilio, showing by his expression that
he understood why such an important point should not be touched
on lightly, did not come back to it—and only every now and then
assumed a concentrated and even severe expression.

Having had coffee, the two friends set out—on foot, of course—for
Hausen, a small village lying not far from Frankfurt and surrounded
by forests. You can see the whole Taunus mountain range from there,
as if in the palm of your hand. The weather was wonderful; the sun
was warm and bright, but not scorching; a fresh breeze rustled briskly
in the green leaves; the shadows of the high, round, little white clouds
skidded smoothly and quickly in small patches over the earth. The
young men soon had made their way out of town and struck out
boldly and gaily along the well-kept road. They went into a forest,
and wandered around there for a long time; then had a hearty lunch
in a village inn; then climbed some mountains, enjoyed the views,
rolled stones down and clapped their hands as they watched them
hop, amusingly and surprisingly, like rabbits, until some man passing by below, invisible to them, cursed them out in a strong, ringing
voice. They lay stretched out on the short, dry moss that was a yel-
low-lavender color; they drank beer at another inn, then chased each

other, and made a bet to see who could jump farther. They found an
echo and talked to it; sang, hallooed, wrestled; broke off twigs, put
ferns in their hats—and even danced. Tartaglia took part in all this
as best he could: he did not throw stones, to be sure, but he rolled
head-over-heels after them, howled when the young man sang—and
even drank beer, though with obvious dislike: a student, to whom he
had once belonged, had taught him this art. Besides, he did not obey
Emilio well—quite unlike his obedience to his master Pantaleone—
and when Emilio commanded him to "speak" or "sneeze," he just
wagged his tail and hung out his tongue.

The young men also chatted together. In the beginning of their
walk, Sanin, as the older and, therefore, more reasonable, began to
talk about fate and predestination and what is the import and significance of a man's calling, but the conversation very soon took a less
serious direction. Emilio began questioning his friend and patron
about Russia, about how duels are fought there, asking if the women
there are beautiful, and if one can learn Russian quickly, and what
he felt when the officer aimed at him. And Sanin, in his turn, asked
Emilio about his father, his mother, about their family business in
general, in every way trying to avoid mentioning Gemma's name—
and thinking only of her. Strictly speaking, he was not thinking even
about her but about the next day, about that mysterious day tomorrow, which would bring him inconceivable, unprecedented happiness! It was as if a curtain, a light, delicate curtain were hanging,
gently swaying, in front of his mind's eye; and behind that curtain he
sensed...sensed the presence of a young, motionless, divine countenance with a tender smile on its lips and austerely—feignedly austerely—lowered eyelashes. And this countenance was not Gemma's
face, but the face of happiness itself! And now, at last, his hour has
struck, the curtain has been raised, the lips open, the eyelashes are
lifted—the divinity has seen him—and now there is light, as from the
sun, and joy, and endless delight! He thinks about that tomorrow—
and his heart again becomes ecstatically still in the thrill of longing
and of an expectation being continually reborn!

And this expectation, this longing does not interfere with anything. It goes along with his every gesture—and interferes with

nothing. It does not interfere with his dining splendidly with Emilio in a third inn, and only now and then the idea flashes in his mind, like a sudden bolt of lightning—what if anybody in the world knew? This longing does not keep him from playing leapfrog with Emilio after dinner. The game takes place on a wide, open, green meadow… and what was Sanin's astonishment, his embarrassment, when, to the accompaniment of Tartaglia's wild barking, his legs spread wide and, flying like a bird over the hunched-up Emilio, he suddenly sees in front of him, on the very edge of the green meadow, two officers, whom he immediately recognizes as his antagonist of yesterday and his second, messieurs von Dönhof and von Richter! Each of them puts his monocle on and looks at him and smirks…Sanin lands on his feet, turns away, hurriedly puts on his coat that he had thrown down, says a curt word to Emilio, who also puts on his jacket, and they both leave at once.

They got back to Frankfurt late.

"I'm going to get scolded," Emilio said to Sanin as he was bidding him good-bye, "but it doesn't matter! Because I had such a wonderful, wonderful day!"

Returning to his room in the hotel, Sanin found a note from Gemma. She set a rendezvous with him for the next day, at seven in the morning, in one of the public parks that surround Frankfurt on all sides.

How his heart quivered! How glad he was that he had so unquestioningly obeyed her! And, good Lord, what was promised…what wasn't promised by this unprecedented, unique, impossible—and absolutely certain tomorrow?

He kept staring at Gemma's note. The long, graceful flourish of the letter G, the first letter of her name, standing at the bottom of the page, reminded him of her beautiful fingers, her hand…He reflected that he had never once touched that hand with his lips…"Italian girls," he thought, "despite what's said about them, are shy and stern…And Gemma all the more! A queen…a goddess…pure and virginal marble…"

"But the time will come—and it's not far off…"

That night in Frankfurt there was one happy man…He was asleep, but he could have said about himself, in the words of the poet: "I sleep…but still my wakeful heart does not…" It was beating as softly as the wings of a butterfly clinging to a flower and bathed by the summer sun.

XXVII

Sanin woke up at five o'clock, was already dressed by six, and at half-past six was walking up and down in the public park within sight of the small arbor mentioned by Gemma in her note.

The morning was quiet, warm, and overcast. Once in a while it seemed as if it were just about to start raining, but the outstretched hand felt nothing, and only by looking at the sleeve of the clothing could the traces of tiny drops, like the smallest beads, be noticed; and even that soon stopped. The wind—it was as if there had never been any wind in the world. Each sound did not fly across the air but spilled out around itself; in the distance, a whitish mist became ever so slightly thicker; the air was filled with the smell of mignonette and white acacia blossoms.

In the streets the shops were not yet open but pedestrians were already appearing; from time to time a solitary carriage rattled by… There was no one walking in the park. A gardener was unhurriedly scraping the path with a shovel, and a decrepit old woman in a black cloth cloak was hobbling along across an alley. Sanin could not for even a moment take that poor creature for Gemma—yet the heart in him shrank, and he intently followed the retreating black spot with his eyes.

Seven! the clock in the tower droned out.

Sanin stopped. Really, wasn't she coming? A cold shiver suddenly ran all through his body. The same shiver went through him again a moment later, but for a different reason. Sanin heard light footsteps behind him, the light noise of a woman's dress…He turned around: it was she!

Gemma was coming from behind him along the path. She had on a greyish mantilla and a small dark hat. She glanced at Sanin, turned her head aside—and, having come up even with him, quickly walked past.

"Gemma," he said, barely audibly.

She nodded to him slightly and kept walking on ahead. He followed her.

He was gasping. His legs hardly obeyed him.

Gemma passed the arbor, turned right, passed a small, flat fountain in which a sparrow was busily splashing, and, going behind a bed of tall lilac, sat down on a bench. The place was agreeable and concealed. Sanin sat down beside her.

A minute went by, and neither he nor she said a word; she even did not look at him—and he looked not at her face but her folded hands, in which she was holding a little parasol. What was there to say? What was there to say that, by its meaning, could be compared to their just being here, together, alone, so early, so close to each other?

"You…aren't angry with me?" Sanin said finally.

It would have been hard for Sanin to have said anything stupider than this…he was aware of it himself…But, at least, the silence had been broken.

"Me?" she asked. "Why? No."

"And you believe me?" he went on.

"What you wrote?"

"Yes."

Gemma lowered her head and said nothing. The parasol slipped out of her hands. She hurriedly caught it before it landed on the path.

"Ah, believe me, believe what I wrote you!" exclaimed Sanin; all his timidity had suddenly disappeared, and he started talking heatedly: "If there's truth in this world, sure, sacred truth, it is that I love you, love you passionately, Gemma!"

She threw a sidelong, momentary glance at him, and again nearly dropped her parasol.

"Believe me, believe me," he kept repeating. He begged her, reached his hands out toward her, and did not dare touch her. "What do you want me to do…to convince you?"

She glanced at him again.

"Tell me, Monsieur Dmitri," she began, "the day before yesterday, when you came to try to persuade me—I suppose you still didn't know...didn't feel..."

"I felt," Sanin put in, "but I didn't know. I fell in love with you the first moment I saw you—but didn't understand at once what you meant to me! Besides, I'd heard that you were engaged...And as for what your mother asked me to do, well, first of all, how could I refuse? And, secondly, I think I told you what she wanted me to in such a way that you could have guessed ..."

There was a sound of heavy footsteps, and a rather portly gentleman with a traveling bag over his shoulder, obviously a foreigner, came out from behind the lilac and, with the unceremoniousness of a passing tourist, looked the pair seated on the bench up and down, coughed loudly, and went on.

"Your mother," Sanin began as soon as the sound of the heavy footsteps had died away, "told me that your refusal would cause a scandal" (Gemma frowned slightly); "that I myself had been in part responsible for improper rumors, and that...consequently...the obligation lay on me—to a certain degree—of persuading you not to refuse your fiancé", Herr Klüber..."

"Monsieur Dmitri," said Gemma, and ran her hand through her hair on the side turned toward Sanin, "please don't call Herr Klüber my fiancé. I will never be his wife. I've broken with him."

"You've broken with him? When?"

"Yesterday."

"You told him personally?"

"Him personally. At our house. He came over."

"Gemma! That means you love me?"

She turned toward him.

"Otherwise...would I have come here?" she whispered, and both her hands fell onto the bench.

Sanin seized these helpless hands, lying palms up, and pressed them to his eyes, to his lips...That was when the curtain was raised, the curtain he had imagined he had seen the night before! Here it was—happiness; there was its radiant countenance!

He raised his head—and looked at Gemma straight and boldly.

She, too, looked at him, from a little bit above him. The gaze of her half-closed eyes barely flickered, swimming with light, blissful tears. But her face was not smiling…no! It was laughing a blissful but soundless laughter.

He wanted to draw her to his breast, but she held back and, without stopping that same soundless laughter, shook her head to say no. "Wait," her happy eyes seemed to be saying.

"O Gemma!" exclaimed Sanin, "could I have thought that thou" (the heart in him quivered, like a string, when for the first time his lips said this intimate word) "—that thou would love me!"

"I didn't expect it myself," said Gemma quietly.

"Could I have thought," Sanin went on, "could I have thought, driving up to Frankfurt, where I expected to stay just a few hours, that I would here find the happiness of my whole life!"

"Your whole life? Really?" Gemma asked.

"My whole life, forever and ever!" exclaimed Sanin in a new burst of passion.

The gardener's shovel suddenly started scraping two paces away from the bench on which they were sitting.

"Let's go home," Gemma whispered; "let's go together—you want to?"

If at that moment she had said to him: "Throw yourself into the sea—*do you want to?*" she would not have finished before he would have already been flying headlong into the deep.

They left the park together and headed for the house, not through the streets of the city but through the suburbs.

XXVIII

Sanin walked sometimes beside Gemma, sometimes a little behind her, did not take his eyes off her and did not stop smiling. And she seemed to be hurrying on—seemed to be pausing. To tell the truth, both of them—he all pale, she all pink from excitement—moved forward as if dazed. What, they had done together, a few moments before—this giving of one's soul to another—was so strong and new and awesome; everything in their lives had been reordered and changed so suddenly, that they both could not collect themselves, and were aware only of the whirlwind which had caught them up, like that night whirlwind which had almost thrown them into each other's arms. Sanin walked along and felt that he was even looking at Gemma differently: he instantly noticed several peculiarities in her walk, in her gestures—and good Lord! how endlessly dear and charming they were to him! And she felt that he was looking at her *that way.*

Sanin and she had both fallen in love for the first time; all the miracles of first love absorbed them. First love is the same as a revolution: the monotonously regular structure of established life is smashed and broken in a moment, youth; stands on the barricade, its bright banner waves on high—and no matter what lies ahead for it—death or a new life—it sends everything its ecstatic greetings.

"What's this? Isn't that our old friend?" said Sanin, pointing his finger at a muffled figure which was little by little making its way along on one side, as if trying to remain unnoticed. In his excess of bliss, he felt a need to talk to Gemma not about love—that was something already decided, sacred—but about something else.

"Yes, it's Pantaleone," Gemma answered gaily and happily. "He probably left the house on my heels; even yesterday he followed every step I took....He has figured it out."

"He has!" repeated Sanin in delight. What could Gemma have said that would not have made him delighted?

Then he asked her if she would tell him in detail everything that actually had happened the day before.

And she immediately began telling it all, hurrying, getting mixed up, smiling, letting out little sighs, and exchanging brief bright glances with Sanin. She told him how, after the conversation the day before yesterday, her mother had kept trying to get something positive out of her; how she had put off Frau Lenore by promising to let her know her decision within twenty-four hours; how she had finally succeeded in getting that delay—and how hard it had been; how Herr Klüber had showed up completely unexpectedly, more prim and starched than ever; how he had expressed his indignation at the childishly unforgivable, and for him, Klüber, deeply insulting (that was exactly how he put it) prank of the Russian stranger—"he meant your duel"—and how he demanded that *you* immediately be forbidden the house. 'Because,' he added"—and here Gemma slightly mimicked his tone and manner—" 'it casts a shadow on my honor; as if I didn't know how to stand up for my own fiancée if I found it necessary or useful! Tomorrow all Frankfurt will know that a stranger fought with an officer over my fiancée—how does that look? It stains my honor!' Mama agreed with him—imagine!— but at this point I suddenly told him that he was worried about his honor and his person for nothing, was feeling insulted by rumors about his *fiancée* all for nothing—because I wasn't his fiancée any longer, and was never going to be his wife! I confess I would have liked to have talked to you first…before refusing him finally, but he had come…and I couldn't hold back. Mama even cried out in fright, and I went into the other room and brought him back his ring—you didn't notice, I took his ring off two days ago—and gave it to him. He was very offended, but since he's terribly conceited and boastful, he didn't say much—and left. Of course, I had to put up with a great deal from Mama, and it was very painful for me to see how grieved she was—and I thought I'd been a little hasty, but, after all, I had your note—and even without it I already knew…"

"That I love you," put in Sanin.

"Yes…that you loved me."

That is how Gemma talked, becoming confused and smiling, and dropping her voice or falling silent completely whenever someone came toward her or went past. And Sanin listened ecstatically, delighting in the very sound of her voice, as the evening before he had delighted in her handwriting.

"Mama is extremely upset," Gemma began again, and her words came very quickly one after another; "she doesn't at all want to consider the fact that Herr Klüber might have become repulsive to me, that I was marrying him not for love but because of her insistent beggings. She suspects…you; that is, frankly speaking, she's sure that I've fallen in love with you—and it's even harder for her because only the day before yesterday nothing of the sort had entered her head and she had even asked you to try to persuade me...And it was an odd commission, wasn't it? Now she calls you a sly one, a cunning man, says that you betrayed her confidence, and predicts that you'll deceive me..."

"But, Gemma," exclaimed Sanin, "didn't you tell her..."

"I didn't tell her anything! What right did I have, without having talked to you?"

Sanin threw up his hands.

"Gemma, I hope that now, at least, you'll tell her every thing; take me to her...I want to show your mother I'm not a deceiver!"

Sanin's chest heaved from an onrush of magnanimous and passionate feelings.

Gemma looked at him with wide eyes.

"You really want to go to Mama now with me? To Mama, who's certain that...that everything between us is impossible—and never can be?" There was one word which Gemma did not dare speak out....It seared her lips, but Sanin said it all the more willingly.

"Marry you, Gemma, be your husband—I know of no greater happiness!"

He knew no limits either to his love or his magnanimity or his determination.

Having heard those words, Gemma, who had stopped for just a moment, went on still faster...She seemed to want to run away from this too great and unexpected happiness!

But suddenly her legs gave way under her. From around the corner of an alleyway, a few steps from her, appeared Herr Klüber wearing a new hat and a new long, full, pleated overcoat, as straight as an arrow and as curly as a poodle. He noticed Gemma, noticed Sanin—and somehow snorting inwardly and bending back at his supple waist, he strode forward dandily to meet them. Sanin was disgusted, but, glancing at Klüber's face, to which its owner tried, as best he could, to lend an expression of contemptuous amazement and even condolence—glancing at that ruddy, commonplace face, he suddenly felt a surge of anger, and stepped forward.

Gemma seized his arm and, with calm decisiveness giving him hers, looked her former fiancé straight in the face...He squinted, shrank back, scooted to one side, and, muttering through his teeth: "The usual ending to the song!" *(Das alte Ende vom Liede!)*, went off in that same dandyish, slightly bouncy gait.

"What did he say, the scoundrel?" Sanin asked, and wanted to rush after Klüber, but Gemma restrained him and went on with him, not taking her arm out of his.

The Roselli confectioner's shop appeared in front of them. Gemma stopped once more.

"Dmitri, Monsieur Dmitri," she said, "we aren't there yet, we haven't yet seen Mama....If you want to think it over, if—You're still free, Dmitri."

In response, Sanin pressed her arm very tightly against his chest, and drew her on.

"Mama," said Gemma, going with Sanin into the room where Frau Lenore was sitting, "I've brought the real one!"

XXIX

If Gemma had announced that she had brought home with her cholera or death itself, Frau Lenore, one must suppose, would not have received the news with greater despair. She immediately sat down in a corner, her face to the wall, and burst into tears, almost wailing, just like a Russian peasant woman over the coffin of her husband or her son. At first Gemma was so confused that she did not even go up to her mother, and stood, like a statue, in the middle of the room; and Sanin was completely lost, almost to the point of tears himself! This inconsolable weeping went on for a whole hour: a whole hour! Pantaleone thought it better to lock the outside shop door so that no stranger would come in—since it was still early. The old man himself was perplexed; at any rate he did not approve of the haste with which Gemma and Sanin had acted, but he would not criticize them and was ready to give them his support in case they needed it—he really hadn't liked Klüber! Emilio considered himself an intermediary between his friend and his sister—and was almost proud of how well everything had turned out! He was completely unable to

understand what Frau Lenore was so upset about, and in his heart
he then and there decided that women, even the very best of them,
suffer from a lack of quickness of wit! It was worse for Sanin than
for anyone else. Frau Lenore's voice rose to a howl and she waved
him away as soon as he approached her; standing at a distance, he
several times tried vainly to shout out: "I'm asking for your daughter's hand!" Frau Lenore was especially annoyed at herself for having
been so blind—for having seen nothing! "If my Giovann' Battista
were alive," she kept repeating through her tears, "none of this would
have happened!" "Lord, what is this?" thought Sanin. "After all, it's
really absurd!" He did not dare look at Gemma, nor did she have the
courage to look at him. She just patiently looked after her mother,
who at first pushed even her away...

Little by little the storm at last quieted down. Frau Lenore
stopped crying, let Gemma lead her out of the corner where she had
crouched, seat her in a chair by the window, and give her a glass of
water with *fleur d'orange;* she let Sanin—not come near...oh no!—
but at least stay in the room (before she had kept demanding that he
go away), and did not interrupt him when he was talking. Sanin at
once took advantage of the calm that had set in—and displayed an
astounding eloquence: he could hardly have set out his intentions
and his feelings with such ardor and such conviction before Gemma
herself. These feelings were the most sincere, these intentions the
most honorable, like Almaviva's in *The Barber of Seville.* He did not
conceal, either from Frau Lenore or from himself, the unfavorable
side of his intentions, but these were only seeming disadvantages!
True, he was a foreigner, they had met him only recently, they knew
nothing positive either about him personally or about his means, but
he was prepared to bring all the necessary proofs to show that he was
an honest and respectable man, and not poor; he would call as his
witness the most unquestionable testimony of his fellow-country-
men! He hoped that Gemma would be happy with him and that he
would be able to make her separation from her family a happy one...
The mention of separation—just that word "separation"—almost
ruined the whole things. Frau Lenore started trembling all over
and became all wrought-up. Sanin hastened to point out that the

separation would be only temporary—and that, after all, perhaps, there would not be any.

Sanin's eloquence was not lost on Frau Lenore. She began looking at him, though still with sadness and reproachfulness, at least no longer with her former aversion and anger; later, she let him even come and sit down beside her (Gemma was sitting on the other side); then she began reproaching him—not merely with her eyes, but in words, which signified a certain softening of her heart; she started complaining, and her complaints became quieter and quieter and softer and softer; they alternated with questions, sometimes to her daughter, sometimes to Sanin; then she let him take her hand and did not take it away immediately; then she started crying again—but already with quite different tears; then she smiled sadly and regretted the absence of Giovann' Battista, but now in a different sense than before…Another moment went by, and both criminals—Sanin and Gemma—were on their knees at her feet and she was laying her hands on their heads in turn; still another moment went by, and they were embracing her and kissing her; and Emilio, his face radiant with joy, ran into the room and flung himself into the tightly packed group.

Pantaleone glanced into the room, grinned and frowned simultaneously, and, having gone into the shop, unlocked the street door.

XXX

The transition from despair to sadness, and from sadness to "quiet resignation" took place rather quickly in Frau Lenore, but this quiet resignation did not take long in turning into secret delight, which was, however, in every way possible covered up and kept back for the sake of propriety. Sanin had been to Frau Lenore's liking from the very first day of their acquaintance; once used to the idea that he would be her son-in-law, she no longer found anything about it especially unpleasant, though she did consider it her duty to keep a somewhat hurt—or rather, worried expression on her face. Besides, everything that had happened in the last few days was so extraordinary...One thing after another! As a practical woman and as a mother, Frau Lenore considered it also her duty to subject Sanin to various questions; and Sanin who, setting out that morning for a rendezvous with Gemma, had had no thought at all of marrying her—to be sure, he had not been thinking of anything then, but was just abandoning himself to the bent of his passion—Sanin took up his role, the role of fiancé, with complete readiness and, one might say, excitement, and responded to all the questions fully, in detail, and willingly. Having made sure that he was a real nobleman by birth—and having been even a little surprised that he was not a prince—Frau Lenore assumed a grave expression and "warned him ahead of time" that she was going to be completely and informally frank with him, because her sacred obligation as a mother required this of her! To which Sanin replied that he had expected nothing else of her, and earnestly begged her not to spare him!

Then Frau Lenore remarked to him that Herr Klüber (having said this name, she lightly sighed and pressed her lips and hesitated an instant)—Herr Klüber, Gemma's *former* fiancé, now had an income of eight thousand guldens and each year that sum would rapidly increase—but his, Herr Sanin's, income was how much?

"Eight thousand guldens, " repeated Sanin slowly. "In our money, that's about fifteen thousand rubles...My income is a lot less. I have a small estate in Tula province...With good organization and supervision, it might yield—and certainly ought to yield—about five or six thousand...And if I go into the government service, I can easily get a salary of about two thousand."

"Government service in Russia?" exclaimed Frau Lenore. "Then that means I have to part with Gemma!"

"It's possible to get assigned to the diplomatic corps," Sanin put in. "I have a few connections...Then the service is abroad. Or this, too, is something that could be done: sell the estate and use the money for some useful enterprise, for example, for the improvement of your shop." Sanin felt that he was saying something foolish, but an incomprehensible courage had taken possession of him! He would glance at Gemma who, from the time the "practical" conversation had started, had been constantly getting up, walking around the room, and sitting down again—he would glance at her, and there would be nothing in his way, and he would be ready to arrange everything, this moment, in the best possible way—if she only did not worry!

"Herr Klüber also wanted to give me a small amount for fixing up the shop," said Frau Lenore, after a little hesitation.

"Mother! For God's sake! Mother!" exclaimed Gemma in Italian.

"You have to talk about these things in advance, my child," Frau Lenore answered her in the same language.

She again turned to Sanin and started questioning him about the Russian laws in regard to marriages, and if there were any obstacles to entering into matrimony with Catholics, as in Prussia? (At that time, in '40, all Germany still remembered the quarrel of the Prussian government with the Arch bishop of Cologne over mixed marriages.) When Frau Lenore heard that, by marrying a Russian nobleman, her daughter herself would become a noblewoman, she expressed a certain pleasure.

"But don't you have to go to Russia first?"

"Why?"

"How else?" To get the permission of your sovereign!"

Sanin explained to her that that wasn't necessary at all…but that, perhaps, before the wedding, he indeed ought to go to Russia for just a very short time (he said this—and his heart contracted painfully; looking at him, Gemma under stood that it had, and blushed and became lost in thought), and that he would try to use his stay in his own country to sell his estate…at least, he would bring back the necessary money.

"I'd also like to ask you to bring me back some good Astrakhan lambskin for a cape," said Frau Lenore. "From what I hear, they're amazingly good there and amazingly cheap!"

"Certainly, with the greatest pleasure—for both you and for Gemma!" exclaimed Sanin.

"And a little silver-embroidered Morocco cap for me," put in Emilio, poking his head in from the next room.

"All right, I will…and for Pantaleone, some slippers."

"But what's all this for? What for?" remarked Frau Lenore. "We're talking about serious things now. Now, here's another thing," the practical lady added: "You say: sell your estate. But how will you do that? You'll sell the peasants, too, is that it?"

It was as if Sanin had been jabbed in the side. He remembered that, in talking with Signora Roselli and her daughter about serfdom—which, according to what he had said, aroused deep indignation in him—he had repeatedly assured them that he would never sell his peasants for any reason, for he considered such a sale an immoral act.

"I'll try to sell my estate to a man whom I know to be good," he said, not without hesitation, "or perhaps the peasants themselves will want to buy themselves off."

"That's best of all," Frau Lenore agreed. "Because selling living people…"

"*Barbari!*" muttered Pantaleone, who appeared in the door way behind Emilio, shook his topknot, and vanished.

"It's bad!" Sanin thought to himself, and glanced furtively at Gemma. She did not seem to have heard what he had just been saying. "Well, never mind!" he thought.

The practical conversation went on like this almost until dinner. Toward the end, Frau Lenore calmed down completely—and was even calling Sanin, Dmitri, affectionately shaking her finger at him, and promising to revenge his perfidy. She kept asking him questions in great number and detail about his relatives, because "that's very important, too," requested also that he describe the marriage ceremony as performed in the Russian church—and was already delighted with Gemma in a white dress and with a gold crown on her head.

"You know, she's as beautiful as a queen," she said with maternal pride. "Why, there's not even a queen like her in the whole world!"

"There's no other Gemma in the whole world!" Sanin chimed in.

"Yes; that's why she's—Gemma!" (Gemma, of course, in Italian means a jewel.)

Gemma flung herself on her mother and kissed her…It seemed that only now she breathed freely—that the weight that had been making her despondent had been lifted from her heart.

And Sanin suddenly felt so happy, his heart was filled with such childlike gaiety at the thought that they had come true, they had come true, those dreams which he had recently abandoned himself to here in these very rooms, his whole being was so full of joy, that he immediately went into the shop—he absolutely wanted, whatever might be, to do some business behind the counter, as he had a few days before…."I have full right to do it now," he seemed to be saying. "I'm one of the family now!"

And he actually went behind the counter and actually did some business, that is, he sold a pound of candy to two little girls who came in, giving them two pounds instead of the one and charging only half the price.

At dinner, he, as fiancé, sat officially beside Gemma. Frau Lenore continued her practical considerations. Emilio was laughing all the time and pestering Sanin to take him along to Russia. It was decided that Sanin would leave in two weeks. Only Pantaleone looked somewhat sullen—so much so that even Frau Lenore chided him: "And you were a second, too!" Pantaleone looked scowlingly at her.

Gemma was silent almost the entire time, but her face had never been more beautiful and bright. After dinner she called Sanin out into the garden for a moment and, stopping by that same bench where she had been sorting the cherries two days before, she told him: "Dmitri, don't be angry with me, but I want to remind you once more that you don't have to feel yourself obligated—"

He did not let her finish…

Gemma turned her face away.

"And about what Mama brought up—remember?—about the difference of our religion, well, here!…"

She seized the little garnet cross which was hanging around her neck on a thin cord, jerked it hard, broke the cord, and handed him the little cross.

"If I'm yours, then your faith is mine, too!"

Sanin's eyes were still moist when he and Gemma returned to the house.

By evening, everything was back in its old routine. They even played a little *tresette.*

XXXI

Sanin woke up very early the next day. He felt himself at the peak of human well-being, but it was not that which kept him from sleeping; the question, the vital, fateful question—how could he sell his estate as soon and as advantageously as possible—disturbed his peace of mind. All different sorts of plans kept crisscrossing in his head, but nothing was yet clear. He went out of the house to get a breath of fresh air. He wanted to come before Gemma with a ready project—not otherwise.

What figure was that, rather heavy and thicklegged, but quite properly dressed, walking along in front of him, swaying slightly and hobbling a little? Where had he seen the back of that head, with tow-colored, curly hair, that head seemingly planted right onto the shoulders, that soft, fatty back, those puffy, loose-hanging hands? Was that really Polozov, his old boarding-school friend whom he had lost track of these five years now? Sanin overtook the figure going along in front of him, turned…A broad, yellowish face, little piglike eyes with white brows and lashes, a short, flat nose, thick lips, seemingly glued together, a round, hairless chin—and that sour, lazy, and distrustful expression of the whole face—yes, really: it was he, it was Ippolit Polozov!

"Can this be my lucky star at work again?" flashed through Sanin's thoughts.

"Polozov! Ippolit Sidorych! Is that you?"

The figure stopped, lifted its tiny eyes up, held still a moment—and, at last ungluing its lips, said in a wheezy falsetto:

"Dmitri Sanin?"

"The very same!" exclaimed Sanin and shook one of Polozov's hands; covered with tight, ash-grey lad gloves, they hung as lifelessly as before beside his bulging thighs. "Have you been here long?" Where did you come from? Where are you staying?"

"I came from Wiesbaden yesterday," Polozov answered, in no hurry, "to get things for my wife—and I'm going back to Wiesbaden today."

"Oh, yes! So you're married, and they say to such a beauty!"

Polozov looked to one side.

"So they say."

Sanin laughed. "I see you're still the same—phlegmatic, as you were in school."

"What would I change for?"

"And they say," Sanin added with special stress on the word "say," "that your wife is very rich."

"They say that, too."

"But don't you yourself know, Ippolit Sidorych?"

"I, my friend Dmitri…Pavlovich?—yes, Pavlovich!—don't interfere in my wife's business."

"Don't interfere? Not in anything?"

Polozov again turned his eyes away.

"Not in anything, my friend. She takes care of herself—and I of myself."

"Where are you going now?" asked Sanin.

"Now I'm not going anywhere; I'm standing in the street talking to you; but when you and I've finished, why, I'll go back to my hotel and have some lunch."

"With me along—would you like that?"

"You're talking about lunch, now, that is?"

"Yes."

"Please do; it's much more cheerful to eat together. You're not a great talker, are you?"

"Hardly."

"Very good."

Polozov moved on. Sanin set out beside him. And the thought occurred to Sanin—Polozov's lips became glued together again, he wheezed and swayed along without talking—the thought occurred to Sanin: how did this idiot manage to catch a beautiful and rich wife? He was neither rich, nor eminent, nor intelligent; in school he was known as a dull and thick-headed boy, as a sleepyhead and a glutton—and had the nickname "The Slob." Miracles never cease!

"But if his wife's very rich—they say she's the daughter of some tax-farmer—then wouldn't she buy my place? Though he says he never interferes in any of his wife's affairs, a man can't really believe that! And besides, I'll put a moderate, reasonable price on it. Why not try? Maybe my lucky star is still working...Done! I'll give it a try!"

Polozov led Sanin into one of the best hotels in Frankfurt, in which he had, of course, the best room. The table and chairs were piled high with cartons, boxes, packages..."All things bought, my friend, for Maria Nikolaevna!" (that was Ippolit Sidorych's wife's name). Polozov sank down into an armchair and moaned, "What heat!" and undid his tie. Then he rang for the headwaiter and carefully ordered the most enormous lunch. "And have the carriage ready at one! You hear, exactly at one!"

The headwaiter bowed obsequiously and servilely with drew.

Polozov unbuttoned his vest. Merely by the way he raised his eyebrows, huffed and puffed and wrinkled his nose, one could see that talking would be a big burden for him and that he was wondering, not without a certain alarm, whether Sanin would make him wag his tongue, or whether he himself would undertake the labor of starting a conversation.

Sanin realized his friend's frame of mind and therefore did not burden him with questions, limiting himself to the most essential: he learned that he had been in government service two years (in an uhlan regiment! He must have looked really good in a little short tunic!), had gotten married three years ago, and had been abroad now for more than a year with his wife, "who's now getting cured of something in Wiesbaden"—and then was going to Paris. On his part, Sanin expatiated very little on his past life, on his own plans; he launched right in on the main thing—that is, started talking about his intention of selling his estate.

Polozov listened to him silently, only from time to time glancing up at the door through which the lunch was due to appear. It finally came. The headwaiter, accompanied by two other servants, brought in several dishes under silver covers.

"Your estate is in Tula province?" said Polozov, seating himself at the table and tucking his napkin into his shirt collar.

"It is." "Efremov district...I know."

"You know my Alekseevka?" asked Sanin, also sitting down at the table.

"Of course I do." Polozov stuffed a bite of omelette with truffles into his mouth. "Maria Nikolaevna, my wife, has an estate nearby... Open this bottle, waiter! The land is good enough—only the peasants have cut down your forest. Why are you selling?"

"I need the money, old man. I'd let it go cheaply. Now, you could buy it...Just the thing."

Polozov downed a glass of wine, wiped his mouth with his napkin, and again started chewing, slowly and noisily.

"Mm—yes," he said finally. "I don't buy estates: no capital. Push the butter over. But maybe my wife would. You have a chat with her. If you're not asking too much—she's not against that sort of thing... Oh, these Germans—real asses! Don't know how to cook fish. Now, what's easier? And they keep on saying: 'Got to unite the *Vaterland*.' Waiter, take this foul stuff away!"

"Does your wife really take care of running the place herself?" asked Sanin.

"Herself. Now, these chops are good! I recommend them to you. I told you, Dmitri Pavlovich, that I never interfere in my wife's business—and now I tell you it again."

Polozov kept on chomping away.

"Hm...But how can I have a talk with her, Ippolit Sidorych?"

"Very simply, Dmitri Pavlovich. Go to Wiesbaden. It's not far from here...Waiter, haven't you any English mustard? No? Pigs!...Only don't waste any time. We're leaving the day after tomorrow. Please, let me pour you a glass: this wine has bouquet—it's not vinegar."

Polozov's face became animated and flushed; it became animated only when he was eating—or drinking.

"Really...I don't know how I can do it," Sanin muttered.

"But what's suddenly gotten into you?"

"There is something, old man."

"And you need a lot of money?"

"A lot. I—how'll I tell you? I'm thinking of—getting married."

Polozov put his glass on the table, the glass he had just raised to his lips.

"Getting married!" he said in a voice hoarse from amazement, and folded his puffy hands on his stomach. "So suddenly?"

"Yes—soon."

"Your fiancée's in Russia, of course?"

"No, not in Russia."

"Where then?"

"Here, in Frankfurt."

"And who is she?"

"A German girl; that is, no—an Italian. She lives here."

"With money?"

"Without."

"It must be a very powerful love?"

"How ridiculous you are! Yes, powerful."

"And you need money for that?"

"Well, yes…yes, yes."

Polozov downed his wine, rinsed his mouth and washed his hands, carefully wiping them on the napkin, took out a cigar and lit it. Sanin looked at him in silence.

"There's only one way," mumbled Polozov at last, throwing his head back and blowing smoke out in a fine stream. "Go see my wife. If she wants to, she'll solve all your troubles at once."

"But how can I see her—your wife? You say you're leaving the day after tomorrow?"

Polozov shut his eyes.

"You know what?" he said finally, rolling the cigar in his lips and sighing. "Go home now, get your things together as quick as you can, and come back here. I'm leaving at once—my carriage is big—I'll take you along. That's the best thing. But now I'm going to have a little nap. Once I've eaten, old man, I've got to have a nap. It's nature's demand—and I'm not against it. And don't you bother me."

Sanin thought and thought about it—and suddenly raised his head: he had decided!

"All right, I agree, thank you. I'll be here at twelve-thirty, and we'll go to Wiesbaden together. I hope your wife won't be angry…"

But Polozov was already wheezing. He mumbled: "Don't bother me!" moved his feet, and fell asleep like a baby.

Sanin once more glanced over his massive figure, his head, neck, his chin raised high—round and like an apple—and, leaving the hotel, quickly set off for the Roselli confectioner's shop. He had to forewarn Gemma.

XXXII

He found her in the shop along with her mother. Frau Lenore, her back bent over, was measuring the space between the windows with a small folding foot-rule. On seeing Sanin, she straightened up and greeted him cheerfully, but not without a little embarrassment.

"After what you said yesterday," she began, "my head's been spinning with ideas about improving our store. Now here, I think, we ought to put two little cupboards with little mirrored shelves. It's very fashionable now, you know. And then—"

"Wonderful, wonderful," Sanin interrupted; "that all must be thought out. But come here, I want to tell you something." He took Frau Lenore and Gemma by the arm and led them into the next room. Frau Lenore became nervous and dropped the foot-rule. Gemma at first was nervous, too, but she looked more closely at Sanin and relaxed. His face, worried indeed, at the same time expressed an animated daring and decisiveness.

He asked both women to sit down and he stood in front of them— and, waving his arms and ruffling his hair, told them everything: his meeting with Polozov, the proposed trip to Wiesbaden, the possibility of selling his estate.

"Imagine my good luck!" he exclaimed finally. "The thing's taken such a turn so that perhaps I won't even have to go to Russia! And we can have the wedding much sooner than I thought!"

"When do you have to go?" asked Gemma. "Today, in an hour; my friend has hired a carriage—he'll take me."

"Will you write us?"

"Right away! Just as soon as I've talked to this lady, I'll write at once."

"This lady, you say, is very rich?" asked the practical Frau Lenore.

"Extremely! Her father was a millionaire, and left her everything."

"Everything—just to her? Well, that's your good luck. Only be careful not to sell your place too cheap! Be sensible and firm. Don't get carried away! I understand your wanting to become Gemma's husband as soon as you can—but caution comes first! Don't forget: the more you sell your estate for, the more there is for the two of you, and for your children."

Gemma turned away, and Sanin again waved his arms.

"You can rely on my caution, Frau Lenore! But I'm not going to bargain. I'll tell her the actual price: if she gives it—fine; if not—never mind about her."

"Do you know her—this lady?" asked Gemma.

"I never saw her in my life."

"And when are you coming back?"

"If our business doesn't work out, the day after tomorrow; if it all goes fine, maybe I'll have to stay an extra day or two. In any case, I won't linger a minute. I'm leaving my heart here! But I've lost track of the time talking to you, and I still have to run back to the hotel before leaving…Give me your hand for good luck, Frau Lenore—we always do that in Russia."

"The right or the left?"

"The left-it's closer to the heart. I'll be here the day after tomorrow—with my shield, or on it! Something tells me I'll come back the victor! Good-bye, my dears, my darlings…"

He embraced and kissed Frau Lenore, and asked Gemma to go into her room with him, for just a moment, since he had something very important to tell her.…He simply wanted to say good-bye to her alone. Frau Lenore understood this—and showed no curiosity as to what this important thing was…

Sanin had never been in Gemma's room. All the charm of love, all its fire and ecstasy and sweet terror blazed up in him and burst into his soul the moment he stepped across the sacred threshold… Deeply moved, he glanced around, fell at the feet of the beloved girl, and pressed his face against her waist…

"Are you mine?" she whispered. "Will you come back soon?"

"I'm yours…I'll come back," he kept repeating breathlessly.

"I'll be waiting for you, my darling!"

A few moments later Sanin was running along the street toward his hotel. He did not even notice that Pantaleone rushed out of the shop door right behind him, all disheveled, and kept shouting something at him, and was shaking his upraised hand, seeming to threaten him.

At exactly a quarter of one Sanin appeared at Polozov's. The carriage, hitched to four horses, was already standing at the hotel gate. On seeing Sanin, Polozov merely said: "Ah! you decided to go?" and, having put on his hat, his coat, and his galoshes, and having stuffed cotton in his ears, although it was summer, he went out onto the steps. On his orders, the waiters had lined the inside of the carriage with his numerous purchases, had surrounded his seat with silk pillows, little bags, and parcels, put a hamper of provisions at his feet, and tied his trunk to the box. Polozov tipped everyone generously—and respectfully, supported from behind by the obliging doorman, he climbed, groaning, into the carriage, settled down, patted everything around him down well, took out a cigar and lit it— and only then beckoned to Sanin with his finger, as if to say: "Now you climb in, too!" Sanin took a seat beside him. Polozov, through the doorman, told the coachman to drive carefully if he wanted a tip; the footboards came up with a crash, the doors slammed shut, the carriage rolled off.

XXXIII

From Frankfurt to Wiesbaden is now less than an hour by rail; in those days the express post could do it in about three hours. Horses were changed five times. Polozov half dozed, and swayed back and forth, holding his cigar in his teeth and talking very little; he did not look out the window once, he was not interested in scenic views and even announced: "Nature is the death of me!" Sanin, also, was silent and also did not admire the view: he was in no mood for it.

He was completely absorbed in thoughts and memories. At the stations, Polozov carefully paid his fare, noted the time on his watch and rewarded the drivers a little or a lot, depending on their zeal. At the halfway point, he took two oranges out of the food hamper and, having chosen the better one, offered Sanin the other. Sanin looked hard at his traveling companion and suddenly broke into a laugh.

"What are you laughing at?" asked the latter, carefully taking the skin off the orange with his short white nails.

"What at?" Sanin repeated. "At this trip of yours and mine."

"What about it?" Polozov asked, putting into his mouth one of those longitudinal sections into which the inside of an orange is divided.

"It's very strange. Yesterday, I must say, I thought as little about you as about the emperor of China—and today I'm riding along with you to sell my estate to your wife, about whom I haven't the least idea."

"All kinds of things happen," replied Polozov. "Just live a bit longer—you'll get to see everything. For example, can you imagine me riding along as an orderly officer? But I did, and the Grand Duke Mikhail Pavlovich gave the order: 'At a trot, at a trot for that fat cornet! Trot faster!'"

"Tell me, please, Ippolit Sidorych, what's your wife like? What sort of disposition has she? It's important for me to know."

"It's all right for him to order: 'Trot!'" Polozov put in with sudden vehemence, "but what about me...how's it for me? So I thought: keep your ranks and your epaulettes—the hell with them! Yes...You were asking about my wife? What about my wife? A human being, like everybody. Don't get her back up—she doesn't like that. Most important, talk a lot...so she has something to laugh at. Tell her about your love, now—but rather amusingly, you know."

"What do you mean, rather amusingly?"

"Why, just that. You were just telling me you're in love, want to get married. Well, now, describe it all to her."

Sanin was offended. "What do you find amusing in that?"

Polozov merely rolled his eyes. Juice from the orange ran down his chin.

"Your wife sent you to Frankfurt to shop?" Sanin asked a little while later.

"She did."

"For what kind of things?"

"The usual: toys."

"Toys? You have children?"

Polozov even moved back from Sanin.

"Heavens! Why would I have children! Women's *colifichets...* Finery. Toilet articles."

"Do you know anything about all that?"

"I do."

"Why did you tell me, then, that you never have anything to do with what your wife does?"

"In other things I don't. But this—it's nothing. Out of boredom, I can do that. And, besides, my wife trusts my taste. I'm clever at bargaining, too."

Polozov was beginning to talk jerkily; he was already tired.

"And your wife's very rich?"

"Rich enough, yes, indeed. Only mostly for herself."

"However, I think you can't complain, can you?"

"That's why I'm her husband. The idea of my not taking advantage of it! And I'm a useful fellow for her! With me she's in clover! I'm convenient!"

Polozov wiped his face with a foulard handkerchief and ' puffed heavily. "Spare me," he seemed to say, "don't make I me talk. You see how hard it is for me."

Sanin left him alone, and sank into thought again.

The hotel in Wiesbaden in front of which the carriage stopped really looked like a palace. Little bells immediately started ringing somewhere inside; a great bustle and fuss arose; handsome servants in black dress coats began jumping about at the main entrance; a doorman covered with gold opened the carriage doors with a flourish.

Like some victorious hero, Polozov got out of the carriage and started going up the staircase, sweet-smelling and covered with carpeting. A man, also excellently dressed, but with a Russian face, flew down to meet him—his valet. Polozov remarked to him that henceforth he would always take him along, for, in Frankfurt the night before, he, Polozov, had been left for the night without hot water! The valet's face showed he was horrified, and, deftly bending down, he took off his master's galoshes.

"Is Maria Nikolaevna in?" Polozov asked.

"Yes, sir. She's dressing. She'll be dining at Countess Lasunskaia's."

"Ah! At her place...Wait! There are things in the carriage; take them all out yourself arid bring them in. And you, Dmitri Pavlovich," Polozov added, "get yourself a room, and come in in three-quarters of an hour. We'll have dinner together."

Polozov went waddling off, and Sanin asked for a room that was inexpensive, and, having put his things in order and rested a little, set out for the enormous suite occupied by his Serene Highness (*Durchlaucht*) Prince von Polozóff.

He found this "prince" sitting in state in a most luxurious velvet armchair in the middle of a most splendid drawing room. Sanin's phlegmatic friend had already managed to have a bath and garb himself in a very rich satin dressing gown; he had put a raspberry-colored fez on his head. Sanin drew near him and for a while looked him up and down. Polozov sat motionless, like an idol; he did not even turn his face to one side, did not even raise an eyebrow, did not make a sound. The spectacle was truly magnificent! Having admired him for a minute or two, Sanin was just about to say something, to break this holy silence, when suddenly the door of the next room opened and there appeared on the threshold a young, beautiful lady in a white silk dress with black lace, and diamonds on her hands and around her throat—Maria Nikolaevna Polozova herself. Her thick blond hair fell down on both sides of her head—braided, but not pinned up.

XXXIV

"Oh, excuse me!" she said with a half-embarrassed, half-mocking smile, instantly catching the end of one braid in her hand and fixing her big, grey, bright eyes on Sanin. "I didn't think you'd come yet."

"Sanin, Dmitri Pavlovich, my childhood friend," said Polozov, without, as before, turning to him and without getting up, but pointing to him with his finger.

"Yes...I know...You already told me. I'm very pleased to meet you. But I wanted to ask you to do something, Ippolit Sidorych. My maid's somehow so scatter-brained today..."

"Put up your hair?"

"Yes, yes, please. Excuse me," Maria Nikolaevna repeated with the same smile as before, nodded to Sanin, and, quickly turning around, disappeared behind the door, leaving the fleeting but pleasing impression of a charming neck, marvelous shoulders, and a marvelous figure.

Polozov rose and, waddling heavily, went out through the same door.

Sanin did not for an instant doubt that his presence in "Prince Polozov's" drawing room had been perfectly well known to the mistress herself; the whole gambit was to show off her hair, which was, indeed, very fine. Sanin was even inwardly glad of this little trick of Madame Polozova's. "If," he thought, "she wanted to impress me, to show off in front of me, maybe—who knows?—she'll be complaisant about the price of the estate, too." His heart was so filled with Gemma that all other women had no significance for him at all: he hardly noticed them; and this time he confined himself to the thought: "Yes, I was told the truth: this lady's quite some thing!"

But if he had not been in such an exclusively spiritual state, he would probably have put things differently: Maria Nikolaevna Polozova, née Kolyshkina, was a very remarkable person. Not that she was a real beauty: traces of her plebeian origin were even rather obvious in her. Her forehead was low, her nose somewhat fleshy and turned-up; she could not boast either of delicate skin or elegant hands and feet—but what did all this signify? Any man who ran into her would have stopped, not before a "sacred thing of beauty," to use Pushkin's phrase, but before the fascination of a powerful, half-Russian, half-gypsy, blooming, woman's body—and would not have stopped involuntarily!

But Gemma's image protected Sanin, like that triple armor of which the poets sing.

Some ten minutes later Maria Nikolaevna appeared again accompanied by her husband. She went up to Sanin—and she walked in such a way that some crackpots in that—alas!—now long-gone time went out of their minds just from the way she walked. "When this woman comes toward you, it's as if she were carrying all the happiness of your life to meet you," one of them used to say. She went up to Sanin and, holding her hand out to him, said in her soft and seemingly restrained voice, in Russian: "You'll wait for me, won't you? I'll be right back."

Sanin bowed respectfully, but Maria Nikolaevna had already disappeared behind the portière of the main door and, on her way out, had again looked over her shoulder and again smiled, and again left behind that previous, pleasing impression.

When she smiled, not one or two but three little dimples appeared on each cheek, and her eyes smiled more than her lips, than her long, bright red, delicious lips with two tiny moles on the left side of them.

Polozov stumbled into the room, and again parked himself in the armchair. He kept silent as before, but a strange ironic grin from time to time came over his colorless and already wrinkled cheeks.

He looked old, though he was only three years older than Sanin.

The dinner with which he entertained his guest would, of course, have satisfied the most exacting gourmet, but to Sanin it seemed endless and unbearable. Polozov ate slowly, "with feeling, with intelligence, without haste," intently bending over the plate, sniffing almost every bite, at first rinsing out his mouth with the wine, then swallowing it, and smacking his lips…Over the entree he suddenly started talking—but about what? About merino sheep, of which he was planning to order a whole flock—and in such detail, with such tenderness, using affectionate diminutives. Having drunk a cup of boiling-hot coffee (he had several times reminded the waiter, in a teary, irritated voice, that yesterday he had been served coffee as cold as ice!) and having bit off the end of a Havana cigar with his crooked, yellow teeth, he dozed off, as was his habit. Sanin, delighted, began walking back and forth on the soft rug with noiseless steps and dreamed about how he and Gemma would live together and with what news he would go back to her. Polozov, however, woke up earlier than usual, as he himself remarked; he had slept only an hour and a half. And, after drinking a glass of seltzer water with ice and swallowing some eight spoonfuls of jam—of Russian jam, which was brought him by his valet in a dark green, real "Kiev" jar, and without which, according to what he said, he could not live—he fixed his puffy eyes on Sanin and asked him if he didn't want to play a little Old Maid. Sanin willingly agreed; he was afraid that Polozov might again start talking about dear little lambs, about lovely little ewes, and about curly little sheep with cute, fat tails. The host and the guest both went into the living room, the waiter brought in some cards, and the game began, though not for money, of course.

Maria Nikolaevna, returning from Countess Lasunskaia's, came on them at this innocent pastime.

She burst out laughing loudly as soon as she entered the room and saw the cards and the open card table. Sanin jumped up, but she exclaimed:

"Sit down and play. I'll change right away and join you," and again disappeared, rustling her dress and pulling off her gloves as she went.

Indeed, she soon returned. She had changed her smart dress for a loose, silk, lavender gown with open, hanging sleeves; a thick, twisted cord was around her waist. She sat down by her husband and, having waited until he was the Old Maid, said to him: "Now, Dumpling, that's enough!" (Sanin glanced at her in amazement at the word "dumpling," but she smiled cheerfully, answering his glance by a glance and showing all the dimples in her cheeks.) "That's enough; I can see you want to go to sleep; kiss my hand and go off to bed, and Mr. Sanin and I will have a little chat together."

"I'm not sleepy," said Polozov, rising cumbrously from his chair, "but going to bed, now—why, I will, and I'll kiss your hand." She offered him her palm, without ceasing to smile or taking her eyes off Sanin.

Polozov also glanced at him, and left without saying good-night.

"Now, tell me, tell me," said Maria Nikolaevna animatedly, at once putting both her bare elbows on the table and impatiently tapping the nails of one hand with those of the other. "Is it true you're getting married, as I've heard?"

Having said this, Maria Nikolaevna even bent her head a little to one side to look into Sanin's eyes more intently and more piercingly.

XXXV

Madame Polozova's familiar manner would at first probably have embarrassed Sanin—although he was no tyro and had been about a good deal—had he not seen this very familiarity and over-freeness as a good portent for his undertaking. "We'll humor the whims of this rich lady," he decided to himself, and answered her just as casually as she had asked her question.

"Yes, I am."

"To whom? A foreigner?"

"Yes."

"You just met her? In Frankfurt?"

"That's right."

"And who is she? May I ask?"

"You may. She's a confectioner's daughter."

Maria Nikolaevna opened her eyes wide and raised her eyebrows.

"Oh, that's charming," she said slowly, "that's marvelous! I didn't think there were any more young men like you left in the world. A confectioner's daughter!"

"That surprises you, I see," Sanin remarked, not without some dignity. "But, first of all, I don't have any of those prejudices—"

"*First of all,* it doesn't surprise me a bit," Maria Nikolaevna interrupted. "I haven't any prejudices, either. I'm the daughter of a peasant myself. Well? I beat you there, didn't I? It surprises me and delights me that here is a man who isn't afraid of loving. Because you love her, don't you?"

"Yes."

"She's very good-looking?"

Sanin winced slightly at this last question...But this was not the time to give in.

"You know, Maria Nikolaevna," he began, "that for every man the face of the woman he loves seems better than all others, but my fiancée is really beautiful."

"Actually? In what way? The Italian? The classic?"

"Yes, she has very regular features."

"You don't have her portrait with you?"

"No." (At that time, there was no mention even of photographs. Daguerreotypes were just beginning to be popular.)

"What's her name?"

"Gemma."

"And yours?"

"Dmitri."

"Patronymic?"

"Pavlovich." "You know what," said Maria Nikolaevna in the same slow voice. "I like you very much, Dmitri Pavlovich. I'm sure you must be a good man. Give me your hand. Let's be friends."

She pressed his hand hard with her strong, beautiful, white fingers. Her hand was somewhat smaller than his—but much warmer, and smoother, and softer, and more full of life.

"Only you know what occurs to me?"

"What?"

"You won't be angry? No? She's your fiancée, you say. But really—really was that absolutely necessary?"

Sanin frowned.

"I don't understand you, Maria Nikolaevna."

Maria Nikolaevna laughed softly and, shaking her head, tossed back the hair that had fallen onto her cheeks.

"He is delightful, absolutely," she said half-thoughtfully, half-absent-mindedly. "A knight! Now, after this, just try to believe those who say that the idealists are all dead!"

Maria Nikolevna spoke Russian the whole time with a surprisingly pure, true Moscow accent—the way the people talk, rather than the nobility.

"Most likely you were brought up at home, in an old-fashioned, God-fearing family?" she asked. "You're from which province?"

"Tula."

"Well, then we're neighbors...But you know who my father was?"

"Yes, I do."

"He was born in Tula...A Tula man. Well, good enough..." (Maria Nikolaevna deliberately pronounced "good enough" exactly as the shopkeepers do—"gudnuf.") So, now let's get down to business."

"That is...What's this getting down to business? What do you mean by that?"

Maria Nikolaevna half-closed her eyes.

"But what did you come here for?" (When she half-closed her eyes, their expression became very tender and a little derisive; when she opened them wide, something evil came through their bright, almost cold, gleam—something threatening. Her thick, slightly raised, really sable-like eyebrows lent her eyes a special beauty.) "You want me to buy your estate? You need money for your wedding? Isn't that right?"

"Yes, I do."

"And do you want much?"

"I would be satisfied with a few thousand francs to start with. Your husband knows my estate. You can ask his advice; I would take a very reasonable price."

Maria Nikolaevna swung her head to the right and to the left.

"*First of all,*" she began slowly, tapping the lapel of Sanin's frock coat with the ends of her fingers, "it's not my habit to consult with, my husband, except for clothes—he's splendid at that for me; and *secondly,* why do you say you'll set a very reasonable price? I don't want to take advantage of the fact that you're very much in love now and prepared to make all kinds of sacrifices....I won't accept any sacrifices from you. What? Instead of encouraging your—well, how'll I say it best?—noble feelings, say, shall I try to fleece you? That's not the way I do things. When it comes down to it, I don't let people off easy—only not in that way."

Sanin could not understand at all whether she was making fun of him or speaking seriously, and merely thought to himself: "Oh, indeed with you one must keep his eyes open."

A servant came in with a Russian samovar, a tea service, cream, rusks, etc., on a large tray, set all this bliss out on the table between

Sanin and Madame Polozova, and went out.

She poured him a cup of tea.

"You don't mind?" she asked, putting the sugar into his cup with her fingers, though the sugar-tongs were lying right there.

"Heavens!…From such a beautiful hand…"

He did not finish the sentence and almost choked over a mouthful of tea, and she watched him intently and serenely.

"I mentioned a very reasonable price for my estate," he went on, "because, since you're now abroad, I can't expect you to have much ready cash and, finally, I myself feel that the sale…or purchase of an estate under such conditions is something out of the ordinary, and I must take that into consideration."

Sanin became embarrassed and confused, but Maria Nikolaevna quietly leaned against the back of her chair, folded her hands, and kept looking at him in the same intent and serene way. He finally fell silent.

"Never mind, go on, go on," she said, as if coming to his rescue. "I'm listening to you—I like listening to you: go on."

Sanin started describing his estate, how many acres it had, where it was, what kind of farmland and forest it had, and what profits one could get from it—he even mentioned the picturesque setting of the manor house; but Maria Nikolaevna kept looking and looking at him, more and more brightly and intently, and her lips just barely moved, without smiling: she was biting them. Finally he felt completely awkward: he fell silent a second time.

"Dmitri Pavlovich," Maria Nikolaevna began—and sank into thought…"Dmitri Pavlovich," she repeated, "you know what? I'm sure that the purchase of your estate is a very profitable bit of business for me and that we'll agree on the terms, but you must give me…two days—yes, two days. After all, you can be separated from your fiancée for two days, can't you? I won't keep you any longer, against your will—I give you my word. But if you need five, six thousand francs right away, I'm ready to lend them to you with great pleasure—and we'll settle later."

Sanin got up. "I must thank you, Maria Nikolaevna, for your kind and heart-warming readiness to help a person practically unknown to you…But if this is what's most convenient for you, I'd prefer to wait for your decision about my estate—I'll stay here two days."

"Yes, that's most convenient for me, Dmitri Pavlovich. But will it be very hard for you? Very? Tell me."

"I love my fiancée, Maria Nikolaevna, and being separated from her is not easy for me."

"Ah, you're an angel!" said Maria Nikolaevna with a sigh. "I promise not to torment you too much. You're going?"

"It's late," Sanin observed.

"And you have to rest after the trip, and after the game of Old Maid with my husband. Tell me—you're a close friend of Ippolit Sidorych, my husband?"

"We were at the same boarding school."

"And even then he was like this?"

"What does 'this' mean?" asked Sanin.

Maria Nikolaevna suddenly laughed, laughed until her whole face was red, put her handkerchief to her lips, got up from her chair—and, swaying as if very tired, went up to Sanin and held out her hand to him.

He said good-bye and started for the door.

"Please come very early tomorrow, do you hear?" she called after him. He glanced back as he was leaving the room and saw that she had again sunk into the armchair and thrown both hands up behind her head. The loose sleeves of her gown had fallen down almost to her shoulders—and it could not be denied that the pose of those arms, that her whole figure was fascinatingly beautiful.

XXXVI

The lamp in Sanin's room burned long after midnight. He was sitting at a table and writing "his Gemma." He had told her everything, described the Polozovs to her—husband and wife—expatiated more about his own feelings, and ended with setting a meeting with her in three days!!! (with three exclamation marks) . Early in the morning he took this letter to the mailbox and then went for a walk in the

Kurhaus garden, where music was already being played. There were few people yet; he stood for a while in front of the arbor where the orchestra was, listened to a pot-pourri from *Robert le Diable,* and, having had some coffee, set out along a lonely side alley, sat down on a bench, and became lost in thought.

The handle of a parasol tapped him briskly, and rather hard on the shoulder. He gave a start....In front of him, in a light, greyish-green Barèges dress, a white tulle hat and suede gloves, fresh and pink as a summer morning, but with the languor of a peaceful night's sleep still in her movements and her eyes, stood Maria Nikolaevna.

"Hello," she said. "I sent for you today, but you had already gone out. I've just had my second glass—I have to drink the water here, you know—God knows why...am I not healthy? So now I have to take a walk for a whole hour. Do you want to be my companion on the walk? And then we'll drink some coffee."

"I already have," said Sanin rising, "but I'm very glad to walk with you."

"Well, let me have your arm...Don't be afraid: your fiancée isn't here—she won't see you."

Sanin gave a forced smile. He had an unpleasant feeling every time Maria Nikolaevna reminded him of Gemma. However, he leaned toward her hurriedly and obediently. Maria Nikolaevna's hand came slowly and softly down onto his arm, and slid along it, and seemed to cling to it.

"Let's go—this way," she said to him, putting up her opened parasol over her shoulder. "In this park I feel I'm at home,: I'll take you to the good places. And you know what" (she often used these three words) : "you and I won't talk about that purchase now; we can discuss it thoroughly after lunch; but now you must tell me about yourself—so that I'll know with whom I'm dealing. And afterwards, if you want, I'll tell you about myself. Do you agree?"

"But, Maria Nikolaevna, what can there be of interest for you..."

"Wait, wait. You didn't understand me correctly. I don't want to flirt with you." Maria Nikolaevna shrugged her shoulders. "He has a fiancée like an antique statue, and I'm going to flirt with him? But you have something to sell—and I'm a buyer. Now, I want to know what kind of goods you've got. Well, show me—what are they? I want to know not only what I'm buying, but also from whom I'm buying. That was my father's rule. Well, begin…Well, if not from childhood—well, now, have you been abroad long? And where were you until now? Only go slower, we're in no hurry."

"I came here from Italy, where I spent several months."

"Obviously you feel a special attraction for everything Italian? It's strange you didn't find your beloved there. You like art? Paintings? Or music perhaps more?"

"I like art…I like everything beautiful."

"Music, too?"

"And music, too."

"I don't like it at all. I like only Russian songs—and then only in the country, in spring—with dancing, you know…The red calicoes, the strings of beads around the heads, the young grass in the pasture, the smell of smoke…It's wonderful! But we weren't talking about me. Go on, tell me more."

Maria Nikolaevna walked on, but kept constantly looking at Sanin. She was tall—her face came almost up to the same level as his.

He started telling about himself—reluctantly at first, clumsily, but then he warmed up, and was even chatty. Maria Nikolaevna listened very sensibly; besides, she herself seemed so candid that she inevitably provoked candor in others. She had that great gift of "intimacy"—*le terrible don de la familiarité,* which Cardinal Retz speaks of. Sanin talked about his travels, about life in Petersburg, about his youth…Had Maria Nikolaevna been a society lady with refined manners, he would never have opened up like that, but she herself called herself a good fellow who wouldn't put up with any formalities; that was exactly how she described herself to Sanin. And at the same time there was something catlike in the way this "good fellow" was walking along beside him, lightly rubbing up against him and glancing up into his face; was walking along in the guise of a young female creature giving off that enticing and tormenting, that quiet and searing air of seduction with which only Slav natures—and only some of them; not those of pure blood, but only those with mixed blood—are able to plague us sinful, weak men!

Sanin's walk with Maria Nikolaevna, Sanin's talk with Maria Nikolaevna, lasted over an hour. And they did not stop once—they kept walking and walking along the endless alleys of the park, sometimes going up a hill and admiring the view as they went, sometimes going down into a dale and becoming hidden in impenetrable shade—and all the time arm in arm. At moments, Sanin even became annoyed: he had never taken such a long walk with Gemma, with his sweet Gemma…and here this lady had gotten hold of him—and he could do nothing about it.

"Aren't you tired?" he asked her more than once.

"I never get tired," she replied.

From time to time they met others out for a walk; they almost all bowed to her—some respectfully, others even obsequiously. To one of them, a very handsome, smartly dressed, dark-haired man, she called from a distance, in the very best Parisian accent: *"Comte, vous savez, il ne faut pas venir me voir—ni aujourd'hui, ni demain."* He silently took off his hat and bowed very low.

"Who's that?" asked Sanin, from the bad habit of "being curious," peculiar to all Russians.

"That? A little Frenchman—there are a lot of them running around here…He's one of my admirers also. However, it's time for coffee now. Let's go home. You, I'm sure, have become hungry. My lord and master, I suppose, has unbuttoned his eyes now."

"My lord and master! Unbuttoned his eyes!" Sanin repeated to himself…"And she speaks such excellent French…What a queer one!"

Maria Nikolaevna was not wrong. When she got back to the hotel together with Sanin, her "lord and master," or "dumpling," was already sitting, with the inevitable fez on his head, in front of a table all set.

"I've been waiting and waiting for you!" he exclaimed, making a sour face. "I was about to have coffee without you."

"It doesn't matter, it doesn't matter," Maria Nikolaevna retorted gaily. "Are you angry? That's good for you: or you'll stiffen up completely. Here, now, I've brought a guest. Ring quickly! Let's drink some coffee; coffee—the very best coffee—in Saxony cups, on a snow-white tablecloth!"

She slipped off her hat and gloves, and clapped her hands.

Polozov glanced at her scowlingly.

"Why are you feeling so good today, Maria Nikolaevna?" he said in a low voice.

"That's none of your business, Ippolit Sidorych! Ring! Dmitri Pavlovich, sit down—and have some coffee a second time! Ah, how much fun to give orders! There's no other such pleasure in the world!"

"When they're obeyed," her husband again muttered.

"Exactly, when they're obeyed! That's what makes it fun for me. Especially with you. Isn't that right, Dumpling? And here's the coffee."

On the enormous tray with which the waiter had appeared there was also a theater playbill. Maria Nikolaevna immediately snatched it up.

"A drama!" she said indignantly; "a German drama. It doesn't matter: that's better than a German comedy. Order a box for me—a *baignoire*—or no…better the *Fremden-Loge*," she said to the waiter. "You hear: the *Fremden-Loge* positively!"

"But if the *Fremden-Loge* is already taken by His Excellency the City Manager *(seine Excellenz der Hen Stadt-Direktor)*?" the waiter was bold enough to reply.

"Give His Excellency ten thalers—but be sure the box is mine! You hear!"

The waiter submissively and sadly bowed his head.

"Dmitri Pavlovich, you'll go to the theater with me? German actors are dreadful, but you'll go?…Yes? Good! How kind you are! Dumpling, you're not going?"

"Whatever you say," said Polozov into the cup which he had raised to his mouth.

"You know what: stay here. You always sleep in the theater—and you understand German badly, besides. You do this instead: write an answer to the steward—you remember, about our mill…about the peasants' grinding. Tell him I won't, I won't, and I won't! There's something to keep you busy all evening…"

"Yes'm," responded Polozov.

"Well, that's splendid. You're my clever boy. And now, gentlemen, since we've started talking about the steward, let's discuss our main business. Just as soon, now, as the waiter clears the table, you'll tell us all, Dmitri Pavlovich, about your estate—what price you're selling it for, how, and what, how much deposit you want in advance—in short, everything!" ("At last," thought Sanin, "thank God!") "You've already told me some things—described your orchard, I remember, marvelously—but Dumpling wasn't there. Let him listen a bit—he always has something to mumble about! It's very pleasant for me to think that I can help you get married—besides, I've already promised you to get down to business with you after breakfast, and I always keep my promises, don't I, Ippolit Sidorych?"

Polozov rubbed his face with his palm.

"The truth is the truth: you don't deceive anybody."

"Never! and I never will. Well, Dmitri Pavlovich, state your case, as we say in the Senate."

XXXVII

Sanin started "stating his case"—that is, describing his estate again, a second time, but no longer touching on the beauties of nature—and from time to time referring to Polozov for confirmation of "facts and figures" introduced. But Polozov merely grunted and shook his head—approvingly or disapprovingly, God Himself, probably, would have had a hard time saying. Maria Nikolaevna, however, did not need his help. She showed such commercial and administrative abilities as one could only wonder at! She knew perfectly all the ins and outs of running an estate: she asked about everything precisely, went into every detail; everything she said hit its mark, put the dot on every "i." Sanin had not expected such an examination: he was unprepared. And this examination lasted a whole hour and a half. He experienced all the feelings of a defendant sitting on a narrow bench in front of a harsh and penetrating judge. "It's a cross-examination!" he whispered miserably to himself. Maria Nikolaevna kept laughing softly all the time, as if she were joking, but that made things no easier for Sanin; and when during the "cross-examination" it turned out that he did not completely clearly understand the meaning of the words "re-allotment" and "tillage," he even broke into a sweat.

"Well, fine!" Maria Nikolaevna decided at last. "Now I know your estate...as well as you do. What price do you want per peasant?" (At that time, the price of estates was, of course, figured according to the number of peasants.)

"Well...I think...I can't take less than five hundred rubles," Sanin said with difficulty. (O Pantaleone, Pantaleone, where are you? Now's the time for you to shout out again: *Barbari!)*

Maria Nikolaevna raised her eyes on high, as if considering it.

"Why not?" she said finally. "That price seems to me harmless enough. But I stipulated two days and you must wait until tomorrow. I think we'll agree, and then you can say how much you want down. But now *basta cosí!*" she put in, noticing that Sanin was about to make an objection. "We've spent enough time on filthy lucre...*à demain les affaires!* You know what: I'll let you go now" (she glanced at the little enamel watch tucked into her belt) "...until three. You must be allowed to rest. Go play a little roulette."

"I never play games of chance," Sanin remarked.

"Really? You're perfection. However, I don't play, either. It's silly to throw money to the wind. But go into the gambling hall, look at the faces. Some really amusing ones turn up. There's one old woman there with a *ferronnière* and a moustache—marvelous! There's one of our princes there—he's good, too. A majestic figure, a nose like an eagle's, bets a thaler and secretly crosses himself under his vest. Read the journals, walk around—in short, do what you want...But I'll be expecting you at three...*de pied ferme.* We'll have to eat dinner a little earlier. The theater among these silly Germans starts at six-thirty." She held out her hand. *"Sans rancune, nest-ce pas?"*

"Heavens, Maria Nikolaevna, what have I to be annoyed at you for?"

"For having tormented you. Wait a bit, I haven't really yet," she added, half-closing her eyes and all her dimples appeared at once on her crimsoned cheeks. "Until later!"

Sanin bowed and went out. A merry laugh rang out behind

him—in the mirror which he was passing at that moment this scene was reflected: Maria Nikolaevna had pushed her husband's fez down over his eyes, and he was helplessly struggling with both hands.

XXXVIII

Oh, how deeply and joyfully Sanin sighed as soon as he found himself in his own room! Indeed, Maria Nikolaevna had spoken truthfully—he needed to rest, to rest from all these new acquaintances, encounters, conversations, from the smoke and fumes which had gotten into his head, into his soul—from this unforeseen, unasked-for intimacy with a woman so alien to him! And when was all this happening? Practically the day after he had learned that Gemma loved him, that he had become her fiancé! Why, it was a sacrilege! A thousand times in his thoughts he begged forgiveness from his pure, chaste darling—although actually he could not accuse himself of anything; a thousand times he kissed the little cross she had given him. Had he had no hope of speedily and successfully finishing the business for which he had come to Wiesbaden, he would have rushed back again headlong to his dear Frankfurt, to that dear, already kindred home, to her, to her adored feet...But there was nothing he could do! He had to drain the cup to the bottom, had to get dressed, go have dinner—and then go to the theater....If only she would let him go as soon as possible tomorrow!

One other thing bothered him, made him angry: he thought of Gemma with love, with tender emotion, with grateful delight, of his life together with her, of the happiness which lay ahead of him in the future—and meanwhile this strange woman, this Madame Polozova, constantly drifted along...no! not drifted along—loomed up—thus Sanin put it with special vindictiveness—*loomed up* before his eyes, and he could not get free of her image, could not stop hearing her voice, remembering what she said—could not help but sense even that special scent, delicate, fresh, and penetrating, like the smell of yellow lilies, that came from her clothes. This lady was clearly making a fool of him, getting around him this way and that...Why? What did she want? Was it just the whim of a spoiled, rich, and most likely immoral woman? And that husband! What kind of creature was he? What were his relations with her? And why were these questions creeping into his head, when he, Sanin, really had nothing to do with either Polozov or his wife? Why couldn't he drive that importunate image away even when he was turned body and soul to another, as bright and clear as the daylight of God's world? How dared—through those other, almost divine features—*these* slip through? And they didn't just slip through—they grinned impudently. These grey, predatory eyes, these dimples on the cheeks, these snakelike braids—was it all now really as good as stuck to him; and couldn't he, wasn't he able, to shake it off, to throw it all away?

Nonsense! Nonsense! It'll all disappear tomorrow anyway without a trace…But would she let him go tomorrow?

Yes…He put all these questions to himself—but when it was getting near three o'clock, he put on his black dress coat and, having walked in the park a little, headed for Polozov's.

In their living room he found an embassy secretary, a German, very tall, blond, with a horse-like profile and his hair parted in the back (that was still something new then), and…oh, wonders! whom else but von Dönhof, that same officer with whom he had fought just a few days before! He had not at all expected to run into him here—and involuntarily he was confused, but exchanged hellos with him nonetheless.

"You know each other?" Maria Nikolaevna asked, by whom Sanin's embarrassment had not gone unnoticed.

"Yes…I've already had the honor," said Dönhof, and, bowing slightly in Maria Nikolaevna's direction, added in a low voice, with a smile: "The same man…Your com patriot…the Russian…"

"Impossible!" she exclaimed, also in a low voice, shook her finger at him, and immediately started saying good-bye both to him and to the lanky secretary who, from all the signs, was head over heels in love with her, for he gaped every time he looked at her. Dönhof left immediately, with courteous acquiescence, like a friend of the family who at a hint understands what is being asked of him; the secretary rather balked, but Maria Nikolaevna showed him out without further formalities.

"Go on to your sovereign lady," she told him (in Wiesbaden at that time there lived a certain *principessa di Monaco,* who strikingly resembled a poor cocotte). "Why should you stay with such a plebeian as me?"

"Please, madam," the hapless secretary asserted, "all the *principesse* in the world…"

But Maria Nikolaevna was merciless—and the secretary went out, along with his hair-do.

Maria Nikolaevna had that day dressed up very much to her "advantage," as our grandmothers used to say. She had on a pink, glacé silk dress with sleeves *à la Fontanges* and a big diamond in each ear. Her eyes were shining no less than the diamonds: she seemed in high spirits and good form.

She seated Sanin beside her and began talking to him about Paris, where she was planning to go in a few days, about the fact that she was fed up with the Germans, that they were stupid when they tried to be witty, and ineptly witty when they were being stupid; then suddenly, as they say, pointblank—*à brûle pourpoint*—asked him if it was true that he had fought a duel the other day over a certain lady with that same officer who had just been there?

"How do you know that?" a surprised Sanin muttered.

"The world is full of talk, Dmitri Pavlovich; but I know you were right, a thousand times right, and behaved like a knight. Tell me— this lady—was your fiancée?"

Sanin slightly frowned…

"Well, I won't, I won't," Maria Nikolaevna said quickly. "It's unpleasant for you; forgive me, I won't! Don't be angry!" Polozov appeared from the next room with a page from a newspaper in his hands. "What do you want? Or is dinner ready?"

"Dinner will be served in a minute, but look here, now, what I read in *The Northern Bee*…Prince Gromoboi's dead."

Maria Nikolaevna looked up.

"Ah! May he rest in peace! Every year," she turned to Sanin, "in

February, for my birthday, he used to decorate all the rooms with camellias for me. But it's still not worth living in Petersburg in the winter for that. Why, I suppose he was over seventy, wasn't he?" she asked her husband.

"He was. His funeral is described in the paper. The whole court was there. And here's a poem by Prince Kovrizhkin about it."

"Well, that's wonderful."

"If you want me to, I'll read it. The Prince calls him a man of counsel."

"No, don't. What kind of a man of counsel was he! He was simply Tatiana Iurevna's man. Let's go have dinner. The living must think of the living. Dmitri Pavlovich, your arm."

The dinner was, like that the day before, marvelous, and passed very animatedly. Maria Nikolaevna knew how to tell stories—a rare talent in a woman, especially in a Russian woman. She did not hold back her expressions, and her fellow-countrywomen, especially, got a good going over from her. Sanin often had to burst out in hearty laughter at her witty and pointed remarks. Maria Nikolaevna hated bigotry most of all, and pompous phrases and lies…She found them almost everywhere. She seemed to boast, to be proud of the low-class environment in which her life had begun; she told rather strange stories about her relatives and family from the days of her childhood; called herself a poor peasant woman no worse than Natalia Kirillovna Naryshkina.[6] It became obvious to Sanin that she had experienced much more in her life than the majority of women of her age.

Polozov kept on eating thoughtfully, drank intently, and only now and then glanced either at his wife or at Sanin with his whitish, seemingly blind, but actually very perceptive, eyes.

"Oh, you're my clever boy!" exclaimed Maria Nikolaevna, turning to him; "how well you did everything I ask you to in Frankfurt! I'd kiss your little forehead, but you don't much like that from me."

"I don't," replied Polozov, and cut a pineapple with a silver knife.

---

6   The mother of Peter the Great, the second wife of Tsar Aleksei Mikhailovich, came from a very poor family.

Maria Nikolaevna glanced at him and tapped her fingers on the table.

"So our bet's on?" she said meaningfully.

"It's on."

"Right. You'll lose."

Polozov thrust his chin out.

"Well, this time, no matter how much you count on yourself, Maria Nikolaevna, I think you're going to lose."

"What's the bet about? May I ask?" asked Sanin.

"No…you can't now," replied Maria Nikolaevna—and laughed.

It struck seven. The waiter announced that the carriage was at the door. Polozov saw his wife out and then immediately dragged himself back to his chair.

"Mind now! Don't forget the letter to the steward!" Maria Nikolaevna shouted to him from the hall.

"I'll write it, don't worry. I'm a careful man."

XXXIX

In 1840 the theater in Wiesbaden was terrible, even from the outside, and its company of actors, by their pompous and shabby mediocrity, by their assiduous and cheap routine, were not a hair's breadth above that level which even now can be considered normal for all German theaters, and the epitome of which is the Karlsruhe company under the "illustrious" direction of Herr Devrient. Behind the box taken for "Her Serene Highness Madame von Polozóff" (God knows how the waiter managed to get it; maybe he actually had bribed the Stadt-Direktor!)—behind this box there was a small vestibule with sofas around the walls; before going into it, Maria Nikolaevna asked Sanin to put up the screen separating the box from the theater.

"I don't want them to see me," she said, "or they'll be coming up here right away."

She seated him beside her, his back to the orchestra, so that the box would seem empty.

The orchestra started playing the overture from *The Marriage of*

Figaro…The curtain went up, the play had begun.

It was one of those numerous, home-grown products in which well-read but talentless authors, in carefully chosen but lifeless language, diligently but awkwardly would try to advance some "profound" or "crucial" idea, present a so-called tragic conflict, and bring on boredom…as deadly as Asian cholera. Maria Nikolaevna listened patiently to half an act, but when the young lead, having found out about the betrayal of his beloved (he was dressed in a brown frock coat with "puffs" and a velveteen collar, a striped vest with mother-of-pearl buttons, green trousers with patent-leather shoe-straps, and white chamois gloves), when this lead, pressing his two fists to his chest and thrusting his elbows out in front at a sharp angle, started howling exactly like a dog, Maria Nikolaevna could take no more.

"The worst French actor in the worst little provincial town plays better and more naturally than the biggest German celebrity," she exclaimed indignantly, and moved into the little vestibule. "Come here," she said to Sanin, patting the sofa beside her. "Let's talk."

Sanin obeyed. Maria Nikolaevna glanced at him.

"Why, I see you're as meek as a lamb! Your wife'll have an easy time of it with you. That clown," she went on, pointing to the howling actor with the end of her fan (he was playing the role of a private tutor) "reminded me of my youth: I was once in love with a teacher, too. That was my first—no, my second flame. The first time I fell in love with a lay brother of the Donskoi Monastery. I was twelve. I used to see him only on Sundays. He wore a velvet cassock, sprayed himself with *eau de lavande,* and as he made his way through the crowd with the censer would say to ladies in French, '*Pardon, excusez,*' and never looked up, and his eye lashes were—like that!" Maria Nikolaevna marked off half her little finger with her thumbnail and held it up to Sanin. "My teacher was called Monsieur Gaston! I have to tell you he was terribly learned and a very severe man, a Swiss—and with such an energetic face! His sideburns were as black as pitch; he had a Greek profile—and his lips seemed cast of iron! I was scared to death of him! This is the only man whom I've ever been afraid of in my whole life. He was my brother's tutor, my brother who later died—drowned. A gypsy has predicted a violent death for me, too, but that's absurd. I don't believe it. Can you imagine Ippolit Sidorych with a dagger?"

"You can die from other things besides a dagger," Sanin remarked.

"It's all absurd! Are you superstitious? I'm not a bit. And what's going to happen has to happen. Monsieur Gaston lived in our house, right over my head. I used to wake up in the night and hear his footsteps—he went to bed very late—and my heart would stop beating in awe…or from some other feeling. My father himself could hardly read and write, but he gave us a good education. Do you know I understand Latin?"

"You? Latin?"

"Yes—me. Monsieur Gaston taught me. I read the *Aeneid* with him. It's a boring thing—but there are good spots in it. You remember when Dido and Aeneas are in the woods…"

"Yes, yes, I do," Sanin said quickly. He himself had long ago forgotten all his Latin and had only a vague idea of the *Aeneid*.

Maria Nikolaevna glanced at him, the way she usually did, somewhat from one side and looking upward.

"Don't think, though, that I'm very learned. Ah, good Lord, no! I'm not learned, and I have no special talents. I can hardly write—really; I can't read out loud, nor play the piano, nor draw, nor sew—nothing! That's what I'm like—this is all there is!"

She spread her arms.

"I'm telling you all this," she continued, "first of all, in order not to listen to those fools" (she pointed toward the stage where at that moment, instead of the actor, an actress was wailing, with her elbows, too, stuck out), "and secondly, because I'm in debt to you: you told me about yourself yesterday."

"You asked me to," Sanin observed.

Maria Nikolaevna suddenly turned around to him.

"And you don't want to know just what kind of woman I am? However, I'm not surprised," she added, again leaning back on the sofa cushions. "A man who is getting ready to get married, and for love, and after a duel…Why would he be thinking of anything else?"

Maria Nikolaevna became lost in thought and began biting the handle of her fan with her large but even, milk-white teeth.

It seemed to Sanin that his head was again filling up with the fog and fumes which he could not get free of—for two days now.

The conversation between him and Maria Nikolaevna was being carried on in a low voice, almost in a whisper—and that irritated and excited him even more...

When was it all going to end?

Weak people never end anything themselves—they always keep waiting for an end.

On stage someone sneezed; this sneezing had been introduced into the play by the author as the "comic relief" or "element"; there was, of course, no other comic element in it, and the audience was delighted with this moment and laughed.

This laughter, too, irritated Sanin.

There were moments when he really did not know whether he was angry or delighted, bored or having a good time. Oh, if Gemma could have seen him!

"Really, it's strange," said Maria Nikolaevna suddenly. "A man tells you, and in such a calm voice: 'I'm going to get married'; but nobody'll tell you calmly: 'I'm going to throw myself in the water.' And what's the difference between them? It's strange, really."

Annoyance seized Sanin.

"The difference is enormous, Maria Nikolaevna! For some, throwing yourself in the water isn't terrible at all: they can swim; and besides...as far as the strangeness of marriages goes...if it's a question of that..."

He suddenly fell silent and bit his tongue.

Maria Nikolaevna struck her palm with her fan.

"Finish it, Dmitri Pavlovich, finish it—I know what you wanted to say. If it's a question of that, my dear lady, Maria Nikolaevna,' you wanted to say, 'one can't imagine a marriage stranger than *yours*... why, I've known your husband well, since childhood!' That's what you wanted to say, you swimmer!"

"Please," Sanin began...

"Isn't it true? Isn't it true?" Maria Nikolaevna said insistently.

"Well, look me in the eye and tell me that I didn't speak the truth!"

Sanin did not know where to look.

"Well, all right: it's true, if you absolutely insist on knowing," he finally said.

Maria Nikolaevna nodded.

"Exactly...Indeed. Well, and have you asked yourself, you swimmer, what might be the reason for this strange...action on the part of a woman who is not poor...and not stupid...and not bad-looking? That doesn't interest you, perhaps; it doesn't matter. I'll tell you the reason, but not now; just as soon as the intermission is over. I'm always worried that somebody might come in..."

Maria Nikolaevna had barely managed to get out the last word when the outer door actually opened halfway—and a head stuck itself into the box—reddish, oily, perspiring, still young but already toothless, with straight long hair, a pendulant nose, huge ears like a bat, with gold-rimmed glasses on inquisitive and dull little eyes and with a *pince-nez* on top of the glasses. The head looked around, noticed Maria Nikolaevna, grinned wretchedly, started nodding....A stringy neck stretched out behind it....

Maria Nikolaevna waved her handkerchief at it:

"I'm not in! *Ich bin nicht zu Hause, Herr P...! Ich bin nicht zu Hause...*Shoo, shoo!"

The head was taken aback, gave a forced laugh, and said, as if sobbing, in imitation of Liszt at whose feet it had at one time groveled:

"*Sehr gut! sehr gut!*"—and vanished.

"What fellow is that?" asked Sanin.

"That? A Wiesbaden critic. A *literat* or a *lohn*-lackey, whichever you please. He's in the hire of the local contractor, and therefore he has to praise everything and be ecstatic about everything, but he himself is filled with foul bile which he doesn't dare let out. I'm afraid: he's a terrible gossip, he'll run now and tell everybody that I'm in the theater. But it makes no difference."

The orchestra played a waltz, the curtain went up again...On stage, the face-making and whimpering started again.

"Well, now," began Maria Nikolaevna, sitting down on the sofa again, "since you're caught and have to sit with me, instead of enjoying the closeness of your fiancée—don't turn your eyes up like that and don't be angry—I understand you and have already promised you I'll let you go, as free as the wind, but now listen to my confession. You want to know what I love most of all?"

"Freedom," prompted Sanin.

Maria Nikolaevna put her hand on his.

"Yes, Dmitri Pavlovich," she said, and her voice sounded special, sounded unquestionably sincere and serious, "freedom, more than anything else and before anything else. And don't think I'm boasting about it—there's nothing to boast about in it—only that's the way it is, and it always was and will be like that for me to the day I die. In childhood, I suppose, I saw my fill of slavery and suffered from it. Well, Monsieur Gaston, my teacher, opened my eyes. Now, perhaps, you understand why I married Ippolit Sidorych; with him I'm free, completely free, like the air, like the wind…And I knew that before the wedding, I knew that with him I'd be a free Cossack!"

Maria Nikolaevna fell silent for a moment and tossed her fan to one side.

"I'll tell you something else: I'm not against thinking things over… it's amusing, and, besides, that's what our mind is for, but about the consequences of what I myself do—I never think, and when I have to, I'm not sorry for myself—not the tiniest bit: it's not worth it. I have a saying: *"Cela ne tire pas à conséquence"*—I don't know how to say it in Russian. And indeed: why *tire pas à conséquence?* Because nobody's going to ask me for an accounting here—in this world; and there" (she raised her finger and pointed up)—"well, *there*—let them arrange things as they can. When I'm judged *there*, I won't be *me!* Are you listening to me? You're not bored?"

Sanin was sitting bent over. He raised his head.

"I'm not at all bored, Maria Nikolaevna, and I'm listening to you with interest. Only I…confess…I'm asking myself, why are you telling me all this?"

Maria Nikolaevna shifted slightly on the sofa.

"You're asking yourself…Are you so slow? Or so modest?"

Sanin raised his head still more.

"I'm telling you all this," Maria Nikolaevna continued in a calm tone, which, however, did not completely correspond to the expression on her face, "because I like you very much. Yes, don't be surprised, I'm not joking; because, after having met you, I would be unhappy thinking that you had an unpleasant memory of me...or even not unpleasant—that makes no difference to me—but a false one. And therefore I lured you here, and have stayed alone with you, and have been talking to you so frankly...Yes, yes, frankly. I'm not lying. And mind, Dmitri Pavlovich, I know you're in love with another woman, that you're planning on marrying her...Do justice to my disinterestedness! However, here's your chance to say in your turn: *Cela ne tire pas à conséquence!*"

She laughed, but her laughter suddenly broke off—and she remained still, as if her own words had astounded her very being; and in her eyes, usually so merry and bold, flashed something like timidity, even like sorrow.

"A snake! Ah, she's a snake!" thought Sanin meanwhile, "but what a lovely snake!"

"Give me my lorgnette," Maria Nikolaevna said suddenly. "I'd like to see if that *jeune première* is really so ugly. Really, one might think that the government gave her the job with the moral aim that the young men do not get too infatuated."

Sanin handed her her lorgnette, and she, taking it from him, quickly, but hardly audibly, seized his hand with both of hers.

"Don't be so serious," she whispered with a smile. "You know what: nobody can put chains on me, but I don't put chains on anybody, either. I love freedom and don't admit obligations—and not just for myself. And now move aside a little, and let's listen to the play."

Maria Nikolaevna turned her lorgnette on the stage and Sanin started looking there, too, sitting beside her in the semidarkness of the box, and breathing in, involuntarily breathing in the warmth and fragrance of her luxurious body and just as involuntarily turning over in his own mind everything she had told him during the evening, especially during the last few minutes.

XL

The play lasted more than an hour longer, but Maria Nikolaevna and Sanin soon stopped looking at the stage. A conversation started up again between them, and it went along the same lines as before; only this time Sanin was less silent. Inside, he was angry both at himself and at Maria Nikolaevna; he tried to show her the whole superficiality of her "theory," as if she cared about theory! He started arguing with her, which secretly delighted her very much: if he argues, he's either giving in, or will give in. He had taken the bait, he was yielding, he had stopped being shy of her! She kept retorting, laughing, agreeing, thinking deeply, attacking...and meanwhile his face and hers grew close together, his eyes no longer looked away from hers. These seemed to be wandering as if circling over his features, and he was smiling back at her—politely, but smiling. He was also playing into her hands in that he was indulging in abstractions, discussing the honesty of reciprocal relations, obligation, the sanctity of love and marriage....It is a well-known fact that these abstractions are very useful as a beginning, as a starting point...

People who knew Maria Nikolaevna well used to assert that when something tender and modest, something practically virginally coy suddenly broke through her strong and sturdy being—although you wondered where it came from—then, yes, then things took a dangerous turn.

It apparently was taking this turn for Sanin, too...He would have felt scorn for himself if he had managed to concentrate for even a moment, but he did not manage either to concentrate or to scorn himself.

She was losing no time. And this all was happening because he was very good-looking! Willy-nilly one must say: "How can you know when you'll find something or lose something?

The play was over. Maria Nikolaevna asked Sanin to throw her shawl over her shoulders and did not stir while he wrapped her truly regal shoulders with the soft material. Then she took his arm, went out into the corridor—and almost screamed: right by the door of the box, like a ghost, stood Dönhof, and the filthy little figure of the

Wiesbaden critic was peeping out from behind his back. The oily face of the *literat* was radiant with vindictiveness.

"Wouldn't you like me, madam, to fetch you your carriage?" The young officer turned to Maria Nikolaevna with a quiver of barely restrained fury in his voice.

"No, thank you very much," she replied, "my servant will get it. Stay here!" she added in a commanding whisper, and quickly went off, drawing Sanin after her.

"Go to hell! What are you hanging around me for?" Dönhof suddenly barked at the *literat*. He had to let off steam on somebody!

"*Sehr gut! Sehr gut!*" muttered the *literat* and cleared out.

Maria Nikolaevna's servant, who had been waiting for her in the lobby, found her carriage in no time at all and quickly got into it; Sanin jumped in after her. The doors slammed shut and Maria Nikolaevna dissolved in laughter.

"What are you laughing at?" Sanin inquired.

"Ah, I'm sorry, please…but it just occurred to me: what if Dönhof and you fight a duel again…over me? Wouldn't that be amazing?"

"You know him very well?" asked Sanin.

"Him? That boy? He runs errands for me. Don't you worry!"

"I'm not worrying at all."

Maria Nikolaevna sighed.

"Ah, I know you're not. But listen—you know what: you're so sweet, you can't refuse me one last request. Don't forget—in three days I'm leaving for Paris, and you're going back to Frankfurt… When will we ever meet!"

"What's your request?"

"You know how to ride, of course?"

"Yes."

"Well, it's this. Tomorrow morning I'll take you with me and we'll go riding together outside of town. We'll have excellent horses. Then we'll come back, finish our business—and amen! Don't be surprised, don't tell me it's just a whim, that I'm mad—that may all be true—but just tell me: I agree!"

Maria Nikolaevna turned her face to him. It was dark in the carriage, but her eyes flashed in that very darkness.

"All right, I agree," said Sanin with a sigh.

"Ah! You sighed!" Maria Nikolaevna mimicked him. "That I means: once you've started, you can't stop. But no, no...You're charming, you're good—and I'll keep my promise. Here's my hand, without a glove on, my right hand, my business hand. Take it and believe its handshake. What kind of woman I am I don't know, but I'm an honest person, and one can do business with me."

Sanin, without himself being very well aware of what he was doing, raised this hand to his lips. Maria Nikolaevna gently drew it back and suddenly fell silent—and remained silent until the carriage had stopped.

She started getting out...What is that? Did it only seem so to Sanin, or did he really feel on his cheek a quick and burning touch?

"Until tomorrow!" Maria Nikolaevna whispered to him on the steps, all lit up by the four candles of a candelabrum held high on her arrival by the gold-braided doorman. She kept her eyes down. "Until tomorrow!"

Returning to his room, Sanin found a letter from Gemma on the table. He instantly was frightened—and then immediately pretended to rejoice, in order all the more quickly to conceal his fright from himself. It consisted of several lines. She was delighted with the good "beginning of the business," advised him to be patient, and added that everyone at home was well and looking forward with delight to his return. Sanin thought the letter rather dry; however, he picked up a pen, paper—and threw it all down. "Why write? I'll be going back tomorrow myself—it's time, it's time!"

He went to bed at once and tried to get to sleep as soon as he could. Had he stayed up and kept awake, he surely would have started thinking about Gemma—and for some reason he was...ashamed to think about her. His conscience was stirring. But he reassured himself with the thought that tomorrow everything would be over, once and for all, and that he would have parted forever from this extravagant lady—and would forget all this nonsense!

Weak people, talking to themselves, eagerly use energetic expressions.

Et puis...cela ne tire pas à conséquence!

XLI

That is what Sanin was thinking, going to bed, but what he thought the next day when Maria Nikolaevna knocked on his door impatiently with the coral handle of her riding crop, when he saw her on the threshold of his room—with the train of a dark blue riding habit over her arm, with a little, man's hat on her thickly braided locks, with a veil thrown back over her shoulder, with an inviting smile on her lips, in her eyes, over all her face—what he thought then—about that history is silent.

"Well? Are you ready?" her cheerful voice rang out.

Sanin buttoned up his coat and silently picked up his hat. Maria Nikolaevna glanced at him brightly, nodded her head, and quickly ran downstairs. And he ran after her.

The horses were already standing in the street in front of the entrance. There were three: a golden-chestnut, thoroughbred mare, with a dry-skinned muzzle that showed its teeth, black bulging eyes, legs like a deer, a little lean, but beautiful and fiery—for Maria Nikolaevna; a powerful, broad, rather heavy horse, jet-black without markings—for Sanin; the third horse was for the groom. Maria Nikolaevna leaped nimbly onto her mare, who started pawing and wheeling around, raising her tail and lowering her crupper, but Maria Nikolaevna (an excellent horsewoman) held her in place. They had to say good-bye to Polozov, who, in his inevitable fez and his dressing gown wide open, appeared on the balcony and from there waved his little cambric hand kerchief, without smiling at all, though, but rather frowning. Sanin, too, mounted his horse; Maria Nikolaevna saluted good-bye to Polozov with her crop and then struck her horse with it on its arched, smooth neck: it reared up on its hind legs, jumped forward, and set off at a smart, curbed gait, trembling in all its sinews, champing at the bit, nipping the air, and snorting. Sanin rode behind and kept his eyes on Maria Nikolaevna: her slender, supple body, tightly but easily held in by her corset, swayed self-confidently, dexterously, and gracefully. She turned her head around and beckoned to him with her eyes alone. He caught up to her.

"Now, you see how good it is," she said. "I'm telling you for the last time before we part: you're charming and you won't be sorry."

Having said this, she nodded her head several times, as if wishing to confirm it and make its meaning felt.

She seemed so happy that Sanin was simply amazed; there appeared on her face even that sedate expression which children have when they are very, very pleased.

They rode at a walk to the nearby tollgate and then set out at a good trot along the highway. The weather was marvelous, real summer weather; the wind streamed to meet them and pleasantly sang and whistled in their ears. They felt wonderful: consciousness of youth and health and of free and impetuous forward motion took possession of them both; it grew with each moment.

Maria Nikolaevna reined in her horse and again went at a walk; Sanin did as she did.

"This," she began with a deep, contented sigh, "this is all it's worth living for. If you've succeeded in doing what you want—what seemed impossible—well, then, enjoy it, right to the last drop!" She drew her hand across her throat. "And how good you then feel you are! Take me, now—how good I feel! I think I could embrace the whole world. Well, no, not the whole world! I wouldn't hug that one, now." With her riding crop she pointed to a poorly dressed old man making his way along the side of the road. "But I'm ready to make him happy. Here, take this," she shouted out loudly in German, and threw her purse at his feet. The rather heavy little bag (there was no such thing as a coin-purse in those days) struck the road with a thud. The passer-by stopped, astounded, and Maria Nikolaevna burst out in a loud laugh and galloped off.

"Do you enjoy riding so much?" asked Sanin, having caught up to her.

Maria Nikolaevna immediately reined in her horse hard again: she did not stop it any other way.

"I just wanted to get away from his gratitude. Whoever thanks me spoils my pleasure. Because I did that not for him, but for myself. How dare he thank me?...I didn't hear what you were asking me."

"I was asking...I wanted to know why you're so cheerful today?"

"You know what," said Maria Nikolaevna: either she had again not heard Sanin or else she did not think it necessary to answer his question. "I'm terribly fed up with that groom who keeps dangling along after us and who, I imagine, is thinking only about when the lady and gentleman will go home. How will we get rid of him?" She quickly took a little notebook out of her pocket. "Send him to town with a note? No…that's no good. Ah! I have it! What's that up ahead? An inn?"

Sanin took a look where she was pointing.

"Yes, I think it is."

"Splendid. I'll tell him to stay at this inn and drink beer until we come back."

"But what will he think?"

"What do we care! Besides, he won't even think; he'll be drinking beer—and that's all. Well, Sanin (she called him for the first time by just his last name), onward, at a trot!"

On reaching the inn, Maria Nikolaevna called up the groom and told him what she wanted him to do. The groom, a man of English origin and English temperament, silently raised his hand to the vizor of his cap, jumped down from his horse, and took it by the bridle.

"Well, now we're free as the birds!" exclaimed Maria Nikolaevna. "Where shall we go—north, south, east, west? Look—I do what the King of Hungary does at his coronation" (she pointed with her crop to all four corners of the world). "It's all ours! No, you know what: see, how wonderful the mountains are—and that wonderful forest! Let's go there, to the mountains!

"In die Berge, wo die Freiheit thront!"

She turned off the highway and galloped along a narrow, untrodden path which really seemed to lead to the mountains.

Sanin galloped after her.

XLII

This path soon turned into a little footpath, and finally disappeared completely, cut off by a ditch. Sanin advised going back, but Maria Nikolaevna said: "No! I want to go to the mountains! Let's go straight, as the birds fly," and made her horse jump the ditch. Sanin also jumped over. A meadow began on the other side of the ditch, at first dry, but then wet, and then completely swampy: the water seeped through everywhere and stood in puddles. Maria Nikolaevna rode her horse deliberately through these puddles, laughed loudly and kept repeating: "Let's just be children!"

"You know," she asked Sanin, "what it means to go puddle-hunting?"

"Yes," replied Sanin.

"My uncle was a huntsman," she went on. "I used to go out on horseback with him in the spring. It was marvelous! And now here you and I are, too—puddle-hunting! It's just that I see you're a Russian man and you want to marry an Italian girl. But that's your business. What's this? Another ditch? Hup!"

The horse jumped across—but the hat fell off Maria Nikolaevna's head, and her curls tumbled down over her shoulders. Sanin was about to get down from his horse and pick up the hat, but she shouted to him: "Don't touch it, I'll get it myself." She bent down low from the saddle, caught the veil with the handle of her crop, and indeed got the hat and put it on her head, but did not put up her hair, and again dashed off with a whoop. Sanin tore along beside her, jumped over ditches, fences, streams, fell in and scrambled out, rushing downhill, rushing uphill, and all the time looking at her face. What a face it was! It seemed all wide open: the eyes wide open, avid, bright, and wild; the lips, the nostrils, also wide open and breathing greedily; she stared straight, fixedly, in front of her, and it seemed that that soul wanted to possess everything it saw—the earth, the sky, the sun, and the air itself—and that there was just one thing it regretted—there weren't enough dangers—it would have overcome them all! "Sanin," she cried, "it's like Bürger's *Lenore*! Only you're not dead, are you? Not dead?...I'm alive!" Daring forces had come into play. This is no horsewoman putting her horse to a gallop—this is a young female Centaur galloping—half-beast and half-god—and the sedate and well-bred countryside, trampled underfoot by her wild revelry, is amazed!

Maria Nikolaevna finally stopped her foaming, mud-spattered horse: it was swaying under her, and Sanin's powerful but heavy stallion was gasping for breath.

"Well? Pleasant?" Maria Nikolaevna asked in a sort of wonderful whisper.

"Yes!" Sanin replied ecstatically. His blood, too, had taken fire.

"Wait, there's more!" She held out her hand. The glove on it was torn.

"I said I'd take you to the woods, to the mountains…There they are, the mountains!" Indeed: some two hundred paces from the place where the dashing riders had stopped, the mountains began, covered with a tall forest. "Look: there's a path. Let's go on. Only, at a walk. We have to rest the horses."

They set out. Maria Nikolaevna threw her hair back with one strong sweep of her hand. Then she glanced at her gloves and took them off. "My hands will smell of leather," she said, "but that doesn't make any difference to you, does it?"

Maria Nikolaevna smiled, and Sanin smiled too. This mad gallop had somehow finally brought them close together and made them friends.

"How old are you?" she suddenly asked.

"Twenty-two."

"Really? I'm twenty-two, also. It's a good age. Put them together, and old age is still a long way off. But it's hot. Am I all red in the face?"

"Like a poppy."

Maria Nikolaevna wiped her face with her handkerchief.

"Once we get into the woods, it'll be cool there. It's such an old forest—like an old friend. Do you have friends?"

Sanin thought a moment.

"Yes…just a few. No real ones."

"Well, I have, real ones, but no old ones. Here's a friend too—my horse. How carefully she carries one! Oh, but it splendid here! Am I really going to Paris the day after tomorrow?"

"Are you?" Sanin chimed in.

"And you to Frankfurt?"

"I'm going to Frankfurt for sure."

"Well, go ahead! But today is ours…ours…ours!"

The horses reached the edge of the forest and went into it. The shade covered them, wide and soft on all sides. "Oh, it's heaven here!" exclaimed Maria Nikolaevna. "Let's go deeper, farther into this shade, Sanin!" The horses quietly went "deeper into the shade," swaying slightly and snorting. The little path they were riding along turned suddenly to one side and ran into a rather narrow ravine. The smell of heather, ferns, pine resin, last year's dank leaves was collected in it, thick and drowsy. A strong freshness came from the cracks in the huge, brown rocks. Round knolls covered with green moss rose up on both sides of the little path.

"Stop!" cried Maria Nikolaevna. "I want to sit down and rest on this velvet. Help me down."

Sanin jumped off his horse and ran over to her. She leaned on his shoulders, instantly jumped off onto the ground, and sat down on one of the mossy knolls. He stood in front of her holding the reins of both horses in his hands.

She looked up at him…

"Sanin, do you know how to forget?"

Sanin recalled yesterday's happenings…in the carriage.

"Is that a question…or a reproach?"

"Since the day I was born I've never reproached anyone for anything. Do you believe in the magic of love potions?'

"What?"

"In the magic of love potions—you know, what they sing about in our songs. In the popular Russian folk-songs."

"Ah! That's you're talking about…" Sanin said slowly.

"Yes, that. I believe…and you will, too."

"Love potions…magic…" Sanin repeated. "Anything's possible in this world. Before, I didn't believe—now I do. I don't recognize myself."

Maria Nikolaevna thought a moment and looked around.

"I somehow feel I know this place. Take a look, Sanin, behind that wide oak—is there a red wooden cross there, or not?"

Sanin took a few steps to one side.

"There is."

Maria Nikolaevna smiled.

"Oh, fine! I know where we are. We're not lost yet. What's that tapping? A woodcutter?"

Sanin glanced into the thicket.

"Yes…a man is cutting up dead wood there."

"I must tidy up my hair," said Maria Nikolaevna. "He might see me—and not like it." She took off her hat and started braiding her long plaits, silently and seriously. Sanin continued to stand in front of her…Her graceful body was clearly outlined under the dark folds of her habit, to which here and there little moss fibers were sticking.

One of the horses suddenly gave a start behind Sanin's back: he himself shook involuntarily, from head to foot. Everything in him was confused—his nerves were as taut as violin strings. There was good reason for his having said he did not recognize himself…He really was bewitched. His whole being was filled with one idea, one desire. Maria Nikolaevna glanced at him piercingly.

"Well, now everything's in order," she said, putting on her hat. "You're not going to sit down? Here! No, wait…don't sit down! What's that?"

A dull rumble rolled over the tops of the trees, across the forest air.

"Can that be thunder?"

"It seems like it," replied Sanin.

"Oh, this is a holiday, simply a holiday! That was all we needed!" A hollow rumble resounded again, rose up and fell with a crash. "Bravo! *Bis!* Remember, I told you yesterday about the *Aeneid?* You know, a storm caught *them* in the woods, too. However, we have to get going." She got up quickly. "Bring me my horse…Your hand. Like that…I'm not heavy."

She climbed into the saddle like a bird. Sanin, too, mounted his horse.

"Are you going home?" he asked in an uncertain voice.

"Home!" she replied after a pause and picked up the reins. "Follow me!" she ordered almost coarsely.

She rode out onto the road and, passing the red cross, went down into a hollow, came to a crossroad, turned right, and again went uphill…She obviously knew where she was going—and this path led farther and farther into the forest. She said nothing, did not look around; she moved commandingly forward—and he followed her obediently and submissively, without a spark of will in his sinking heart. It began to drizzle. She hurried her horse—and he did not lag behind her. Finally, through the thick green of low firs, under an overhanging grey cliff, he caught sight of a wretched little warden's hut with a low door in its wattle wall. Maria Nikolaevna made her horse push through the firs, jumped down, and, finding herself suddenly by the entrance to the hut, turned around to Sanin—and whispered: "Aeneas!"

Four hours later Maria Nikolaevna and Sanin, accompanied by the groom dozing in his saddle, returned to Wiesbaden to the hotel. Herr Polozov met his wife, holding in his hand the letter to the steward. Looking at her more closely, however, he showed a certain displeasure—and even muttered:

"Did I really lose the bet?"

Maria Nikolaevna merely shrugged her shoulders.

And that same day, two hours later, Sanin was standing in his room in front of her, like a lost, like a ruined, man…

"Where are you going?"[7] she was asking him. "To Paris—or to Frankfurt?"

"I'm going where you'll be—and I'll be with you until you drive me away," he replied in despair and started kissing the hands of his sovereign-mistress. She freed them, put them on his head, and seized his hair with all her fingers. She slowly twisted and turned his unresisting hair, herself sitting up straight, her lips curled in triumph—and her eyes, wide and bright almost to the point of whiteness, expressed only the merciless dullness and satiety of victory. A hawk, holding in its claws a bird it has caught, has such eyes.

---

7   Maria Nikolaevna now uses the 2nd person singular to Sanin.

XLIII

This is what Dmitri Sanin remembered when, in the quietness of his study, sorting his old papers, he found among them a little garnet cross. The events we have told about rose clearly and consecutively before his mind's eye…But having reached that moment when with such humiliating supplication he turned to Madame Polozova, when he fall at her feet, when his bondage began—he turned away from the images he had conjured up, he did not want to remember any more. Not that his memory had betrayed him. Oh, no! He knew, he knew too well, what followed that moment, but shame was smothering him—even now, so many years later. He was terrified of that feeling of invincible scorn for himself which, he could not doubt, would certainly rush over him and, like a wave, drown all his other feelings, if he did not make his memory be still. But no matter how he turned away from the memories which had come back, he could not stifle them completely.

He remembered the wretched, tearful, lying, pitiful letter he had sent Gemma, a letter that had gone unanswered…To go to her, to return to her—after such deceit, after such a betrayal—no! no! He still had that much conscience and honesty left. Besides, he had lost all confidence in himself, all self-respect: he no longer dared vouch for anything. Sanin also remembered how he later—oh, the shame!—had sent Polozov's servant to Frankfurt for his things, how scared he had been, how he had thought only about leaving for Paris, leaving for Paris as soon as possible; how he, at Maria Nikolaevna's bidding, had played up to Ippolit Sidorych and fawned on him—and been gracious to Dönhof, on whose finger he noticed exactly the same sort of iron ring as the one Maria Nikolaevna had given him!

Then came memories still worse, still more shameful…A waiter brings him a visiting card, and on it is the name of Pantaleone Cippatola, Court Singer to H. H. the Duke of Modena. He hides from the old man, but can't avoid meeting him in the hallway—and there rises before him the angry face under the towering grey topknot; the old man's eyes burn like coals—and he hears the threatening exclamations and curses: *"Maledizione!"*; hears even the terrible words: *"Codardo! Infame traditore!"*

Sanin squints, shakes his head, turns away again and again—and still sees himself sitting on the narrow front seat of a big *dormeuse*. On the comfortable rear seats sit Maria Nikolaevna and Ippolit Sidorych—the four-in-hand is going at a good trot along the streets of Wiesbaden on the way to Paris! To Paris! Ippolit Sidorych is eating a pear which Sanin has peeled for him, and Maria Nikolaevna is watching him and smiling that smile he, a man enslaved, already knows so well—the smile of an owner, of a sovereign...

But good God! There, on the street corner, not far from the exit from town—isn't that Pantaleone there again—and who is with him? Is it really Emilio? Yes, it is, that ecstatic, devoted boy! It wasn't so long ago that his young heart was filled with reverence for his hero, his ideal; and now his pale, beautiful face—so beautiful that Maria Nikolaevna noticed it and put her head out the window of the carriage—this noble face is burning with hatred and scorn; the eyes, so much like *those* eyes! sink into Sanin, and the lips are pressed—and suddenly they open to shout an insult...

And Pantaleone reaches out his hand and points Sanin out—to whom? To Tartaglia standing beside him, and Tartaglia barks at Sanin—and the very bark of the honest dog resounds as an unbearable insult...Hideous!

And then—life in Paris, and all the humiliations, all the foul tortures of a slave who is not allowed to be jealous or to complain and who is finally thrown away, at last, like worn-out clothing....

Then—the return home to his own country, the poisoned, devastated life, the petty cares, the petty worries, the bitter and futile repentance, and the just as futile and bitter apathy—the invisible but constant punishment of every minute, like an insignificant but incurable pain, the repayment penny by penny of a debt which can never be settled...

The cup was filled to overflowing—enough!

How did it happen that the little cross which Gemma had given to

Sanin had been preserved; why hadn't he returned it? How had it happened that until that day he hadn't once come across it? He sat for a long, long time in deep thought—and now, taught by the experience of so many years, still could not understand how he could have left Gemma, whom he so tenderly and passionately loved, for a woman he didn't love at all.... The next day he saw all his friends and acquaintances: he told them that he was going abroad.

Bewilderment spread through society. Sanin was leaving Petersburg in the middle of winter, having just rented and furnished an excellent apartment, even having taken a subscription to the performances of the Italian opera in which Madame Patti herself was singing—herself, Patti herself! His friends and acquaintances were bewildered; but in general people can't long be interested in others' affairs, and when Sanin set out for abroad, only his French tailor came to see him off at the railroad station—and at that in the hope of settling a little unpaid bill—*pour un saute-en-barque en velours noir, tout à fait chic.*

XLIV

Sanin told his friends he was going abroad—but he didn't say exactly where: the reader can easily guess that he headed straight to Frankfurt. Thanks to the general expansion of railroads, on the fourth day after he had left Petersburg he was already there. He hadn't visited the city since 1840. The White Swan hotel was still in its old place and flourishing, although no longer considered first-class; the Zeile, the main street of Frankfurt, had changed little; but there was not a trace left of Signora Roselli's house, nor of the street itself where the shop had been. Sanin wandered like a crazy man though the places once so familiar to him—and recognized nothing: old buildings had disappeared; they had been replaced by new streets lined with enormous solid blocks of houses, elegant villas; even the public garden, where his last conversation with Gemma had occurred, was so overgrown and changed that Sanin kept asking himself: was this really the garden? What could he do? How and where could he start inquiring? Thirty years had passed since...It was hardly easy! No matter to whom he turned, no one had even heard of the name Roselli; the proprietor of his hotel advised him to inquire in the public library: there, he said, he'd find all the old papers, but what use he could make of this the proprietor himself couldn't explain. Sanin, in despair, asked him about Herr Klüber. The proprietor knew the name well—but here, too, he was unsuccessful. The elegant clerk, having made himself a name and become a capitalist, was ruined in trade, went bankrupt, and died in jail. This news, however, didn't cause Sanin the slightest grief. He was already beginning to feel that his trip was somewhat rash. But then one day, leafing through the Frankfurt directory he came upon the name of von Dönhof, retired Major *(Major a. D.)*. He immediately took a carriage and went to him—though why did *this* Dönhof have to be *that* Dönhof, and why could even that Dönhof tell him anything about the Roselli family? It didn't matter: a drowning man catches at a straw.

Sanin found the retired major von Dönhof at home—and in the grey-haired gentleman who received him, he at once recognized his former antagonist. And Dönhof recognized him, too, and was even glad to see him: it reminded him of his youth—of his youthful pranks. Sanin heard from him that the Roselli family had long, long ago gone to America, to New York; that Gemma had married a merchant; that he, Dönhof, had a friend, also a merchant, who probably knew the address of her husband, since he did much business with America. Sanin successfully begged Dönhof to go call on his friend and—oh, joy!—Dönhof brought him the address of Gemma's husband, a Mr. Jeremiah Slocum, 501 Broadway, New York. Only, this address was for 1863.

"We'll hope," exclaimed Dönhof, "that our Frankfurt beauty is still alive and hasn't left New York! By the way," he added, dropping his voice, "what about that Russian lady, the one who was staying in Wiesbaden then, you remember—Madame von Bo—von Bosolóff— is she still living?"

"No," replied Sanin, "she died some time ago."

Dönhof looked up but, having noticed that Sanin had turned away and frowned, said nothing more and left.

That same day Sanin sent a letter to Mrs. Gemma Slocum in New York. In this letter he told her that he was writing her from Frankfurt, where he had come solely in order to find a trace of her; that he was extremely conscious that he had not the slightest right to expect an answer from her; that he in no way deserved her forgiveness, and hoped only that she, in the midst of happy surroundings, had long ago forgotten his very existence. He added that he had made up his mind to remind her of himself as a result of a coincidence which had too vividly aroused his memories of the past; told her about his own life, lonely, without family, joyless; begged her to understand the reasons inducing him to turn to her, not to let him carry to the grave the bitter consciousness of his guilt—long ago atoned by suffering, but not forgiven—and to make him happy by even the briefest news of her life in the new world to which she has gone. "In writing me just one word," Sanin finished his letter, "you will have done a good deed, worthy of your beautiful soul, and I will be grateful to you until my dying day. I have stopped here, at the White Swan" (he underlined these words), "and I'll wait, until spring, for your answer."

He sent off the letter and started waiting. He spent six whole weeks in the hotel, almost without leaving his room—and seeing absolutely nobody. No one could write to him from Russia or from any place else, and that suited him; if a letter came for him, he would know immediately that it was *the one* he was waiting for. He read from morning till night—not journals, but serious books, histories. This continuous reading, this silence, this snail-like, hidden life—all this was right in tune with his frame of mind: and thanks to Gemma for that! But was she alive? Would she answer?

Finally, a letter came for him—with an American stamp—from New York. The handwriting of the address on the envelope was English. He didn't recognize it, and his heart sank. It took him a while to make up his mind to break the seal and open the letter. He glanced at the signature: Gemma! Tears gushed from his eyes: just the fact that she had signed her name, without her last name—was for him a pledge of reconciliation, of forgiveness! He unfolded the thin sheet of dark blue notepaper—a photograph slipped out. He hurriedly picked it up—and froze: Gemma, the living Gemma, young, as he had known her thirty years ago! The same eyes, the same lips, the whole face the same. On the back of the photograph was written: "My daughter, Marianna." The whole letter was very affectionate and simple. Gemma thanked Sanin for not having hesitated to write to her, for having had confidence in her; she did not hide from him also the fact that after his flight she had really lived through some terrible moments, but she added at once that she still considered—and always has considered—her meeting with him good fortune, since this meeting had prevented her from becoming Herr Klüber's wife—and thus, though indirectly, was the reason for her marriage to her present husband, with whom she has been living now for over twenty-seven years, completely happily, in comfort and plenty: everyone in New York knows their house. Gemma told Sanin that she had five children—four boys and a girl of eighteen, engaged to be married, whose photograph she was sending him—because, according to the general opinion, she was just like her mother. The sad news Gemma kept to the end of the letter. Frau Lenore had died in New York, where she had followed her daughter and son-in-law, but she had lived long enough to delight in the happiness of her children and to take care of her grandchildren, Pantaleone, also, was planning to come to America, but he died just before he was to leave Frankfurt. "And Emilio, our darling, incomparable Emilio, died a hero's death for the liberation of his native land, in Sicily, where he went as one of the 'Thousand,' under the leadership of the great Garibaldi; we all bitterly mourned the death of our priceless brother—but, as we shed our tears, we were proud of him and always will be proud of him and hold his memory sacred! His lofty, selfless soul was worthy of its martyr's crown!" Then Gemma expressed her regret that Sanin's life, apparently, had worked out so badly, wished him above all peace of mind and a calm spirit, and said she would be glad to see him, although she was aware how improbable such a meeting was...

We will not attempt to describe the feelings experienced by Sanin on reading this letter. There is no satisfactory expression for such feelings: they are deeper and stronger—and more indefinite than any word. Only music could communicate them.

Sanin replied immediately—and as a present to the bride he sent to "Marianna Slocum from an unknown friend" the little garnet cross, set in a magnificent pearl necklace. This present, although it was very expensive, did not ruin him: over the period of thirty years, since his first stay in Frankfurt, he had managed to accumulate a sizable fortune. In the beginning of May he returned to Petersburg— but hardly for long. It is rumored that he is selling all his estates and is planning to go to America.

"FIRST LOVE IS EXACTLY LIKE REVOLUTION": INTIMACY AS POLITICAL ALLEGORY IN IVAN TURGENEV'S NOVELLA *SPRING TORRENTS*

by Alexey Vdovin and Pavel Uspenskij

WHEN IVAN TURGENEV's novella *Spring Torrents* was published in the first issue of *The Herald of Europe* in 1872, the critics dismissed it as a "trinket," yet another love story that "does not reflect the spirit of the times."[1]

Turgenev finished the novella amidst the Franco-Prussian War (1870–71) and the defeat of the Commune of Paris, yet in private conversations, despite his close interest in the political developments, he insisted on the autobiographical nature of the story.[2] Moreover, in his correspondence, he cunningly dismissed any political implications: "My new story…will hardly please: it is a love story narrated at length, in which there isn't even a social, political or contemporary allusion. If I am mistaken, all the better."[3] Although *Spring Torrents* is often interpreted as an autobiographical novella, such explanation does nothing but establish the correlation between the text and the author's biography. We are instead going to look into poetics, the system of meaning presented in the text in which biographical context plays only a secondary role.

"A love story narrated at length" fits well into the thematic repertoire

---

1   See a review of critics' opinions: Turgenev, Ivan, Polnoe sobranie sochinenii i pisem: v 30 tomakh (Moscow, 1981), 8: 510–11.

2   M.B. Rabinovich, "I. S. Turgenev i franko-prusskaia voina 1870–71 gg.," in M.P. Alekseev, ed., *I. S. Turgenev. Voprosy biografii i tvorchestva* (Leningrad, 1982), 99–108.

3   *Ivan Turgenev, Polnoe sobranie sochinenii i pisem: V 30 tomakh / Pis'ma 11, 1871–1872* (Moscow, 1999), 18: 185; Ralph E. Matlaw, "Turgenev's Art in *Spring Torrents*," *The Slavonic and East European Review* 35, no. 84 (December 1956): 157.

of Turgenev's novellas, which are focused on the twists and turns of first love.[4] *Spring Torrents* is the retrospective narration of a fifty-two-year-old protagonist who, on the threshold of old age, suddenly experiences an almost Proustian moment when he remembers the most intense feelings of his entire life. In 1840, a twenty-two-year old nobleman, Dmitry Sanin, arrives in Frankfurt where, by chance, he meets the Roselli Family (Frau Lenora, her son Emil and her daughter Gemma). Driven by emotional impulses, Sanin falls in love with Gemma, thwarts her engagement to shop manager Karl Klueber and proposes to her. In search for money to arrange the wedding, Sanin goes to Wiesbaden to sell his Russian estate to Madame Polozov and almost succeeds when she suddenly seduces him. Sanin forgets his fiancée, and when he finally overcomes this obsession, he is nothing but an empty shell of a man. At fifty-two, although still lamenting his wasted life, Sanin is filled with hope when he is planning on going to America to take a glance at Gemma, who is now happily married with five children.

The novella can be interpreted as a two-part psychological journey, first to the poetic heights of first love and then to the abyss of moral abomination. Turgenev seems to have combined the plots of his previous stories, *Asya* and *First Love,* with the plot of the Leopold von Sacher-Masoch's notorious novella *Venus in Furs,* which was published shortly before *Spring Torrents* in 1869.[5] This juxtaposition helps to enrich the psychology of the characters. Psychological subtleties are not what distinguish *Spring Torrents,* however. On the contrary, thoughtful readers considered Sanin's transition from sublime love to humiliating obsession odd and unmotivated.[6] Unlike

4   See: V[ladimir] M[arkovich] Markovich, "Povesti Turgeneva o 'tragicheskom znachenii liubvi,'" in V. M. Markovich, *O Turgeneve. Raboty raznykh let* (St. Petersburg, 2018), 469–86.

5   Some scholars believe that Masoch could have influenced Turgenev's works. See: L. Poluboiarinova, *"A teper' eshche i Turgenev!" Istoki, osnovaniia i kliuchevye parametry retseptsii russkogo klassika v Avstrii,* 2nd ed. (St. Petersburg, 2019), 110–11; Michael Finke, *"Sacher-Masoch, Turgenev, and Other Russians,"* in Michael C. Finke and Carl Niekerk, eds., *One Hundred Years of Masochism: Literary Texts, Social and Cultural Contexts* (Amsterdam, 2000), 119–38.

6   See Pavel Annenkov's opinion in his letter to Turgenev on December 14 (26), 1871: "I still don't understand how he could become her minion after having

First Love, in which Turgenev deals with psychological trauma in a pre-Freudian manner, the semantics and poetics of *Spring Torrents* cannot be analyzed in psychological terms only.[7] Instead, Sanin's story can be read in political categories, as plot twists directly correlate to the revolutionary and reactionary discourses. In this article, we explore the political implications in *Spring Torrents* to demonstrate that its intimate story of love and moral fall can be read in the context of "social imaginary" that, in Turgenev's manner, is wrapped in leitmotivs and symbols. Building our hypothesis on an analysis of the poetics of Turgenev's novellas in comparison to his novels, we will demonstrate that, although *Spring Torrents* is not a political treatise, it is so ideologically charged that it can be seen as a sociopolitical allegory of Russia's present and future.

Realistic Prose and Allegory

The allegorical nature of *Spring Torrents* allows us to revisit the question of Turgenev's relation to Realism. According to many scholars, his novels are centered on ideological and socio-historical issues, whereas his minor works appear to be more "intimate."[8]

The "novel–novella" genre dichotomy is crucial in the perspective we are interested in. Since the 1840s, the Russian novel has aimed at representing contemporary social relationships and discourses that mostly thematized the conflict between an individual and the state and historicized this confrontation. In general, starting with Georg Lukács and Mikhail Bakhtin, the novel is considered to be a form or

---

experienced such pure love. It turns out to be tremendously impressive in the novella—true! Yet tremendously disgraceful for Russian nature. Maybe that is exactly what you meant but then how to explain this marvelous picture of his fascinating relationship with Gemma, without even a drop of this putrid poison?" Ivan Turgenev, *Polnoe sobranie sochinenii i pisem: v 30 t.* (Moscow, 1981), 8: 506; (our translation).

7   James L. Rice, "Turgenev's Mother and Other Problems of 'First Love,'" in Simon Karlinsky, James L. Rice and Barry P. Scherr eds., *O Rus! Studia litteraria slavica in honorem Hugh McLean* (Berkeley, 1995), 249–60.

8   For example, the Russian symbolists favored this "intimacy." See: L. Pild, "Turgenev v vospriiatii russkikh simvolistov (1890–1900-e gody)" (PhD diss., University of Tartu, 1999); Marina Ledkovsky, *The Other Turgenev: From Romanticism to Symbolism* (Würzburg, 1973), 125–38.

a genre that is based, by definition, on the idea of socialness ("social polylingualism/polyphony," according to Bakhtin) and claims totality of representation. In the plot, it is manifested both through the representation of significant sociopolitical events and discursive conflicts between the characters (as in Fedor Dostoevskii's *Demons* or Turgenev's *Smoke*), as well as indirectly, with tropes (allegories) and symbols. Here we can recall some well-known examples: the troika from Nikolai Gogol's *Dead Souls* becomes a symbol of Russia; the life of the main character of Ivan Goncharov's *Oblomov* and his way of living become an allegory for pre-reform reality on the eve of modernization; the grandmother in *The Precipice*, an allegory for the traditional Russian way of life.[9] All types of describing ideological and social problems can be combined in the poetics of one novel, as in Dostoevskii's *Demons*, for example.

Starting with the enigmatic Aleksandr Pushkin's *Tales of Belkin*, Russian novellas seem to have been avoiding problems addressed by the novels. They mainly depicted the secluded world of its characters and were focused on their private life experiences. This focus on the limited depiction of events and selectiveness of private experience prevented them from representing broad social panoramas and novel-like ideological conflicts. Clearly, these genre characteristics do not imply that novellas cannot address ideological conflicts and social issues, but particular forms and ways of addressing them are far less obvious. Although there are many remarkable novellas in the literary canon of Russian Realism that directly deal with political and ideological conflicts, ranging from Gogol's *Taras Bul'ba* to Lev Tolstoi's *Hadji Murat*, this genre mostly preferred indirect ways of representing the political sphere.

The "novel–novella" dichotomy is especially important for

---

9   On symbolization in Russian novel see, for example: V. M. Markovich, "I. S. Turgenev i russkii realisticheskii roman XIX veka" [1982] in V.M. Markovich, *O Turgeneve: Raboty raznykh let* (St. Petersburg, 2018), 141–221; on allegory in *The Precipice* see: Ilya Kliger, "Resurgent Forms in Ivan Goncharov and Alexander Veselovsky: Toward a Historical Poetics of Tragic Realism," *The Russian Reivew* 71, no. 4 (October 2012): 655–72; A. Bodrova and S. Gus'kov, "Literatura na sluzhbe imperii, imperiia na sluzhbe literatury: K interpretatsii finala romana 'Obryv,'" *Novoe literaturnoe obozrenie* 164 (2020): 177–94.

Turgenev, the most typical writer for the rise of Russian Realism who was also the most compliant with the genre system of European literature. As is known, his novels directly address ideological and political conflicts, and semantic tension is generated by the clash of their characters' social positions, which, however, does not prevent particular elements of the text from having symbolic meaning, including allegory.[10] Traditional view of Turgenev's novellas suggests that he avoids the political sphere and develops the area of personal experience and ways of narrativization of individual life, often resorting to new writing methods. Consequently, political space is absent in Turgenev's novellas, at least at first glance.

In this regard, the story of *Rudin* is an especially illustrative example. First published in 1856 in *Contemporary,* this text was labeled as a novella (povest'). Tellingly, it had no epilogue in which Rudin dies on the barricades during the Revolution of 1848. Four years later, Turgenev, due to different circumstances, added this political epilogue and since then decisively defined this text as a novel.[11] At first, Turgenev saw this story about particular characters (the first title was "A Genius Person") and estate life as a "novella," however, the introduction of the political aspect that offered a new framework for interpreting its conflict turned this text into a novel and consequently changed the whole system of social and political projections. An intellectual's failure in love in the 1830s was historicized and inscribed in the context of the European revolutionary movement. *Rudin* as a novel differs from *Rudin* as a novella by the causal link established between the protagonist's failed relationship and his sacrificial death on the barricades. This causation, so evident in Turgenev's novels, is absent in his novellas that do not represent the political sphere directly. In any case, this distinction has always been

---

10   In our understanding of Turgenev's novels, we draw on the V. M. Markovich's monographs "Chelovek v romanakh Turgeneva" [1975] and "I. S. Turgenev i russkii realisticheskii roman XIX veka" [1982] reprinted in: V. M. Markovich, *O Turgeneve.* See also: Elizabeth Cheresh Allen, *Beyond Realism: Turgenev's Poetics of Secular Salvation* (Stanford, 1992); Jane T. Costlow, *Worlds Within Worlds: The Novels of Ivan Turgenev* (Princeton, 1990).

11   Ivan Turgenev, *Polnoe sobranie sochinenii i pisem: v 30 t.* (Moscow, 1981), 8: 472–73.

solid enough to study Turgenev's short-form texts separately from his novels.[12]

Recently, this tradition has begun to change. Ilya Kliger has convincingly demonstrated that the secluded world of the characters in *First Love* is, in fact, influenced by sociopolitical concepts such as "will," "power" and "guilt." As a result, its markedly intimate plot becomes a political allegory shaped by the Russian social imaginary.[13] Such an understanding of allegory as a specific form adopted by realistic writing in a modified way opens up space for the comparative analysis of Russian Realism. Political allegory in *Spring Torrents* prompts us not only to reinterpret the poetics of Turgenev's novellas but also to discover other aspects of allegory that make it a suitable literary tool for Realism.

We see allegory as a literary device with dual temporality that converges the concrete and the abstract levels of representation. As is well known from the history of allegory in European literature, the seventeenth–eighteenth century drama revitalized this trope and legitimized the rich variety of juxtapositions of abstract universal concepts and political figures and images.[14] In the nineteenth century Charles Baudelaire's anti-Romantic poetry, having transformed the function of the allegory, depersonalized the experience of the lyrical subject and shifted it to a new mode, different

---

12   Such a picture becomes even more complicated if we remember that Turgenev was not consistent in using generic terms in the 1850s when he was searching for his novelistic style and maneuvering between critics' opinions. See: M. S. Makeev, "'Bol'shaia povest' vmesto romana: Eshche raz o sisteme zhanrov turgenevskoi prozy 1850-kh godov," *Spasskii vestnik* 22 (2014): 99–105.

13   Ilya Kliger, "Scenarios of Power in Turgenev's 'First Love': Russian Realism and the Allegory of the State," *Comparative Literature* 70, no. 1 (March 2018): 42. The same interpretative logic has informed Boris Maslov's allegorical reading of Turgenev's novel Smoke, see Boris Maslov, "'Zhilishche tishiny preobratilos' v ad': O sud'be starorezhimnykh poniatii v Novoe vremia," in Iu. Kagarlitskii, Dmitrii Kalugin, and B. A. Maslov, eds., *Poniatiia, idei, konstruktsii: Ocherki sravnitel'noi istoricheskoi semantiki* (Moscow, 2019), 347–56. Maslov mentioned *Spring Torrents* as a similar case and analyzes it in: Maslov, "Gnezda klochnei i rokovye retsidivy: K istoricheskoi poetike realisticheskikh siuzhetov" in Margarita Vaysman, A. Vdovin, Ilya Kliger, and Kirill Ospovat, eds., *Russkii realizm XIX veka: Obshchestvo, znanie, povestvovanie* (Moscow, 2020), 542–45.

14   See: Walter Benjamin, *Ursprung des deutschen Trauerspiels* (Frankfurt am Main, 1963).

from the post-Romantic melancholy and anticipating the Modernist theory of the unconscious ("the Id").[15] Realistic novels put a lot of effort into tailoring the allegory to the needs of the new way of representing not only reality but also the human psyche and mind.[16] It was the time when a special type of national allegory emerged in world literature.[17]

In *Spring Torrents*, which is a novella and not a novel, not only the title and the epigraph suggest juxtaposing the plot events with the spring high waters, but the narrator himself clarifies the correlation between the waters, Sanin's sexual enslavement and his memory (or, rather, his conscience):

> But, when he came to the moment when…his enslavement had begun—then he turned aside from the images which he had conjured up; he did not wish to remember more.…he was afraid of the feeling of self-contempt which he knew he could not conquer and which he knew beyond doubt would wash over him, and, like a tidal wave, drown all other sensations as soon as he allowed his memory to speak [emphasis added].[18]

In his speech, the narrator superimposes at least two temporal models, one of a personal life (the protagonist's memories and his dependence on a woman) and another, of nature (the high-water

---

15   Hans Robert Jauss, "The Poetic Text within the Change of Horizons of Reading: The Example of Baudelaire's 'Spleen II,'" in Hans Robert Jauss and Timothy Bahti, eds., *Toward an Aesthetic of Reception* (Minneapolis, 1982), 175, 180.

16   In his recent article about Nikolai Gogol's *The Old-World Landowners,* Kirill Ospovat shows how important allegory was in transition from Romanticism to Realism in the 1830–40s. See: Kirill Ospovat, "Realism as Technique: Mimesis, Allegory, and the Melancholic Gaze in Gogol''s 'Old-World Landowners,'" in Yaraslava Ananka and Magdalena Marszałek, eds., *Potemkinsche Dörfer der Idylle: Imaginationen und Imitationen des Ruralen in den europäischen Literaturen* (Bielefeld, 2018), 219–48.

17   Although Fredric Jameson does not study the genesis of this type of novel, his works remain a good starting point for reflection: Fredric Jameson, "*La Cousine Bette* and Allegorical Realism," *PMLA* 86, no. 2 (March 1971): 241–54; Fredric Jameson, "Third-World Literature in the Era of Multinational Capitalism" in *Social Text* no. 15 (Autumn 1986): 65–88.

18   Ivan Turgenev, *Spring Torrents,* trans. Leonard Shapiro (Harmondsworth, 1980), 145. Further quotations are from this edition with page numbers in parenthesis.)

season). Unlike novels in general and Turgenev's novels in particular, his novellas resort to both types of temporality, often overlooking the political events and minimizing the social context by setting the story in the recent past.

In Turgenev studies, these novellas of the 1850–70s are defined as "memory novellas" *(povesti-vospominaniia)* as the narrator is an aged man who recalls the events of his youth.[19] Among them, we can name *Asya* (1858), *First Love* (1860), *Spring Torrents* (1872), *Punin and Baburin* (1874), and *Clock* (1876). Interestingly, political implications are absent from the plot in three of them (*Asya*, *Spring Torrents*, and *First Love*) and can be found only in political metaphors in the narrator's speech or the manifestations of the protagonist's melancholic consciousness. It is always consumed with Baudelairian spleen, be it Sanin's state of mind we have described, or Vladimir's "melancholy of social passivity" in *First Love* analyzed by Kliger.

In these stories, the reason for such a state is heartbreak, lost love, or other kinds of painful romantic experience that disrupts the course of the protagonist's life. Turgenev was one of the first to integrate this zone of characters' subjectivity with sexuality and the unconscious that had not been coined as a term yet.[20]

To introduce this type of subjectivity, Turgenev constantly shifts the story to the recent past, which is always separated from the present by a barrier of social reforms. Yet this gap is never bigger than the life span of one generation, and the protagonist remembers the time of his youth, which distinguishes Turgenev's prose from historic novels. This is how he creates the third—political—type of temporality, in addition to the individual and natural ones.[21] It is not explicitly present but implied through allegory. It is allegory that ties together the intimate and the natural and gives Turgenev's novellas

19   A. B. Muratov, *Turgenev-novellist (1870–80-e gody)* (Leningrad, 1985), 7–15.
20   Although the philosopher Eduard von Hartmann had already described it in the late 1860s and early 1870s.
21   Our classification of temporalities in Turgenev's prose differs from the three-part (mundane–archetypical—cosmic) plot scheme proposed by Iurii Lotman, see Iurii M. Lotman, "Siuzhetnoe prostranstvo russkogo romana," in Iurii Lotman, *O russkoi literature: Stat'i i issledovaniia, 1958–1993* (St. Petersburg, 1997), 728–29.

a political dimension, which opens them to various sociological interpretations.

Love is Like Revolution in a Political Context

There is only one episode in *Spring Torrents* where words from the political and emotional vocabularies are put together. Describing Dmitry's and Gemma's feelings, the narrator points out that

> Sanin and Gemma were in love for the first time, and all the miracles of first love were happening to them. First love is exactly like revolution: the regular and established order of life is in an instant smashed to fragments; youth stands at the barricade; its bright banner raised high in the air, and sends its ecstatic greetings to the future, whatever it might hold—death or a new life, no matter [emphasis added]. (82–83).

This comparison of love to revolution could be interpreted as a Gallicism, as one of the meanings of the French word *revolution* is "turn" or "change."[22] However, the use of political lexis ("barricade" and "flag"), as well as the hint at ecphrasis of Eugene Delacroix's *Liberty Leading the People* (1830) inspired by the July Revolution, precludes this interpretation. Two discourses are superimposed here. We will now examine different motives entwined in the novella which support this political metaphor.

Frankfurt, where the story takes place, was a city-state governed by a Senate from 1815 to 1866. Open to various cultures, it welcomed the Roselli family. Giovanni Roselli, born in Vicenza, moved to Frankfurt in 1815. At this time, his native city, as well as the whole Lombardo-Venetian Kingdom it then belonged to, was

---

22   A semantically close word *révolte* (indeed, "a revolt") formed part of fixed phrases that described psychological states and reactions, such as *la révolte des passions* ("a riot of passions") or *la révolte des sens contre la raison* ("a revolt of passion against reason"). See in one of the most authoritative dictionaries of the time: N. P. Makarov, *Polnyi frantsuzsko-russkii slovar'*, 11-e izdanie (St. Petersburg, 1904), 933. On the origin of the word, see: R. Koselleck, C. Meier, J. Fisch, N. Bulst, "Revolution," in Otto Brunner, ed., *Geschichtliche Grundbegriffe: Historisches Lexikon zur politisch-sozialen Sprache in Deutschland,* vol. 5 (Stuttgart, 1984), 653–788.

seized by the Austrian Empire and overtaken by political reaction and repressions. As a staunch republican and apparently a member of the Carbonari secret society, Roselli decided to move to a safer place.[23]

At the beginning of the novella, Frau Roselli and her children, though revering the memory of the head of the family, are not involved in politics as they are busy managing the unprofitable confectionery.[24] However, they still live up to republican ideals. For instance, Gemma believes that "it was right to sacrifice one's future security" to "such a noble and sacred cause" as the liberation of Italy (25). Frau Roselli regularly describes her as a republican, adding adjectives like "stubborn" or "desperate" (64, 25).

The Roselli's political preferences reveal themselves when they question Sanin about Russia. Mixing stereotyped judgments with genuine interest, Frau Roselli admits that she has been picturing Russia as "a country where the snow lay permanently and everyone went around in a fur coat and served in the army—but that the hospitality was quite extraordinary, and all the peasants were very obedient" (14). The ideas of government power and oppression clearly dominate this image. No wonder that the conversation about Russia revolves around different social categories ("the Cossacks," "the Russian peasant") and political power ("Peter the Great" and "the Kremlin," 14).

The Roselli family's political ideals are mirrored, in a somewhat caricatured way, in Pantaleone. A former actor, he acts out an episode in which he plays Napoleon, who condemns Marshal Bernadotte, played by a poodle, "for treason" (31). Indeed, in 1813, Marshal, the future king of Sweden, took part in a military campaign against France. Given that Napoleon was deemed a "democrat" in Italy, such

---

23   See also: T. B. Trofimova, "Turgenev i Dante (k postanovke problemy)," *Russkaia literatura* no. 2 (2004): 177.

24   It is hard to discard the idea that the Roselli family business has symbolic meaning. The bakery is an ambivalent allusion, firstly, to the words attributed to Marie-Antoinette, "Qu'ils mangent de la brioche" (Let them eat brioches), which played a crucial role in the French Revolution mythology, and secondly, to the problem of hunger among the lower classes at that time. In this case, the bakery is an ironically literalized metaphor.

identification with him highlights Pantaleone's political preferences.[25]

The pro-republican Roselli family contrasts with Gemma's fiancé, Karl Klueber, owner of the draper's and silk mercer's shop. A major capital-holder, he is ironically portrayed as a conceited man who constantly displays his high social status. He is comfortable with the existing social structure and identifies with a position of power: "…well-brought up and superlatively well-washed, this young man was in the habit of obeying his superiors and of issuing orders to his inferiors" (21). Even with his fiancée, Klueber does not change his attitude as he sees the private sphere as public and believes he has the right to dominate his future wife. Sanin notices that during a walk in the countryside "he presented the appearance of a condescending tutor who was conferring both upon himself and his charges modest and polite enjoyment" (34).

Klueber suspects political unreliability in every deviation from the established order of things. After the incident during the walk that results in a duel between Sanin and Dönhof, he goes off on a political speech:

He then vouchsafed several quite sharp and even radical judgements on the subject of the Government's unpardonable policy of pandering to the officers…Such policy gave rise to feelings of dissatisfaction from which it was only a step to revolution—a fact regarding which France served a sad example.…However, he immediately added the observation that he himself had a veneration for authority and would never…, no, never…become a revolutionary. But he could not refrain from expressing his…how should he put it?…disapproval at the sight of such laxity! (40).

The awaking of Sanin's feelings to Gemma is paralleled by a sudden whirlwind "in a completely cloudless sky" (51). A whirlwind is indeed a minor storm, so this metaphor encapsulates both romantic

---

25   Political inclinations also play a role in those episodes in which the members of the Roselli family have to keep a secret. In one of them, Pantaleone, who has to keep silent about Sanin's upcoming duel, reassures him sagely: "In reply, the old man…whispered twice 'Segredezza!'" (48). In another, Sanin asks Emil to deliver a letter, and he assumes "a purposeful and mysterious expression" (73). In both cases, the characters mimic the family tradition playing out the conspiratorial behavior of Giovanni Roselli.

and political turmoil. This motive reemerges one paragraph before the phrase "First love is exactly like revolution" when the narrator comments that the characters "were only conscious of the sudden rush of wind which had swept them away, like the powerful gust which a few nights ago had all but hurled them into each other's arms" (82).

Thus, the tension in the love triangle between Gemma, Sanin, and Klueber has to do with their political beliefs: an opposition between Gemma, a republican, and Klueber, a monarchist, had been a stalemate until Sanin appeared. With her beauty and strong character, Gemma encourages Sanin to be bold and awakens his rebellious spirit so that the freedom prevails, if only temporarily. Still, thirty years later, Gemma is grateful that Sanin thwarted her engagement. In this vein, an illustrative duel between worldviews and political opinions happens when Gemma and Sanin, having just confessed their love to each other, head back to the confectionery and meet Klueber, who fails in this confrontation.[26] The victory is achieved not only on a personal or political level but also on a symbolic one. It is noteworthy, however, that the victorious one is Gemma, whose unflinching "revolutionary" gaze humiliates Klueber while Sanin is overcome with emotions. This is only logical since a Russian nobleman cannot think in political terms, even when he is dragged into a political discourse. We will address Sanin's political beliefs later, but for now, we must point out that this political inaptitude explains his future moral fall.

Moral Fall as Political Reaction in the Russian Context

In the second part of *Spring Torrents* the course of events and, consequently, their political implications change so radically that the plot departs significantly from the story of lost love typical for Turgenev,

---

26 See: "Suddenly her legs swayed beneath her. From round the corner…appeared the figure of Herr Klueber. He saw Gemma and he saw Sanin—and then gave a kind of inward smirk….he walked towards them with an air of bravura. Sanin was momentarily disconcerted. But then he glanced at the Klueber face…and the sight of this pink, common face suddenly threw him into a rage. Sanin stepped forward. Gemma seized his arm…and looked her former betrothed straight in the face. Klueber narrowed his eyes, hunched his shoulders, stepped quickly aside…" (85).

as in *Rudin* or *Smoke*.[27] If the "Frankfurt part" presents the intimate as political and relates first love to revolution, the "Wiesbaden part" shows the inadequacy of such link, at least for Sanin. Turgenev deconstructs the previously suggested implications using only literary devices, such as symbolic parallels, leitmotifs, or free indirect speech. With almost psychoanalytical scrutiny, Turgenev puts his protagonist into situations with Madame Polozov that are parallel to those with Gemma. However, Sanin is shown to be very dependent as he absorbs Madame Polozov's depravity as much as he absorbed Gemma's rebellious spirit.

Only a few scholars have pointed out that various episodes and motives of the second part mirror those of the first.[28] This system of parallels and contrasts unfolds both on the micro and macro levels (for example, Wiesbaden, a resort town famous for gambling is opposed to the free state of Frankfurt). So as not to dwell on this for too long, we have decided to systematize all the motives in a table (see Table 1). It opens with a list of plot parallels and then offers a comparison of some accordant and discordant motives ascribed to the heroines.

Table 1. Mirroring of Motives in *Spring Torrents*

Element/Motive	Sanin—Gemma	Sanin—Madame Polozov
An unexpected delay because of a woman	Sanin is late for the diligence because Emil faints; Frau Lenore detains him	Madame Polozov detains Sanin on purpose
Reason for the delay	Sanin can't marry Gemma until he sells his estate	Sanin can't leave Wiesbaden until he sells his estate

27   See more about this invariable trope that "the protagonist is held up at his beloved and then runs from her" in Turgenev's prose in Jane T. Costlow, "Dido, Turgenev and the Journey toward Bedlam," *Russian Literature* 29, no. 4 (May 1991): 395–408.

28   See: A. B. Muratov, *Povesti i rasskazy I. S. Turgeneva 1867–71 godov* (Leningrad, 1980), 50–55; James Woodward, "Polemics and Introspection in Turgenev's *Vesnie vody*," in Peter Thiergen, ed., *Ivan S. Turgenev: Leben, Werk und Wirkung, Herausgegeben von Peter Thiergen* (Munich, 1995), 234–35.

Element/Motive	Sanin—Gemma	Sanin—Madame Polozov
Rival	Klueber	Polozov (nominal rival), the Count, the Embassy secretary
False rival/ Mediator	Dönhof	Dönhof
The duel	Sanin defends Gemma's honor dueling with Dönhof	Madame Polozov asks Sanin whether he would like to duel with Dönhof again
The peak of the feelings	Love confession (nature), proposal	Sex in a hut (nature), moral fall
Motive accompanying the feelings	A whirlwind (as a metonymy of a storm)	A thunderstorm in the mountains
Heroine's background	Daughter of an émigré, a republican	Daughter of a lowborn tax farmer millionaire, apolitical
Type of feelings	"Republican" equality, chastity	"Mistress–slave" relationship, sexual dominance
Display of feelings	Desire for freedom and equality is not expressed directly	Desire for freedom is expressed directly; equality is renounced
Heroine's overall attitude	Genuine frankness	Artificial frankness
Heroine's attribute (motive)	Hair	Hair
Attitude to music	Gemma loves and appreciates it (Weber and others)	Madame Polozov doesn't like music (except Russian songs)
Attitude to theatre	Gemma watches comedies of Malz	Madame Polozov watches vulgar plays in Wiesbaden
Attitude to literature	Gemma is passionate about Romanticism but not very fond of Hoffmann	Madame Polozov grew up reading the *Aeneid* and remembers Bürger's *Lenore* to Sanin
Attitude to money	Gemma is practical; money isn't symbolically marked	Madame Polozov careless spends her money

Element/Motive	Sanin—Gemma	Sanin—Madame Polozov
A symbolic item	A rose, a garnet cross	An iron ring (every one of Madame Polozov's "slaves" has one)
Intertextual projections	The Romantic cult of the belle dame and her knight; Beatrice	Dido and Aeneas; Medusa
National code	An Italian in Germany (emigration)	A Russian millionaire in a resort town (trip abroad)

As we can see from the table, Madame Polozov is Gemma's opposite and double.[29] Other scholars have interpreted these female characters as two national substances or even two models of national development. In this regard, two of Madame Polozov's characteristics are crucial. First, that she is Russian, and second, that she loves freedom as much as Gemma does, yet for her, it implies sexually enslaving the men around her, which is as far from Gemma's attitude as possible.

Madame Polozov's nationality is constantly highlighted. She likes Russian songs and dances as well as rural, almost bucolic landscapes.[30] In Wiesbaden, she styles her everyday life in a Russian way "with a Russian Samovar" (112). Concerned with her appearance and dressing in European fashion, Madame Polozov still does not miss a chance to demonstrate her braided fair hair as it is yet another way to emphasize her Russianness. Her language is also notably marked as "pure Moscow" speech.[31]

Among all Madame Polozov's Russian traits, her background is the most prominent one. Not only is she a daughter of a millionaire tax farmer, but she also spent her childhood with common people or merchants (this is obscured in the text), which left an indelible mark on her character. She is aware of how it shaped her values:

29   Woodward, "Polemics and Introspection in Turgenev's Vesnie vody," 234.
30   "…the red cotton of the peasants' clothes, the girls' bead head-dresses, the young grass on the common pasture…" (115).
31   See: "Maria Nikolaevna spoke all the time in Russian, in a remarkably pure Moscow form of speech, but as spoken by the lower classes, not gentry" (110).

"Do you want to know what I love more than anything else in the world?"

"Freedom," Sanin prompted…

"Yes, Dmitry Pavlovich," she said, and there was a special note in her voice, a note that suggested solemnity and absolute sincerity. "Freedom more than anything else, and before everything else. And don't imagine that I am boasting about this… but *that's* how it is, and that's how it will be for me…I suppose I saw a great deal of slavery in my childhood, and suffered from it…" (131).

"Slavery" is as important in this abstract as "freedom" because it explains Madame Polozov's behavior. She does no less than act out the situation of inequality and her plebeian origin. Having suffered from it at a young age and liberated herself through inheritance, she now dominates men, both psychologically and sexually.

Madame Polozov's trajectory from commoner to "nouveau riche" explains multiple motives of power which accompany her throughout the narrative. She believes that "there is no greater pleasure in the world" than giving orders (117) and mostly remembers different signs of submission men have shown her. No wonder her desire to dominate correlates with the absolute political power—she compares herself to "the King of Hungary at his coronation ceremony" (139). This comparison becomes clearer in the light of her experience, as only the position of an absolute ruler gives her a sense of absolute safety and frees her from her dreadful past. Her aggressive and destructive behavior pattern is highlighted in various ways. When she succeeds in seducing Sanin, the narrator calls her not only "a sovereign mistress" but also a "hawk clawing at a bird" (144–45). Sanin's new position among other humiliated lovers is described as "vile sufferings of a slave" (149).

Turgenev does not explicitly articulate the equivalence of the intimate and the political that is played out here in the "Russian" setting, yet it is obvious that while Sanin's love to Gemma is compared to a revolution, his cheating as well as Madame Polozov's sexual addiction and desire to dominate are located in the realm of absolute monarchy. The comparison to a Hungarian king can be interpreted not only in a psychological but also in a political way, given that Madame Polozov's demeanor, caused by socio-political reasons, is played out sexually because any political action is impossible and hardly necessary for her. Madame Polozov does not reflect on the political nature of her behavior, or at least the text does not suggest this.

The monarchic "halo" around Madame Polozov allows us to interpret the second part of *Spring Torrents* in political categories. Sanin's moral fall metaphorically correlates to the political reaction after a revolution. We shall point out that when Sanin and Gemma, having experienced the moment of first love like revolution, come to beg Frau Lenora to let them marry and prostrate themselves before her as if worshipping a monarch. The narrator calls them "criminals": "Another instant passed—and both criminals, Sanin and Gemma, were kneeling at her feet" (44). If Roselli, a benevolent republican, pardons them, Madame Polozov, the real monarch in *Spring Torrents*, plays her part the way she should. The negotiations about selling the estate feel like interrogation in court: "He experienced all the sensations of a prisoner on trial, seated on a very narrow bench, before a severe and searching judge. 'Why, this is a cross-examination,' he whispered to himself unhappily" (119). Sanin's behavior with Madame Polozov resembles that of a criminal defendant who chooses the most efficient strategy and decides to "indulge the caprices of this rich lady" (109). Despite his emotionalism, Sanin tries to keep his distance as he can sense the threat emanating from her.

Sanin's submission to Madame Polozov's will is an act of a sexual self-punishment that seems to be inevitable: "...she moved forward imperiously, and he followed, obedient and submissive, drained of every spark of will and with his heart in his mouth" (144). Sanin's moral fall, yet at this point beyond narration, plays a vital role in the dialectics of sex and power in *Spring Torrents*. Sanin thinks that he, a weak man, simply could not resist Madame Polozov's charms. On the allegorical level, however, sex with Madame Polozov and his enslavement turn out to be a form of political reaction. The female monarch punishes her lover for an affair-like revolution by practically raping him, and this rape is something a Russian nobleman has been waiting for, reluctantly yet longingly.

A Story à la russe: Around Sanin, or the Allegorical Signals

The love story in Spring Torrents is so politically charged that it adopts a two-phase structure of "revolution" and "reaction." It is important to consider these concepts as a pair in their interconnectedness. As Jean Starobinski shows, starting with the French Revolution, the word "reaction" quickly became part of the lexicon of European intellectuals and meant both rejecting progressive ideas and depriving various social groups that were excluded from the political process of their newly obtained political rights. Although being a key word in the vocabulary of Karl Marx, Friedrich Engels, and their followers, reaction as a concept remains to a certain extent unclear, its meaning defined by the ideological system of the one who uses it, their understanding of the current political situation, and ideas about how society should be organized that tie it to the idea of progress.[32] At the same time, it can be defined rather clearly by contradiction within a particular discourse.

Given the opposition between the two parts of the plot of Spring Torrents as well as narrative ideological interpretations of the two key episodes in Sanin's life (discussed below), we think that the "revolution—reaction" dichotomy constitutes the allegorical level of the novella. Although we consider it possible to interpret the character of Madame Polozov as a representation of the idea of monarchy, and, given her nationality, Russian monarchy—constant in its suppressive behavior—in particular, we believe that it is more reasonable to see the two plot twists (Sanin's and Gemma's rebellion and subsequent punishment of the nobleman by Madame Polozov) as a traditional pair of interconnected political concepts.

Other arguments, though not directly related to the poetics of Spring Torrents, could also be relevant here. First, Turgenev was

---

32   Jean Starobinski, *Action and Reaction: The Life and Adventures of a Couple* (New York, 2003), 322–51.

apparently familiar with the most important concepts of the current political discourse and did not consider them to be discredited. Secondly, the events of *Spring Torrents* happen on the verge of the Revolutions of 1848, whose immediate discursive interpretation relied on the concept of reaction as key (see, for example, *From the Other Shore* by Aleksandr Herzen). We shall add that European events reverberated in imperial Russia and led to the infamous last period of Nicholas I's reign, the so-called "dark seven years," when censorship pressure on intellectuals and overall destruction of public life were rather severe. In this regard, *Spring Torrents* can be seen as an isolated, particular projection of large-scale historical events.

This consistent correspondence between the intimate and the political allows us to suggest that the novella as a whole is an unambiguous allegory of sociopolitical changes in Russia. Therefore, connotative and allegorical levels of the novella not only orchestrate the plot but also directly answer the unasked, though implied question of whether revolution is possible in Russia.

To illustrate this, we will continue exploring the poetics of the novella, which serves as the main tool to stage the drama of ideology. In this section, we will analyze some motives overlooked by other scholars and identify various aspects of the image of a Russian nobleman. We will look into narrative and style as well as the consciousness of the protagonist and some constant motives and themes, such as family memory, capital, and gender. We will show that, although these elements belong to different levels of the text, they all can be interpreted in relation to the key opposition of "revolution—reaction." In this regard, we can presume that the novella "transmits" multiple parallel allegorical signals.

Description of Sanin and the Style of the Novella

Unlike other characters, we do not know much about Sanin except that he is good-looking. Such a characteristic implies Turgenev's slightly ironic attitude to his protagonist. However, it is crucial to make the following reservations. First, delicate irony never develops into mockery in *Spring Torrents*. There are hints of mockery in the descriptions of Pantaleone and, to a lesser extent, Polozov, but the narrator talks seriously about all other characters. Secondly, behind the mild narrative irony of Sanin's inner speech (and memories of the long gone youth inevitably create a certain ironic distance) hide various grave ideological and worldview problems that Sanin has as a man of the 1840s. For Turgenev, Sanin's personal story is, in a certain way, typical, so it serves as a case to study the specifics of Russian society.

Sanin distances himself from social and political problems, and if he thinks about them, he does it in a trite and superficial way. The only thing he seems to be interested in is art and beauty, although, judging by his mediocre music tastes (115), he has no original aesthetic views. Turgenev highlights this opposition between the aesthetic and the political, saying about Sanin that "he knew little of the disturbing emotions which had raised a storm in the breasts of the best of the younger generation of that epoch" (32). Thus, he counterposes Sanin to the radically minded intellectuals of the 1830s and 1840s, such as Vissarion Belinskii, Aleksandr Herzen, Nikolai Ogarev, and others who were mainly interested in political, philosophical, and historical discussions. Sanin is also opposed to the "new people" of the 1860s (32). The narrator emphasizes his feeble and fragile subjectivity: "...he was rather like a young, newly grafted, curly-headed apple tree in one of Russia's southern orchards in the black earth country" (32–33). The lack of political as well as general subjectivity is his main characteristic. In his relationship with Gemma, Sanin often makes spontaneous and haphazard decisions following romantic stereotypes and patterns he learned from books. The narrator does not miss the chance to accentuate the protagonist's emotionalism.[33] Such characteristics often conclude the chapters, which makes the reader pay particular attention to them. They bring emotional closure to yet another episode that fails to become a moral lesson for Sanin. Having touched upon the descriptions of

---

33   See: "...he...did not want to think of anything, whistled from time to time— and was very pleased with himself"; "he didn't even attempt to try to fathom what was happening inside him—bedlam, and there's an end on it!" (41, 66).

Sanin's non-reflexivity, we must address the problem of style.[34] There is a consensus among scholars that the transition from "Gemma's part" to "Madame Polozov's part" comes with stylistic changes, yet we believe that this is not the case. We do not observe any shifts in lexis or syntax. Moreover, the fact that the motives from the Frankfurt chapters reappear in the Wiesbaden ones suggests that Turgenev did not mean to make any stylistic changes.

However, there is one change we should mention. In the first part, the narrator only pays attention to Sanin's emotionalism and non-reflexivity while in the second part, he explicitly characterizes him as weak.[35] Not aligning with the non-judgmental tone of the first part of the novella, these remarks in the second part turn the protagonist into a subject of the narrator's moral judgment. Sanin's youth is not the only reason for his weakness as his inability to act and think critically has political implications.

Narrative Frame, Obscuring, Trauma

The structure of the novella is modified with a narrative frame, which consists of an exposition in which Sanin suddenly remembers the days of his youth and an epilogue in which he experiences a moral revival and plans to go to America. What does this frame accomplish? First, it makes clear that the protagonist spent thirty years in oblivion so that only fear of death could remind him of the long-gone, yet crucially important events of the past. This frame obscures the events which lie beyond the narrated story, yet their absence highlights the emptiness of the protagonist's life.

Concealment is first used in the second part of the novella when sex between Sanin and Madame Polozov remains undescribed.

---

34 M. L. Gofman, "Veshnie vody," in *Literaturnaia ucheba,* 3 (May 2000): 155–57 [First published: Vozrozhdenie, no. 77 (1958)]; A. Gladilova, "Stil' 'Veshnikh vod' I.S. Turgeneva," *Russkaia rech'* no. 2 (1971): 26–32. Sometimes scholars even see different genre models in the two parts of the novella. See: Harold K. Schefski, "Novelle structure in Turgenev's Spring Torrents," *Studies in Short Fiction* 22, no. 4 (Fall 1985): 435.

35 "Weak people never make an end themselves—but keep waiting for an end"; "When weak people talk to themselves, they are fond of using forceful turns of speech" (129, 136). See also Matlaw, "Turgenev's Art in *Spring Torrents*," 160.

However, this is not the only case. Shortly after Sanin's moral fall, such obscuring motivates the transition from his past to the present. We shall look into in more detail.

But, when he came to the moment when he had turned imploringly to Madame Polozov, when he had so far abased himself, when he had thrown himself at her feet, when his enslavement had begun—then he turned aside from the images which he had conjured up; he did not wish to remember more. Not that his recollection was unclear—oh no! He knew, he knew all too well everything that had happened after this moment, but shame stifled him...he was afraid of the feeling of self-contempt which he knew he could not conquer... (145).

In this abstract sense, obscuring has a different motivation. That which is not narrated is what Sanin does not want to remember. Paradoxically, he remembers the sequence of events quite clearly, yet those areas of his consciousness responsible for image and speech refuse to reproduce it. It is obvious, then, that his traumatic heartbreak is clear as he is not only unable to analyze these life-changing events, but also represses them. The effect of his grief is nonetheless visible as Sanin's memory offers him a "synopsis" of those events. He decides to set off to Frankfurt to search for Gemma. His inner narrative becomes a first step in working through the trauma. Memories of his youth, arranged in a story and interpreted, even if in such shallow way, becomes a way out of the psychological stasis that Sanin was in.

Using the term "trauma" here, we relied on Dominick LaCapra's approach, who distinguishes between *writing trauma* and *writing about trauma* in his *Writing History, Writing Trauma*. He defines *writing trauma* as the "processes of acting out, working over, and to some extent working through in analyzing" traumatic experiences. In contrast, *the writing about trauma* is "an aspect of historiography," which should reconstruct the past "as objectively as possible."[36] Thus, *the writing about trauma* contains the description of traumatic

---

36   Dominick LaCapra, *Writing History, Writing Trauma* (Baltimore, 2001), 186.

events but is not traumatic itself. We claim that *Spring Torrents* might be considered the *writing about trauma* type of text. Turgenev as a historiographer tells a story of a mere nobleman from the 1840s and shows how Sanin's lack of political subjectivity and non-reflexivity lead to the catastrophe. But not only is his story driven by trauma—Madame Polozov is traumatized, too.[37]

What are the connotations of the characters' trauma? First of all, Sanin feels broken and becomes conscious of his moral fall. We believe that this intimate experience has political meaning. Traumatized by serfdom, Madame Polozov makes Sanin play out the collective Russian trauma of the first half of the nineteenth century in his own life—trauma that he experienced and was influenced by, but unlike Madame Polozov, he was unaware of its existence. We shall emphasize that the trauma of serfdom is composed of special problematic components, such as the deformation of people's identities, imbalance of the private and the public, and the erosion of historical memory.[38] The last case refers to the repressions of the opposition movements, from the 1830s groups to the persecuted sect members Turgenev was interested in. Thus, Sanin's quite predictable trauma is related to a wide range of problems that, according to Turgenev, led to Russia's deviation from the "European" path of civilizational development.

Two Types of National Memory

The opposition between Gemma and Madame Polozov in *Spring Torrents* forms part of the major opposition between "Russianness" and "Italianness" which is played out on the third, politically quite productive territory—Germany, that was going through a period of political turmoil in the 1840s and was a source of radical political thought that subsequently led to the Revolution of 1848. These

---

37   *Spring Torrents* is a text about trauma, but it does not allow us to know whether the author was traumatized. We analyze not the psychology of Turgenev, but the novella's poetics.

38   On the Russian serfdom as a cultural trauma see: "Ot redaktsii," *Novoe literaturnoe obozrenie* 5 (2016): i-iv (special issue on serfdom in Russia). On the slavery as a collective trauma see: Eyerman, Ron, *Cultural Trauma: Slavery and the Formation of African American Identity* (Cambridge Mass., 2001), 1–22

two national characters represented by the heroines have much in common. They both remember their heritage and live by it in a foreign environment. They both cherish the memory of their fathers who played a key role in their lives. Finally, they both follow some ideological and political models, though in different ways. Gemma represents republicanism while Madame Polozov pays lip service to the cult of freedom, but her behavior is defined by her desire to rule and dominate that stems from the abovementioned trauma.

Other characters of the novella are also distributed between these two opposed ideologies—a "normal" one and a "biased" one—which sends another allegorical signal. As we have already mentioned, the Roselli family is inspired with republican ideas. Gemma's brother, Emil, dies at the end of the 1850s fighting for freedom with Garibaldi's troops against the Franco-Austrian alliance (151), which reminds us of the death of another character, Rudin. Emilio's death proves that these ideas were successfully passed down in the family. As for Madame Polozov's "sphere of influence," we should consider her husband. Polozov leads neither a political nor sexual life and is described as practically sexless, only being interested in food and sleep. The ideological model of his wife can only cater to such basic needs. In Sanin's case, sex and enslavement and, quite surprisingly, capital, are added to this list.

It is worth noting that Sanin is opposed to the female characters in terms of national memory, which he completely lacks. Having such underdeveloped subjectivity, he is ready to adopt whichever model is available and, with all else being equal, reaches for someone who is traumatized like him, which indeed happens when Madame Polozov enslaves him.

We should ask ourselves what helped him work through his trauma. Memories themselves brought him alleviation. Yet no less important was the following meditation on his life and strengthening of his subjectivity. The second time in Frankfurt, while waiting for Gemma's letter, Sanin buried himself in books: "He read from morning till night, not the journals, but serious books, works of history. This long period of reading, this silence, this hermit life of a snail in its shell were all exactly what best suited his state of mind..." (150).

Sanin's interest in historical books is consistent with the general idea of the novella—it is only possible to develop one's subjectivity through adhering to memory practices and historical memory. It is history and memory, their political interpretation, that allow one to choose biographical trajectories which they deem acceptable. Thirty years later, Sanin does what his peers—"the best of the younger generation of that epoch"—did in the 1830s and 1840s, and this belated immersion in history helps him heal.

Dialectics of Capital

Financial issues form another aspect related to the allegorical nature of the novella. The description of the political sphere correlates with that of capital. The republican-minded Roselli family, which runs a small business, is contrasted with people of great wealth, such as Klueber, who owns a large store, and Madame Polozov, a millionaire. Significantly, capitalism correlates with reactionary ideology (we have already mentioned Klueber's speech against revolution) so that money serves oppression and enslavement: Gemma's marriage to Klueber could have saved her family from bankruptcy, while Madame Polozov's wealth reinforced her sexual dominance. Turgenev's attitude to capital is expressed through plot twists: both Madame Polozov and Klueber die, and the latter dies in prison.

Most interestingly, at the time of the main events of the story, Sanin owns only one estate. However, by the 1870s he is much wealthier, as "in the course of thirty years…he had had time to amass a considerable fortune" (152). There is no direct explanation of how exactly he managed to get rich.

On the connotative level, however, Sanin's enrichment is unequivocally related to his moral fall. Caught in the traumatic circle of enslavement, sex, and capital, Sanin becomes a part not only of the circulation of power and money but also of the collective responsibility. Since Madame Polozov represents politics, it is obvious that Sanin's financial success, being a result of his moral fall, represents the relationship between the Russian people and power. Morally corrupting practices of collaboration guarantee material well-being.

It is no coincidence that the novella ends with an ambiguous remark about the protagonist's business affairs: "They say that he is selling all his estates and is planning to move to America" (152).

Sanin's desire to break out of this vicious circle and move to America—an ambivalent space for a better life, mythical and even utopian, and a democratic state with its dialectics of capital that threatens cultural aristocratism—is obscured here by the indication that free money from sold estates can be potentially invested in the US.[39]

Nevertheless, working through the trauma with the means of individual memory and big history allows Sanin to get out of the vicious circle of power and meaningless life, or at least enables him to hope that he will be able get out as the ending remains open.

Gender Problems

The last allegorical signal relates to gender. Earlier we attempted to show that Madame Polozov is an exemplary representation both of Russian collective trauma of the first half of the nineteenth century and of power. Having discussed the main conceptual structures of *Spring Torrents*, we can put forward our last crucial argument.

In terms of poetics, Madame Polozov, unlike feminine Gemma, is not quite a woman. Femininity is distorted in the descriptions where she refers "to herself as 'good fellow'" and is rendered a "female Centaur."[40] Both descriptions highlight the deceptive appearance of Madame Polozov, the first one not only lexically, but also grammatically, shifting the gender. She is in no way a woman, she is merely

---

39   Rogger, Hans, "America in the Russian Mind: Or Russian Discoveries of America" *Pacific Historical Review* 47, no. 1 (February 1978): 27–51; Saraskina, L. I., "Amerika kak mif i utopiia v tvorchestve Dostoevskogo" in *Teoriia khudozhestvennoi kult'ury* (Moscow, 2011), 13: 195–211

40   "But she referred to herself as 'good fellow' who could not bear any ceremony: it was in these very terms she had described herself for Sanin's benefit. And at the same time, here was the 'good fellow' walking beside him softly like a cat and leaning slightly against him, looking up at him. What is more, the 'good fellow' was cast in the image of a young female creature who simply radiated that destructive, tormenting, quietly inflammatory temptation…" (116); "Wild forces are now at play. Here is no Amazon putting her steed to the gallop—a young female Centaur gallops along, half-beast and half-goddess. The placid and well-bred German countryside lies amazed at the trample of her wild Russian Bacchanalia" (140).

a monster "cast in the image of a young female creature," a rakish "half-beast," an elusive spirit enslaving everyone who falls under its charms. We believe that such an image cannot be reduced to emotional exaggeration or the protagonist's biased perception. Madame Polozov represents something else, and this something is nothing but power.

Thus, the poetics of the novella corresponds on different levels to the allegorical structure of the plot. All parallel signals form a twofold allegory in which one extreme represents "revolution," and another, "reaction."

To summarize, allegory is ambivalent both as a literary device and as a means of producing meaning. First, it puts the plot of *Spring Torrents* in the conceptual arena of nature and existence and exposes the universal historical mechanism—the cycle of revolution and political reaction. Secondly, allegory is related, through ideology and characters' traumas, to a particular period of Russian history and a particular type of personality ("Sanin as a Russian man").

The allegory, which shifts the balance between the symbolic and the allegorical in the Russian Realistic prose, demonstrates that reactionary Russia falls behind Europe, which is revolutionary in spirit. However, Sanin's transformation at the end of the novella brings ambiguity to Turgenev's image of Russia. On the one hand, one can overcome past traumas: the traumatized Russians pass through self-reflection and reshape the national memory, as the generation of the 1840s and "new people" of the 1860s did. On the other hand, Sanin's liberation from the vicious circle of power and his upcoming trip to America suggest that Russia still has a long way to go. In that respect, Turgenev's attitude is rather pessimistic, especially if we consider how the "nature" part of the allegory is projected onto the political context—Russian social dynamics is described as an annual cycle between the implied winter and *Spring Torrents* that, as the epigraph suggests, hurry away.

Again, Turgenev resorted to political allegory not only in one but in four out of five "memory novellas" (all but *Punin* and *Baburin).* We believe that by doing so, he sought to make his novellas more complex in order to address serious social, political, and national problems, therefore turning them into "minor" novels. Indifference to politics displayed by his characters is a mere façade behind which lurks the traumatic Russian past. The protagonist is unable to talk about it in political terms, although it defines his fate.

We do not imply that Turgenev had no adequate political language to describe Russian traumas but only that his characters did not have one to reflect their past. If we were to imagine Sanin or Vladimir from *First Love* talking about politics, such refection in a first-person narrative would inevitably transform the text into journalism or non-fiction. It would need to be a wide political panorama or a history of a generation. Among Turgenev's contemporaries, such a narrative had already been created by Aleksandr Herzen in *My Past and Thoughts,* and it is unlikely that Turgenev would wish to excel him.

Acknowledgements

This study was implemented in the framework of the Basic Research Program at the National Research University Higher School of Economics (HSE University) in 2020. We are grateful to Andrey Fedotov, Boris Maslov, and anonymous reviewers of the *Slavic Review* for their valuable comments and suggestions.

BIOGRAPHICAL TIMELINE

1818–27   Ivan Sergeyevich Turgenev is born on November 9 the second son of noble Russian parents Sergei Nikolaevich Turgenev (1793–1834), a colonel in the Russian cavalry who took part in the Patriotic War of 1812, and Varvara Petrovna Turgeneva (née Lutovinova; 1787–1850), a wealthy heiress.

       Ivan and his brothers Nikolai and Sergei are raised by their mother, a very educated, but authoritarian woman, on the Spasskoe-Lutovinovo family estate that was granted to their ancestor Ivan Ivanovich Lutovinov by Ivan the Terrible, the grand prince of Moscow from 1533 to 1547 and the first tsar of Russia (1547–1584). She surrounds her sons with foreign governesses; thus Ivan becomes fluent in French, German, and English.

       With family, makes trip through Germany and France in 1822.

1827   Family moves to Moscow to provide sons with a formal education.

1833   Studies for one year at the University of Moscow.

1834–37   Studies at the University of Saint Petersburg, focusing on classics, Russian literature, and philology. During this time, father dies from kidney stone disease; younger brother Sergei dies from epilepsy.

1838–41   Studies philosophy, Hegel, and history at the University of Berlin, returning to Saint Petersburg to complete his master's examination. After his studies in Germany he becomes a confirmed believer in the superiority of the West and in the need for Russia to Westernize.

1841   Starts his career in the Russian civil service; over the next four years.

Writes verses and comedies, reads George Sand, and makes the acquaintance of Dostoevsky and the critic Vissarion Belinsky, who becomes his close friend and mentor.

1842   Has a daughter, Paulinette, by a peasant woman at Spasskoye.

1843   *A Rash Thing to Do* (play); *Parasha (long poem)*.

Meets Pauline Viardot a married renowned French mezzosoprano and actress with whom he has a lifelong affair. (Turgenev eventually entrusts Paulinette's upbringing to Viardot.)

Works for the Ministry of Interior for two years, then resigns; his resignation infuriates his mother who reduces his allowance, thus forcing him to support himself.

1846   *Lack of Money* (play); "The Duellist" (short story); "Three Portraits" (short story).

1847   *It Tears Where It Is Thin* (play); "The Jew" (short story); "Pyetushkov" (short story).

Lives abroad.

1848   *A Poor Gentleman* (play).

1849   *Breakfast at the Chief's* (play); *The Bachelor* (play).

1850   *The Diary of a Superfluous Man* (novella); *A Conversation on the Highway* (play).

Returns to Russia.

1851   *A Provincial Lady* (play).

1852   *A Sportsman's Sketches* (stories) is published and establishes Turgenev's reputation as a writer.

Writes obituary praising Nikolai Gogal, which the censor of Saint Petersburg bans; Moscow censor allows publication but Turgenev is imprisoned for a month, then exiled to his country estate for nearly two years ostensibly over the incident but likely as much for his criticism of serfdom.

1854   "Mumu" (short story).

Emigrates to Europe, in part to be near Pauline Viardot.

1855   *Yakov Pasynkov* (novella); *A Month in the Country* (play).

1856   *Rudin* (novel); *Faust* (novella).

1857   *Fortune's Fool* (play).

1858   *Asya* (novella); *Annouchka* (novel).

1859   *Home of the Gentry* (novel).

1860   *On the Eve* (novel); *First Love* (novella); "Hamlet and Don Quixote" (essay).

1861   Serfdom is abolished in Russia; *A Sportsman's Sketches* is credited with having influenced public opinion in favor of its abolition.

Has a major falling-out with Tolstoy over Turgenev's daughter mending clothes for the poor. Turgenev sees it as charitable; Tolstoy calls it pretentious. They exchange demanding letters, leading to Tolstoy challenging Turgenev to a duel. Both avoid it with more letters. Tolstoy later, during his religious phase, apologizes.

1862   *Fathers and Sons* (novel).

1863   Meets and befriends Gustave Flaubert; history of their friendship becomes part of the literary history of the age.

1864   "Enough" (short story).

Pauline Viardot retires from the stage and moves to Baden-Baden; Turgenev follows her and builds a small house there.

1866   "The Dog" (short story).

1867   *Smoke* (novel); "The Brigadier" (short story); "Lieutenant Yergunov's Story" (short story).

1868   "The Unhappy Girl" (short story).

1869   "A Strange Story" (short story).

1870   *King Lear of the Steppes* (novella); "Knock, Knock, Knock" (short story).

The Franco-German War of 1870–71 forces the Viardots to leave Baden-Baden, and Turgenev follows them, first to London and then to Paris.

1871   After the Franco-Prussian War Turgenev and Viardot purchase a villa at Bougival, near Paris, where he lives until his death.

1872   *Torrents of Spring* (novella).

1874   "Punin and Baburin" (short story).

1875   "The Watch" (short story).

1877   *Virgin Soil* (novel).

1878   Elected vice president of the Paris international literary congress.

1879   Receives honorary doctorate from Oxford.

1880   Gustave Flaubert dies on May 8.

1881   *The Song of Triumphant Love* (novella); "A Desperate Character" (short story); "Old Portraits" (short story).

1882   *An Evening in Sorrento* (play); *Poems in Prose* (sketches); *Klara Milich* (novella).

1883   *The Mysterious Tales* (novella); "Klara Milich" (story).

In January, an aggressive malignant tumor is removed but had already metastasized in his upper spinal cord.

On September 3, Ivan Turgenev dies of a spinal abscess in his house in Bougival, near Paris. His remains are taken to Russia and buried with national honors in Volkovo Cemetery in St. Petersburg.

Made in the USA
Columbia, SC
11 February 2025